MACKAY

–

CANADIAN DETECTIVES SERIES

BOOK SET ONE

A SUITABLE EPITAPH

&

AN IMMIGRANT

Roxana Nastase

Scarlet Leaf

Toronto, Canada

2018

All characters in this book are fictive, and any resemblance to real persons, living or dead, places or events is coincidental.

This book doesn't portray the Canadian police system.

ISBN: 978-1-988827-52-0

Toronto, Canada

Dedication:

To Mariana, for her resilient friendship

A SUITABLE EPITAPH

A Suitable Epitaph

Klavdiya was born on the shore of a small lake in Russia forty years ago...

The woman got married in spring when the cherry trees were in blossom. She was eighteen at the time. She got divorced in autumn when the harsh rains washed the soil and the fallen leaves. She was only twenty-three and she had a young boy attached to her skirts.

...

Klavdiya died on the shore of another lake and on another continent... She'd come into the world restless and with a thirst to exceed the limitations of the world she'd been born to and she died without finding her peace.

PROLOGUE – AXEL'S VISION

The woman had been flirting with him for over fifteen minutes before he invited her to accompany him in the garden for some fresh air. Glancing out the patio doors into the darkness, she smiled. That was exactly what she'd been aiming for and she consented freely to follow him outside.

After all he was a very well built man. Maybe quite too well, she thought when she noticed him for the first time. Her mouth watered while her eyes perused the expanse of his broad shoulders and strong hands.

She needed a man. It had been some time since a man's strong hands aroused her. Probably, too long, if she considered the flutter in her belly.

The physical desire had been compelling enough, but the signs hinting to his wealth had been more important and decisive for her. The man was wealthy enough for her tastes. His suit wasn't a cheap imitation but a true Armani. She'd always had an eye for such things.

They strolled leisurely along the gravel path as she clung to his sturdy arm. He murmured some inconsequential things and she didn't bother to listen.

The power she could feel under her fingers was as exciting as the heavy smell of the roses lining the one side of the trail. She smelled romance in the air and smiled.

A few more steps and the roses made way to berry bushes. The smells changed and the heat of the summer night enveloped them in a humid cocoon.

The shingle path disappeared and she stumbled when her foot stepped on cracked soil. Both chuckled although embarrassment powdered her cheeks with a slight blush. He silently provided more support to her and a giddy feeling bubbled in her veins.

When he hastened his steps, she giggled softly and commented playfully on his haste. He was watching the trees, distracted, and didn't give any sign that he'd heard.

That determined her to bring a halt to their fast advancement through the garden. It might have been romantic, yet it didn't seem very wise. She was alone with a man she'd just met and didn't know anything about him.

It was her first time there and she hadn't been aware that the garden grounds were so extensive and secluded. Besides, while she had all intentions to flirt with him, she didn't have any intentions to succumb to his charms that night.

It was never a good idea to give in too soon. She wanted much more than a tumble in the hay and that meant that she had to play hard to get for a while. Men liked the hunt. They enjoyed the scent of their prey and the efforts that came with their chase.

The huge man glanced at her. His eyes showed understanding and he allowed her to move at a slower pace. She was wearing stilettoes and her feet thanked him. When she put on her high heels that evening before the party, she hadn't meant to wear them on that hard ground.

Once they were about forty meters away from the house and in the shadow of the trees lining that side of the garden, the man grabbed her arm and nudged her to a deserted corner. He put enough strength behind his action and the brutal move startled her.

A shiver played on the back of her neck and sent tentacles along her spine and the back of her legs. A spine-chilling feeling replaced her light-hearted mood from before, but she didn't take it lying down.

She tried to reason with him at first. She preferred to assume that maybe he was too anxious to be alone with her and that was why his attitude changed. Her well-chosen words fell on deaf ears though, and she stopped pretending. She began to oppose him but it was as if she'd been trying to stop a river flow.

Indifferent to her pleas, he dragged her for a few more meters. She continued pleading with him because she didn't see any other solution, but her attempts failed. She replenished her efforts to fight him and tried to dig her heels in the ground, but the soil was too dry and she couldn't get any traction. She just stirred a cloud of dust that rushed to find a home in her pores.

Her legs turned to jelly and she barely kept herself upright. Something was definitely wrong with what was going on there. Both her self-confidence and sense of safety had slowly skulked away during the forced walk through the trees.

Tinges of electrical shocks ran through her arms. She panicked and tears burnt her cheeks. She felt ashamed of her weakness and tried to hold them back, but the cold fingers of fear kept squeezing her heart in an iron fist, and her breath became ragged.

Probably sick of her puny attempts to detangle herself from him, he finally stopped and moved to stand before her. Through the stream of her stubborn tears she surveyed the man's stony face with dread. The man wasn't even blinking and that disconcerted her more. He was just staring at her with dead eyes which quashed her hopes.

She tried to say something again, but now she didn't find the strength to push the sounds past her lips. Her throat refused to work and her mouth was drier than the soil she felt under the thin soles of her fancy shoes.

She glanced back to the house with renewed albeit premature expectation but the trees hid it from sight. Her lips quaked when she realized that no one could see or hear her.

A corner of the man's mouth lifted in a satisfied smirk, and that sneer was a splash of cold water over her face. Even though her anxiety was climbing and reaching new heights, she understood that what he felt for her was nothing else but contempt.

That came like a shock. Not the first that evening to be sure, but this one packed the power of a live wire and her mind scattered looking for an explanation.

She'd always been certain that men admired and even worshipped her. She'd basked in their burning glances often enough and she knew that she didn't delude herself.

She stared back at him with tired eyes. She tried to decipher what lay there behind the mask but her intuition had taken cover somewhere and didn't offer any help.

The sturdy man studied her for a few moments and then, he reached out and fisted his hand over her silk blouse. His touch brought her back to the reality which had twisted a pretend romance into a horror movie. Fear bubbled near the surface now and, as her brain scrambled the signals, she was about to burst into a hysterical laughter.

In that frozen moment, that soft blouse which caressed the curve of her breasts became the most important thing in her world. She was very proud of that top as it was one of the symbols she attached to the life she'd built for herself. She'd turned that expensive piece of silk into a tangible proof that she'd exceeded both her and other people's expectations but, more important, that she'd escaped her birth circumstances, which had confined her to the working class.

The sight of that dark and threatening hand on her precious top brought a glimmer of dread but also made her see red before her eyes.

The beefy hand jerked hard and the flimsy blouse fell apart rendered to rags. Her dismay and the pressure of her fury at the sight of her prized chemise ruined ruthlessly, pushed a warlike cry past her quivering lips.

She abandoned any rational thought and jumped the man. Her shoes found soft spots in his shins and made him grunt. Her nails targeted the handsome and ruthless face she'd admired just minutes before and left blood in their wake.

He fought her back. The slap of his backhand unbalanced her. She stumbled back and cried out again and not only because of the pain. This cry echoed the terror that had swiftly creeped into her bones and fried all her neuronal cells. The man was strong and she didn't have the ability to defend herself against that brutal show of force.

Her cry died soon, though. Another man grabbed her throat from behind and his fingers gripped her as a vise and smothered the sound.

She questioned and berated herself. In the heat of the fight she'd failed to hear the other man's steps. Still, she promised herself to go down swinging.

She tried to claw into his skin but he didn't show that he registered any kind of pain. Running on instinct only, she directed her stilettoes to his shins but she couldn't say for sure if she succeeded. His fingers burrowed harder into the delicate skin and left bruises behind that marred the flawless whiteness of her epidermis. Her air pipe constricted and the woman slid slowly into unconsciousness.

Before she blacked out, she had just enough time to feel other fingers knotted in her hair. She was beyond terror and anxiety. Her impotence overwhelmed the solitary corner of her mind that was still functioning. The last thought that passed her mind was that she couldn't buy or fight her way out of that. She'd lost the game and that was her night.

The slight flicker of life in her body just made it interesting for the men around. The third man who'd grabbed her hair, threw her on the hard ground in the shadow of a bush pregnant with red drops. Her skirt climbed up and the whiteness of the exposed skin of her legs lit the darkness.

The three of them were still looming over her. They stared at her fallen body for a few seconds.

One of the attackers smirked with satisfaction, his eyes going from her body to the red berries. The ugliness in his sneer showed that he knew that the beauty of the red fruit went hand in hand with their poison and he found it befitting the situation. The woman was about to get what she deserved. Poison deserved poison.

***

Axel woke up with a jerk and his half-lidded eyes surveyed the bedroom. The light of the moon reflected in the glass panels of the south wall and filled the room with shadows in the corners.

His heart pounded in his chest. For one brief but agonizing moment, he'd feared that he was there with those men, who were still staring at the woman's body, which was lying in the shadow of that bush.

Now, wide awake, he breathed deeply and closed his eyes in relief. He was still in his house.

Axel's relief was short lived. He'd scarcely closed his eyes, that he had another vision of the woman's broken body.

She was lying down on that hard and dry ground which he'd seen in his dream. Now, a monotonous rain whipped her mercilessly and washed the pattern in blood which had been painted on her body, feeding it to the dehydrated soil.

The vision was so in-depth that Axel could even see the rain drops clinging to the woman's eyelashes. The light in her eyes had dimmed at first and then vanished. The lines on her forehead had deepened and marked her passing years on her face.

A few hours earlier, that face had been flawless. Now it was marred with an x high on her left cheekbone and her features showed weariness, pain and despair.

Axel flexed his fingers and wiped his damp palms off on his thighs. Axel's visions weren't always so detailed, but there were exceptions, such as the one that he'd had that night.

When the image finally blurred, Axel exhaled in a whoosh and then breathed in deeply. He wiped his forehead and noticed that his fingers weren't as steady as he knew them.

Axel shook his head and got off his bed and tried to stand. He had to lean on the night table for a few seconds before trying his wobbly legs again.

In the usual course of events, the man wouldn't have needed help to find his bearings. Axel knew his lair as well as the back of his hand and could find his way through the rooms even if he hadn't pulled the curtains aside to have the room bathed in the light of the moon. Still, that night, he needed the support of the walls to reach the bathroom.

There, he leaned on the lavabo and stared at his reflection in the mirror. Staring didn't help though. He turned on the tap and filled his fists with cold water which he liberally splashed over his face.

When the trepidation had left his body, Axel drank a mouthful. His mouth had been dry and his tongue was almost stuck to the roof of the mouth.

It wasn't enough. He brushed his teeth and only then he left the bathroom. He started towards his terrace but hesitated. He was restive and needed something more than to just listen to the owls in the night and the sounds of the lake.

With a shrug, he turned around and left his bedroom. He needed a glass of his best whiskey to wash away the metallic taste of death which still lingered in his mouth. His toothpaste hadn't succeeded in chasing it away. He also needed to make a decision.

Axel didn't know the people in his dream, but he knew the house. He'd seen that garden before. He'd strolled around it many times in the past and knew exactly where to find that pregnant bush.

Now, he had to decide what to say to the police and how. He didn't want to reveal how he knew about the crime but they would ask and he needed to plot a strategy.

CHAPTER 1 – A SUITABLE EPITAPH

Klavdiya was born on the shore of a small lake in Russia forty years ago. The information on Leah's pad didn't show it but it was raining the day Klavdiya came into the world.

The woman got married in spring when the cherry trees were in blossom. She was eighteen at the time. She got divorced in autumn when the harsh rains washed the soil and the fallen leaves. She was only twenty-three and she had a young boy attached to her skirts.

The young woman migrated to Canada the following summer where she'd already found work in a childhood friend's company.

She raised the boy to stand on his own two feet and when he left home to follow his path, she started looking around ready for the hunt.

Finally, it was her time and she wanted a man and the money that came with him. She wouldn't give any man the time of the day unless he met her expectations. He had to be well-dressed, well-behaved and with a rich portfolio.

Klavdiya died on the shore of another lake and on another continent. Her life had completed a full circle. She'd come into the world restless and with a thirst to exceed the limitations of the world she'd been born to and she died without finding her peace.

Leah sat on her haunches and looked at the battered and broken body lying at her feet in the shadow of the bush. She thought that that was a suitable epitaph after all.

She knew that she was harsh in her judgment but what she'd sensed when she touched the lifeless body made her remember a friend's words, *'Some people are just walking calls for trouble. Most of the time, trouble eventually answers their call'*.

Leah shook her head and scolded herself. No one would ever ask for what that woman got.

She stood up and turned off the pad in her hand. Then, she glanced at the coroner who meticulously discarded the surgical gloves and cleaned his hands with disinfectant.

Why he would do that, it was beyond her comprehension. Yet, she'd watched Dr. Connelly perform the same ritual every single time he was called at the scene of a fatal event.

The detective had known him for a number of years and the doctor's little quirks never ceased to astound her. Right from the beginning of their acquaintance, he stirred her curiosity, but he also pulled at her heart.

Leah's empathic skills were highly triggered whenever she looked at that gloomy old man. She'd found out that the doc wasn't a day over sixty, yet whenever she thought of him she had the feeling she would smell an old piece of parchment. That was why she got into the habit of thinking of him as an old man.

"Any word, doc?" she asked the doctor nimbly.

Leah always asked that question. She supposed it was the force of habit. The detective was compelled to inquire even though she knew that he wouldn't answer to her. Doctor Connelly was the only coroner in the force who never hazarded to give COD before completing the post mortem.

Leah turned to him just in time to catch his scowl and a small smile lifted the right corner of her mouth. Leah knew his reactions by heart and could predict them with accuracy. She actually took joy in every one of them and even found a perverse delight in yanking his chain. His answers would always make her day.

"Detective, when I have a COD, you'll be the first informed," he sternly replied with his hawk-like eyes trained on her.

His displeasure was evident in the tight curve of his mouth. His tone might have been stern but he also had a way of dragging his words which made the interlocutor aware of the sarcasm that dripped off his words like molasses in the water.

Yet, Leah felt warmth beneath the clipped words and bestowed him with a catlike smile. Her blue-green irises intensified the effect of her smile and made her seem eerie. The doc shuddered and brusquely turned and left the scene after he barked an order to the two men waiting on the side to take the body away.

Leah glanced at Klavdiya one last time. Now, no sensation came from the body. As the last drop of warmth had left the corpse, the lingering feelings and occasional thoughts from the victim vanished as well.

Leah pictured the victim's body in her mind as a shell and it wasn't for her to take care of that shell. Her role was to vindicate the victim and bring balance back into the world.

One thing that was certain about Leah was that she had a very strong sense of responsibility and she never shrunk her duties. Her innate sense of justice had pushed her on that difficult road to her family's dismay.

Leah came from a long line of empaths. Some of them had stronger abilities than others but all of them were able to sense something and read people based on those readings.

For four generations, already, her family members numbered several psychologists and counsellors, and she'd been expected to follow in their steps. Tradition was very important for her kin. They'd hoped until the last moment and hadn't resigned until she took her oath as a policewoman.

Leah was aware that she'd been a disappointment of sorts for her folks and yet, she knew she would do the same thing all over again if she'd had to choose once more.

She'd chosen to become a detective and to keep her skills hidden. The police work was chaotic enough and she didn't need to add more suspicion and stress to her colleagues' lives.

People wouldn't react favorably if they heard that she knew how they felt and sometimes why they felt the way they did. People needed to take comfort in the knowledge that they could count on the privacy of their thoughts and feelings.

Leah might have been a disappointment to her family in the beginning, but they'd passed over their displeasure fast enough. She knew that they felt a measure of contentment because at best she hadn't chosen another line of work.

There have been cases in their clan when some of the members embraced a life of deceit and cunning. They had the skills and could pull the wool over people's eyes with ease. It wasn't a difficult career for them to pursue. All the cards were up their sleeves.

After the first three years of her career, her parents came to terms with her profession and relented in their efforts to make her change her profession. They also felt that Leah was meant to bring a sort of balance into the world and they were satisfied to see that she had a deep respect for the responsibilities they had to uphold.

CHAPTER 2 – WOMAN VS POLICEWOMAN

The policewoman walked to her car with long strides. Now that she'd finished there, she was in a hurry to get back to the office and check on a few things.

She especially wanted to verify the emergency call that told them where to find the victim. The caller described the surroundings and events with too much accuracy and that couldn't be qualified as a coincidence.

Leah was certain that the man must have witnessed everything first hand and considered the man an obvious suspect. Her palms were itching with the desire to retain him and ask him some questions.

When she opened the car door, Leah noticed that Mark, her partner, was already sprawled in the passenger seat and she grimaced. She'd been looking for him earlier but she hadn't seen him. He had a talent of making himself scarce. What astounded her was that he managed to do his job despite his sneaking and she couldn't understand how.

Mark glanced at Leah and relaxed back in his seat. His hand, which held the pad he was reading when she opened the car door, fell in his lap.

Leah noticed Mark's rebel lock of hair and a twinkle appeared in her eyes. That was so Mark. His distinctive sign, she thought. Had she been asked to describe the officer she'd have begun with that.

Mark was over thirty but that particular lock of hair made him look much younger. He'd always blow it away because it hindered his sight but it had a life of its own and stubbornly fell back on the exact same spot. Mark seemed completely unaware of his behavior. He'd done that so many times that it became a habit he couldn't shake off.

That absent-minded gesture amused Leah and yet puzzled her at the same time. The young woman failed to understand why Mark didn't merely change his haircut to get rid of the pesky lock. It was obvious that it bothered him a lot and in her book when something didn't work it was time for a change.

Leah shook her head and put the thought at rest. It wasn't for her to tell Mark what to do. She'd learned early that people disliked nothing more than unsolicited advice. Besides, they had more pressing things to discuss and she'd already wasted enough time ruminating on things with no relation to the case they had to solve. Time didn't stand still for anyone, Leah recalled.

The woman sat in her car seat and closed the door with a resounding thump. She made a weary face when she heard the sound reverberate inside the car. Leah rarely allowed her dissatisfaction to control her attitude and every slip seemed like a slap in her face.

"Tough day, boss?" Mark asked with a reluctant smile on his lips.

Leah glanced at him and noticed that he seemed unwilling to provoke a discussion or, worse, a scolding, even though Leah rarely showed her claws. That didn't mean she didn't have any. The policeman had felt those claws a few times over the years and, apparently, didn't feel like repeating the experience.

Leah cast a stern look in his direction. While it was true that she outranked him, she never got used to his calling her *'boss'*. She'd asked him to use her name several times and expected him to have learned his lesson by then. The detective was weary of reminding him about it all the time and sometimes, she wondered if he didn't do it on purpose, just to test her restraint. Yet, the strain around his eyes and the vibes that came from Mark disagreed with her assumption and she preferred to let it go.

She looked out the window and saw that the sun had already reached up in the sky, a definite sign that the morning had come to an end. A black bird, maybe a hawk or a raven, sailed above with its wings outstretched and a piercing shout followed.

Leah knew very little about birds, maybe just that they flew and ate worms. Her eyes followed the arrogant bird for a few seconds and then, her eyes swept over the people gathered about twenty paces away from the yellow band.

Leah could read a broad array of feelings from the small crowd. She felt dismay, fear, pity and there it was, smug satisfaction.

It wasn't unexpected. Despite the saying '*Never speak ill about the dead*', there was always at least one person who disliked the dead with a passion and the satisfaction at the news of the victim's demise overrode their common sense.

Leah never frowned upon such a discovery. She understood people better than normal people did and she allowed room for such petty thoughts. She'd come to terms with the knowledge that humankind was actually anything but kind.

Still, there was something else there. The sensation was indefinite. It was just a probing tentacle which touched her mind and aroused her restlessness.

The young woman scanned the faces again carefully with the trained eyes of a police officer. At the same time, she tried to probe their minds, as well, using the skills she'd honed over many years.

A man turned his back to her slowly before her eyes could have reached him and seen his features. He started towards the house and she could see that his fists were clenched in the pockets of his white linen cotton pants. His stride was long and lazy as if he hadn't a worry in the world. Still, Leah would have bet the shirt on her back that tension defined the lines of his back muscles.

Her eyes lingered on his back and she tried to assess him objectively, yet she couldn't note anything distinctive but his curvy raven hair, which reached the collar of his white shirt, and the strong line of his shoulders. She didn't fail to notice the movement of his muscles under the loose shirt, though.

The man reminded her of an elegant and yet, ferocious feline cut loose out in the wild, absorbed in the mission of checking out its personal hunting grounds.

Leah focused on him until he disappeared behind the line of decorative trees. She hadn't watched him with the eyes of a woman and yet, to her distress, she had to admit that, unwillingly, the woman inside her had peeked.

That thought formed a line between her eyebrows and that line deepened when the woman realized that she hadn't felt anything from the unknown man. She'd experienced some tension and the peripheral edges of worry but nothing else.

Now, Leah worried. That had happened to her only once in the past, when she'd been confronted with a psychopath during her first years in the police force.

She'd been puzzled at the time as well but then her mother showed her that the explanation was at hand. It was perfectly normal not to sense a thing from a psychopath. They don't experience any kind of emotions, and therefore there are no vibes for Leah to catch.

She'd made her business to know everything about psychopaths at the time and nothing she'd learned encouraged her when it came to dealing with such people.

That was Leah's main concern here. Her inability to reach out to that man's emotions could mean only one thing and that wasn't very encouraging.

"Shouldn't we be going, Leah?" Mark asked. At the same time, his eyes were surveying the garden. He was trying to find out what had upset Leah so much that she'd frowned like that and forgotten about leaving the premises.

Leah glanced at him and barely managed to hide her surprise when she heard his voice. She'd been so lost in her thoughts that she'd forgotten about Mark.

She glanced back in the direction that the man had taken but of course he'd already disappeared. She showed Mark a crooked smile and nodded.

"Yeah, I think we should be going, Mark," she agreed and then started the car.

Leah followed the alley leading to the other end of the garden, her eyes attentive to the curves in the road. Yet, her mind was still on the man that she couldn't read and that had swiftly disappeared before she could see his face.

CHAPTER 3 – DIRTY DISHES IN THE AFTERMATH OF A PARTY

When she got back to the office with Mark in her tow, the detective squad was full of noises and movement as always. Anyway, Leah had learned to ignore the cacophony of sounds. She would surround herself in a bubble of isolation and concentrate on her own conversations or on the research she had to do at a certain moment. She'd stopped noticing what was going on around anymore. It was just background noise.

She was content, in any case, that by then, smoking on the squad floor had been forbidden. She could still remember the smog and smell that always lingered around a few years back at the beginning of her career. Her eyes would turn red and watery for days and sometimes she had bouts of coughing that required a lot of coercion to go away. She'd drunk so much raw egg yolk that she was afraid she would start cackling one day.

Working in those conditions had never been too easy. Of course, people had grumbled and protested the new rules but to no avail.

Leah respected other people's rights as much as the next person. However, she expected that her rights to breathe clean air be respected as well.

She hadn't gotten involved in any of the arguments at that time, though. She'd known that the new smoking rules would be in force without her contribution and that was why she kept quiet.

It turned out to be a very wise decision. Leah thought that her reserve was the reason everyone still spoke to her.

Those heated discussions divided people that had been friends for eons. They broke into two fighting camps and many of a friendship dissolved and never mended in the aftermath of the boisterous war.

Anyhow, two years back, Leah quietly snuk into one of the corner offices. That was what she thought at least but in reality, her tenacity and audacity in solving cases had helped her advance in the ranks and affirm her competence in the field.

The rank of lieutenant opened the door of that office, not Leah's ability to talk her way in. The policewoman might have entertained the belief that she was an accomplished diplomat but her empathic abilities didn't give her the necessary skills to grease her way up the ladder.

Not that she had too much tact. There were moments when she was far too direct and liked to give people a piece of her mind. People's memories were long and they never forgot.

Once in her office, Leah signaled Mark, who'd followed her, to close the door behind him. She didn't think of hiding something from the detectives in the squad anyway because the entire wall to the squad was glass. Still, that glass was thick enough and represented a barrier of sorts for the omnipresent clamor. She needed that buffer as she wanted to start on the case without any kind of inconsequential interruptions.

The young woman sat down and turned her computer on. As she knew that the computer liked to take its sweet time to run the initial software, she turned her pad on as well and waved Mark to sit in one of the chairs before her desk and do the same.

Her office was functional. There wasn't an object in there that didn't fulfill a practical function. Leah wasn't too fond of frills when it came to her working space. She'd found out that she preferred them at home where certain people didn't have access and couldn't catch a glimpse into her psyche.

Not even a photo warmed the top of her desk. Only three small baskets she regularly filled with snacks softened the Spartan décor. Leah considered them practical. She didn't always have the time to go out and eat during the day.

"So, Mark, let's see what you have there," she invited him to start the discussion.

Mark nodded but first, he leaned over her desk and checked the little baskets with snacks carefully, just to notice that she had filled them with grapes, cashews and peanuts. Now, that was disappointing and the line between his eyebrows deepened.

The day before she'd had a selection of cookies and he'd enjoyed every one of them. The man scowled with dismay, yet absent mindedly took a grape and popped it into his mouth. Only then he turned his attention to his pad, as well.

Leah smiled amused and turned her eyes to the computer so that he wouldn't be embarrassed. She didn't want him to see that she was monitoring his moves.

She found Mark very entertaining with his childlike tastes. She'd changed the type of snacks on purpose. It was her small and petty revenge because the other day, he wiped every single cookie on her desk. She'd only nibbled on one and swiftly there weren't any left.

Leah knew that she was somewhat mean but she enjoyed his reactions and if she provided the snacks, the least he could do was to provide the entertainment.

"I talked with Mr. Papadopoulos, the owner of the house," Mark began, "and I found out that he'd had a party last night. It didn't end till the wee hours of the morning," he made a point to specify and then, he glanced up at her. Leah nodded and that was his cue to continue. He checked on his pad and said, "I understand that he'd had about sixty guests and he couldn't confirm everyone's whereabouts during the party… Given the number, I think it would have been impossible," he observed, glancing at her again.

"Yeah, it would," she agreed softly, although she imagined that a man of Mr. Papadopoulos's means would have had the necessary personnel to keep track of all those guests.

A man with his status wouldn't have allowed anyone to trespass in certain areas of his house. He would have a sizable number of security people on his payroll to secure boundaries.

Mark nodded, satisfied, and continued his report, completely oblivious to Leah's thoughts, "I understand that the victim, Klavdiya, wasn't on the list."

"How come?" Leah asked and leaned forward.

Her curiosity was piqued. That the victim wasn't on the list didn't sound quite right. No one should have been able to crash a party in the circles where Mr. Papadopoulos moved. Even a beautiful woman like Klavdiya would have encountered resistance.

"I meant that her name wasn't on the list," Mark corrected his statement hastily. "She was under *'plus one'*," he thought to add. Leah was very particular about his being very specific.

"Ah, I see," the woman's understanding shone in her eyes. "She came with someone else."

Mark nodded in agreement and looked back at his pad, "A Mr. Angelus..."

"And where was Mr. Angelus when his date was killed?" she asked in a harsh voice.

"He'd left a couple of hours earlier. I mean a couple of hours before the victim was seen in the house the last time," Mark rushed to add.

He knew that Leah didn't like it when her officers weren't precise in details and he'd already slipped once. It wasn't as if she'd been vicious but her eyes drilled into the offender and no one felt comfortable when Leah went into scolding mode. Even his parents' lectures over the years had seemed more bearable.

"Why? Why did he leave without her?" Leah leaned over the desk once more and braced her elbows on the sides of the keyboard.

"Someone said… it was an assumption actually," Mark thought to point out so that he wouldn't mislead her, "that Mr. Angelus and his date had a discussion. She seemed interested in staying and he was interested in leaving… So, he just left…"

"And the host didn't say anything…" Leah noted pensively.

"He didn't because Mr. Angelus never said *'goodbye'*," Mark thought to mention.

"How come?" Leah perched on the edge of her chair and tilted her head to the right inquiringly.

The etiquette in those circles would have required a few polite words before leaving the host's house.

Mark blushed and looked down. Leah mused because she had a good guess about what he needed to say.

She'd heard him pulling a raw one to the boys in the past and he'd never blushed. Or at least, he hadn't blushed before his eyes fell on her.

It looked like her subordinate was concerned about stating some things in her presence as if they'd lived in the Victorian era and he couldn't tarnish her perception of the world.

That was another constant source of amusement for her. It was downright funny albeit a little puzzling for her to see that the thought that she already had a certain perception of the world, which included abominable crimes and far worse things than what he could say in his jokes or reports, never crossed the detective's mind.

Mark was a contradiction in terms. Just a couple of years older than Leah, he either acted like a teenager or like a concerned parent before her and, sometimes, she found it difficult to balance the man's two sides.

Sometimes she even had doubts about his mental balance although he seemed normal enough.

"All right, Mark, just spell it out," she cajoled him into spilling the beans. The smile flourishing on her lips didn't lack some malice, though.

"Well… the host was otherwise engaged…" Mark explained evasively.

"With?" she insisted mulishly.

"With… a beautiful model, with skin rivaling alabaster and such long and shapely legs that would have made Venus weep…" the officer continued and then glanced up at her just in time to see her eyebrows going up. He tapped his finger on the pad and specified, "That's what he said, word for word."

"I see," she murmured. "Do we have any picture of this… modern Venus, Mark? We should get an idea for ourselves," she explained to a mortified Mark.

For a moment, the man had feared that she implied that he already had a picture with the fashion model and he couldn't fathom why she'd think that of him. Leah had sensed his outrage and tried to smooth his feathers.

"No, not really…" Mark stuttered somewhat.

His eyes were focused on the geometrical pattern of the carpet as if he'd found something extremely interesting there, something that hadn't been there for the last two months since the carpet was replaced. Then he glanced back to her and proposed, "We can try on the Internet. I'm sure that there must be a photo with her…"

Leah invited him with a wide gesture, "By all means, be my guest, Mark, find one."

With nimble fingers, Mark opened the browser on his pad and started a search with the model's name. The avalanche of pages dedicated to the woman startled him.

"Should we try only images?" he asked Leah. "There are so many pages with mentions of her…" he shook his head, at a loss of words.

"Let's try just images for the moment," she acquiesced. "We'll go through the rest if there's any need later."

The man clicked on images and the page turned to tens of pictures reflecting the cold beauty of a modern Venus. Leah hadn't missed her target. Her label was more than appropriate.

The detectives looked from one photo to another and everywhere they saw the same impersonal and cold smile. White and perfect teeth, an elegant arch of the lips but no sparkle in the eyes. However, they both had to admit that the host of the party was very close in his description. The modern Venus's skin rivaled alabaster and her limbs were supple and beautifully shaped.

"Now, I do understand Mr. Papadopoulos," Leah said quietly. "He wouldn't have cared if all his guests had left without a word. Not when he busied himself with… such a delightful creature."

Mark didn't think it was necessary for him to add anything more. His boss had already touched on the heart of the matter.

"So, now we know what the host was doing when his guest met her demise. Do you have the list with the others?" the lieutenant asked the officer.

Mark nodded enthusiastically and showed his pad as a proof, "Yes, we do. Mr. Papadopoulos asked his head of security to provide me with the entire list. The name of everyone invited is here and there's a sign next to each of the people that actually came to the party. There were a few that didn't make it," he specified.

"Interesting," Leah replied softly. "I'd have thought that his parties would be irresistible and no one would miss their chance to attend…"

"I suppose…," Mark agreed reluctantly. "Yet, people get sick or…"

She waived his concern away and replied, "We'll see, no worries, Mark. We have to check all of them…"

"Even the people who didn't attend the party?" he asked in a shocked voice. He glanced at his boss with wide eyes, almost ready to pop out of their sockets.

Sixty people meant a lot of people and he didn't see the reason to question everyone. Not to mention that people who were living in that circle didn't comply easily with police's requests for answers.

"All of them," she repeated stubbornly and then grinned at him. "Imagine, Mark, how many people you'd get to bother. Don't tell me you won't enjoy being on this side of the net, as you'll be the one asking questions," she mocked him.

As a matter of fact, she'd had the occasion in the past to read his overt pleasure whenever he interviewed suspects or witnesses. She'd sensed that he sometimes perversely enjoyed having the control over those people and she didn't like it. She'd been waiting for a good while to catch a chance to rub his nose into that.

"But sixty people…," he mumbled completely oblivious of Leah's objective.

His narrowed eyes and the tension lines gathered on his forehead proved that he was concerned only with the huge load of work, which would fall mostly on his shoulders. Hence, the thought that the lieutenant was simply pushing his buttons never occurred to him.

Leah rolled her eyes at his shortsightedness. It was typical for Mark. That was why she was sitting in the lieutenant chair and not Mark. He was a good officer but couldn't perceive the entire picture.

Leah sighed deeply to keep her disappointment under control. She imagined throwing the pad and nailing Mark directly in the middle of his forehead.

Sometimes his skull turned out to be too thick. He'd completely miss the lessons she tried to teach him. In such moments, she felt the urge to give him a good shake and make him open his eyes.

"Well," Leah shrugged with indifference, "you'll take the first thirty and I'll take the remaining thirty," she said as if it had been the easiest task in the world.

Her lips bowed in a smile when she saw the grimace of displeasure on Mark's face. A tinge of guilt probed the edge of her mind but she muffled it. He deserved it.

"I have plans," he mumbled and his fingers unwittingly began a staccato on the desk top.

"What was that?" she tilted her head and feigned that she hadn't heard him.

"Nothing, nothing," he hastily said. "Maybe we should bring Josh and Anna into this," he said, grasping at straws.

"Oh, I intend to," Leah assured him nonchalantly. "Josh can follow up with Venus here and…"

"Why?" Mark wailed before he could control himself.

Leah's eyebrows raised on top of her forehead as the shock at the man's whimper made her incapable of uttering a syllable.

She eyed him with circumspection. The officer definitely didn't have a good day. He had jumped out of the frying pan into the fire.

"I beg your pardon?" the lieutenant inquired sitting straighter in her chair

She'd expected him to try and convince her to let him handle the model. He was a man after all and no man would have handed over to another man his chance to interact with such a fine specimen of a woman.

Apparently, her expectations were far off. The wail that came from her subordinate was something she'd never heard before.

The emotions coming from him were a total mess. For a few seconds, their force made her incapable of reading anything. His despair, hopelessness and regret enveloped her and she scowled.

Sometimes it wasn't such a good thing that she could feel what others felt. The intensity of Mark's present feelings overwhelmed her and made her palms clammy.

"Mark, look at me," Leah looked directly at him and asked in a flat voice.

She knew that talking without passion was a better way to make him listen to her.

She waited patiently until Mark finally glanced at her and then she continued in the same flat voice, "If you become so volatile when you hear that I'm thinking of assigning another officer to speak to her, it's better that you don't. Your interview with this woman wouldn't be of any use to us and I'm pretty sure that you'd see that as well if you stopped whimpering and started thinking hard… You'd just make an ass of yourself, Mark…"

Leah looked at his bowed head and patted the back of his hand reassuringly. There were times when she had the feeling that men needed more reassurance than their counterparts.

Mark didn't look up and didn't reply. She sensed his mortification and shook her head. A brief smile played on her lips for a few moments.

After a brief moment of reflection, she observed, "I'm afraid that even Josh might not be a good choice for this task... Anna will interview the model," she decided and then, she turned to the desktop and entered her password.

Mark understood that the discussion was over and he was smart enough not to pursue it further. He knew that whenever Leah made a decision, there was no way to dissuade her and he didn't dream of trying.

The lieutenant was easy to work with as long as people didn't step over the boundaries she'd set out. He'd learned that the hard way and didn't care for another lesson.

"Do you want me to send you the guest list? How do you want to divide the names between us?" Mark asked subdued.

The lieutenant's explanation had chastised him enough. He still couldn't believe that he'd reacted like an untried teenager and that before his boss. The officer was afraid that the embarrassment wouldn't go away soon and he had the urge to smack himself over the head for his stupidity. Repeatedly.

"Yes, please, do," she replied absent-mindedly and opened the search option in her software. "It might be easier if I took the names directly from the list instead of having you spelling the names for me... Mark, go into the squad room and call Anna and Josh in. They should be there by now," she continued without sparing a glance to Mark.

She pretended to read something very interesting in her office email and didn't take her eyes off the monitor until she noticed that Mark had left the office.

Leah would have loved to be able to block all those embarrassing feelings that came from Mark wave after wave. She felt sorry for the man but some part of her couldn't stop thinking that it was shameful that a thirty-year old man wasn't able to control himself and that his reactions put her in such a bad position in the process.

She resented him because of that although she had to admit to herself that he wasn't aware of what was going on and blaming him was unproductive.

The detective shook her head and pushed those thoughts to the back of her mind. She had other things to do and she turned her focus to the search. She began with Klavdiya's name and in a few seconds, the data populated the screen.

The information about the woman confirmed some of the things she'd already read before the body turned stone cold.

The woman was born in Russia indeed although the name of the locality blinking on the screen didn't say anything to Leah. She'd never been too fond of geography and in school, she studied just enough to graduate, and nothing more.

Curiosity made her open another browser and google the town's name. She found out that indeed the small town was Rostov, an old town situated in Yoroslavy Oblast. It had been erected on the shore of the lake Nero. Huh, that was an interesting name for a lake, she thought, her curiosity in over drive. She made a mental note to check it later. She had other things to verify right then.

Leah had had her mental readings confirmed more than once over the years, yet, the policewoman in her still had doubts and needed to double check every piece of information. She couldn't afford to leave anything to chance when catching a killer hung in the balance.

The detective returned to the data displayed in the police software search and checked the civil status of the woman. Leah learned that indeed the victim was divorced and had one son. She immigrated to Canada when she was very young where she built a steady life for both of them.

She worked for the same company during the entire life she spent in the adoptive country even though she'd enjoyed a very low increase in salary along the years. The figures showed that she'd had only a two percent increase in pay every year and that increase wouldn't have accounted for inflation. That she'd never looked beyond that to find a new job was telling.

When she touched her hand, Leah had sensed that Klavdiya Alekseyeva was a creature of habit. She wouldn't have left the comfort of a cushy job, even though it didn't pay too much. The woman wouldn't have tried to find something better or something more challenging. She might have harbored such notions now and then but she wouldn't have acted upon those feelings because Klavdiya wasn't the type of person who'd challenge the status quo.

The officer didn't find any notable relationships listed in her search and turned to the victim's son. She hoped that she could unearth something helpful in his profile.

Daniel Alekseyev was twenty-one now and appeared to have been a self-sufficient young man for the last three years. He'd been listed at a different address than Kavdiya's ever since he turned eighteen.

So, he wasn't a momma's boy, at least on paper, Leah concluded. Still, she needed to meet him face to face to be sure.

His profile also showed constancy in his work habits. Apparently, Daniel had worked for the same company for the last six years. He'd started out as a part time employee while in high-school and continued with a full-time job afterwards, although he attended college at the same time. His choice in studies showed that he intended to continue working for the same company after graduation.

The young man appeared to have inherited his mother's contentment with respect to his work and didn't entertain any ideas of changing the direction of his career.

At least he'd had more substantial pay increases over the years, Leah observed when she checked the income tab. In some ways, that set him apart from his mother somewhat.

Leah opened the tab listing relationships and noticed that he'd just got married. The young woman who became his wife had shared his dwelling for the last three years.

The wedding, apparently celebrated with all the trimmings, had taken place exactly a month earlier. His mother's death would have marked the one-month anniversary and that piqued Leah's attention.

That wasn't the only reason that made the detective turn her nose to the news of Daniel's marriage. She doubted that someone at that age could discern between lust or infatuation and the real deal.

In her opinion, strong relationships needed time, even a few years to develop and sustain the proof of time, although there were some exceptions to the rule, she admitted. But those were few and far between.

Leah shrugged, unwilling to explore the idea in more depth and returned to her search. She noted Daniel's home and work addresses and phone numbers to contact him that very day.

After a furtive glance at her watch, she decided that she would visit him at work after a couple of hours. He needed to be notified about his mother's demise, after all, and she didn't want him to hear the news from mass media.

Leah changed the parameters of her search to check Klavdiya's employer, Larissa Petrova.

She'd had the time to read only the information under the civil status tab when she heard the door open. She looked up and saw Anna, Mark and Josh gathered in the doorway.

"We knocked at the door, boss, a couple of times but you didn't appear to hear so...," Mark explained their invasion in her personal space and accompanied his words with wide gestures.

Uncertainty rang in his voice and Leah frowned. She disliked his hesitation.

She expected respect but not fear and Mark left the impression that he had his boundaries somehow messed up. Leah didn't have time to set him straight right then so she waved his concerns away and invited them to sit.

As she rarely worked with more than two or three people, she kept the number of seats in the office minimal. She had exactly three chairs.

She'd skipped over the offer of a sofa or anything on those lines. If she needed to sleep, she could go home. When she worked, she didn't need the flat surface of a couch to invite her to slack off in her job.

The officers sat down with their pads in hand and Leah smiled. She'd trained them well. Long gone were the days when one of them would come with their hands in their pockets as if she'd invited them to a friendly chat.

"I've already started on checking the victim and her close connections," she began and glanced from one to the other.

They nodded in unison and her smile widened. She glanced back at her screen and her fingers tapped on the keyboard.

"I've divided the list between us. I think we should go with two teams at all times, or almost at all times," she corrected herself and leaned back in her chair. "Anna, I want you to interview our model, Sybil Miller, alone. I have the feeling that taking Josh with you for this interview would hamper the results," she explained and glance slyly at Josh who grimaced.

She sensed that Mark had already told Josh about the beautiful model and he'd hoped that he would have a chance to be in the same room with her. Josh had seen photos with her before and had hot dreams featuring Sybil many a night.

Leah considered the wisdom of saying something caustic about his hopes and ambitions but decided against opening her mouth on the subject. She'd have had a hard time explaining how she knew about his most intimate desires.

"I divided the remaining of the list in two and already sent your list to your emails," she explained to Anna and Josh. "I need answers, and I need them soon. Find out who saw the victim, when and with whom. Don't forget, if she went out into the garden with someone, we need that person's name, description and so on," she pointed out and tapped her finger on the desk.

Leah looked from one to the other and then she added, "You know how to do your job. You don't need a refresher course right now," she concluded and noticed with satisfaction that all of them nodded in earnest.

The three detectives stood up and turned to the door when Leah said, "You're with me, Mark."

Mark scowled before he turned to her. He liked working with Leah. Usually. Yet, that day he'd made too many mistakes and he didn't feel comfortable around her. He'd have liked a couple of days to regroup. Anna and Josh left the office and Mark looked after them with longing.

Leah, always leaning back in her chair, observed him with amusement. She knew that he'd liked to have left her office as well.

"All right, Mark. We have to go," she said and locked her computer screen.

She stood up and retrieved her pad off the desk. She also picked up her handbag although she didn't enjoy having to carry it around.

The days were hot now though and wearing a jacket was out of question. Without the large pockets of her jacket, she didn't have anywhere to pile the things she needed. Hence, she had to carry that bag with her everywhere.

Mark opened the door for Leah and followed her into the squad room. People were milling around and the sound of several voices assaulted the two detectives like a shock wave. Leah hurried her step and she didn't stop before reaching her car.

"We'll take my car, Mark. It's more practical," she said and the officer didn't reply although she knew well that he didn't like it when she was driving.

Mark might have had some broad views regarding male and female roles. Yet, driving didn't enter those views. The idea that a woman would chauffeur him around wasn't very palatable to him, and Leah had sensed that frequently. Since she loved driving, she didn't care much about his misogynistic opinions.

CHAPTER 4 – SKELETONS IN THE CLOSET

As directed by the navigational control, Leah parked behind a small building and picked up her things before she got out of the car. The heat wave hit her and stole her breath. The humidity in the air clung onto her skin with clammy fingers. Sweat dripped along the back of her neck and between her breasts.

Mark had already climbed out of the car and was surveying the building, his hands fisted in the pockets of his trousers. He was whistling a merry tune while counting the floors and she resented that the man didn't seem to mind the high temperatures.

The building was almost hidden in a pocket of trees. It wasn't one of the sky-scrapers they would see downtown. Still, the buildings around the area had around seven or even ten floors while that one was low rise. Mark counted four floors, main floor included.

"Kind of isolated," Leah observed, and Mark nodded pensively.

"Probably they don't need visitors here," he replied.

"I don't think they do," she agreed. "I understand that they create and test computer games. I imagine there's a constant market for such products," she added inquiringly.

"You can't even imagine," Mark said. "I have two nephews and they are crazy about this sort of thing. My sister complains all the time about the money she spends on new games."

"Well, they're not for me," Leah shrugged.

She'd never found a reason behind punching away on the keyboard just to evade a dwarf or a dragon or whatever. The computer was a tool for her and she understood to use its potential but she wouldn't care to stare at a screen and play at make believe. Her life was full as it was and she'd always resisted the pressure of her peers and never got involved in futile entertainment.

They climbed the stairs and entered the lobby of the building. Instantly, the cool air inside stole their breath. The difference between the stuffy atmosphere outside and the arctic air inside the building came as a shock to their bodies. Leah shivered and took a squint at Mark. He didn't fare better than she did and that soothed her pride.

At the beginning of her career, she'd been frequently judged because she was a female. She couldn't forget people's biased behavior and double standard. That was why she'd promised herself never to let her gender come into question, even though she was aware that there were some natural differences between men and women. She still tried hard to compensate.

Changes took place all over the police force and women gained more terrain during the last few years. She still had to put up with oblique glances when the crime scene was excessively gruesome or when her temper got the best of her.

She could read in the men's mind the idea that she might fall apart or that she was bitchy because it was that time of the month and hormones obstructed her reasoning.

It was true that sometimes during those periods she lost her patience faster, but hormones didn't account for other times. She was plain angry because someone had screwed up or because someone had chosen not to listen to her orders.

Leah shook the upsetting thoughts away and made a bee line to the front desk where a young woman, almost a teenager, was buttoning on a keyboard with a vengeance. At the same time, she was answering the calls that came through the headset she had perched over her thick purple hair.

Once she reached the reception desk, the detective cleared her throat to make their presence noted. Mark stopped right behind her and his emotions assaulted her. She became aware that the young woman mesmerized him.

The receptionist took her eyes off her monitor for a second and offered them a smile that could have rivaled Sybil's.

Leah didn't need to bother and read Mark's thoughts or feelings to know what he was thinking. His sudden gasp explained everything.

The man was spellbound. The young woman's freshness and beauty surprised and awed him. Leah had to admit jealously that the woman delivered a serious punch to any man who was still alive.

That favorable impression lasted only one second. The woman gestured to them to wait and returned to her keyboard.

Now, it was Leah's turn to be impressed. She couldn't believe the receptionist's gumption. She just glanced at them, smiled and then returned to her game. Leah was sure she was playing a video game considering how she used that keyboard.

"Miss," the detective called out in a sharp voice and had the pleasure to see the young woman's head snap up. "We don't have the time to wait for you to finish that game," she continued harshly.

The receptionist narrowed her eyes but didn't reply. She pushed the keyboard aside and with a cold smile now, she asked, "What can I do for you?"

Leah noticed that her willingness to help had turned as cold as the Arctic, yet she didn't care. She didn't care for the tinges of disappointment that came from Mark either. He wasn't supposed to make conquests during work hours anyway.

"We need to speak to Daniel Alekseyev," the detective replied with clipped words. The sunlight reflected in her green-bluish eyes and highlighted her coldness.

Still, Leah and Mark had to admire the receptionist. She didn't seem impressed with the detective's frigid appearance and kept a businesslike attitude.

She matched Leah's cold demeanor and inquired, "Are you having an appointment?"

The policewoman replied, "No, we aren't. Yet, we don't need one," she added and her smug smirk disconcerted the young woman who seemed baffled for the first time. Leah was positive that no one had ever given her such a reply before.

"How come?" the younger woman retorted with belligerence after only a few seconds of hesitation and her self-confidence earned Leah's respect.

She wouldn't have expected to see such a young individual recover so fast. That girl was something else and Leah made a note to get to know her better if she had the chance. Meanwhile, she dug into her handbag and took out her police ID and badge.

Although the receptionist's sudden curiosity and trepidation were palpable, the only exterior sign of her excitement was a slight dilation in her pupils. She nodded briefly and then she dialed an extension, her eyes always on the two detectives.

"Mr. Alekseyev, the police are here to see you," she said in the most professional tone she could muster and Leah's mouth sketched a smile.

"I understand, sir," the woman replied to something she was told and disconnected the call. She looked at Leah and said, "He'll be downstairs in a couple of minutes. Would you have a seat?" she waved towards the seating area near the far corner of the lobby where the sun played the various colors of the chairs and brightened the floor.

"We'll wait here," Leah responded and leaned onto the front desk bracing herself on an elbow.

She turned her head to the other corner of the lobby where a multitude of potted plants were competing for sunlight. The thought that someone got the things wrong and placed the flowers where the waiting area should have been crossed her mind.

A glance at Mark made her aware that he was trying to make nice with the girl at the front desk but he didn't have too much luck. The young woman had already returned to the game on her monitor and stopped paying attention to them.

Leah mused when she perceived the man's frustration but only for a moment. She reprimanded herself severely.

Lately, she'd been out of sorts somewhat and started taking pleasure in seeing Mark suffer or make mistakes. That wasn't something she should have been comfortable with and she frowned, angry with herself.

She heard the elevator doors open and turned towards the sound just in time to see a casually dressed young man emerge from the elevator. His gait was athletic and showed that the man liked to exercise on a regular basis and keep in shape.

He might have been computer addicted, as his profile implied, yet he still seemed to find time for other things and that spoke of a balanced life regimen.

The lieutenant envied him. She'd never had the ability to balance things. Either she would overdo some or underdo others but she would never get them quite right. She lacked the skill to find the right dose in everything.

Leah also noticed that Daniel Alekseyev took after his mother. The young man had the same white skin set off by disheveled curly black hair. He was looking at her with his mother's hazel and slightly slanted eyes.

Initially, when she saw Klavdiya for the first time, Leah had thought that her negligent hairstyle was the result of long hours of exhausting styling. Now, she wondered if the victim hadn't just been lucky to have been gifted with a willful head of hair which just worked in her favor.

Keeping her eyes on Daniel, she noticed that there were some differences between mother and son, as well. Daniel's chin was square and shadowed by the beginning of a hopeful beard. That detail made him look stronger than Klavdiya. The woman's weak chin didn't recommend her as a strong character in Leah's eyes.

The man's eyes showed concern and worry. Leah knew that she had to tell him what happened and probably shake his world in the process. She didn't enjoy that part of her job but it was hers nonetheless and she took her responsibilities seriously.

Leah, with Mark in tow, walked slowly towards Daniel and extended her hand, "I'm Lieutenant Leah MacKay and this is my colleague, detective Mark Dion."

The man didn't bother to introduce himself. Probably, he thought that they already knew who he was. He shook their hands and a courteous smile fluttered on his lips.

Yet, Leah perceived the tension he tried to hide and she decided not to prolong the unpleasant moment.

"Is there somewhere where we could speak without being interrupted, Mr. Alekseyev?" she asked him with a glance in the direction of the receptionist who conveniently forgot about her game and was eying them with unmasked curiosity.

Daniel tilted his head and seemed to ponder her suggestion for a moment. Then he proposed, "Let's go in one of the meeting rooms on the first floor. No one will disturb us there and it is quiet."

He turned to the woman at the reception and asked her, "Jen, would you verify and see which meeting room is free for the next hour?"

The receptionist replied softly, "Of course, Mr. Alekseyev," and turned to her keyboard. Deftly, she checked the schedule and informed him with a warm smile, "The Willow room is free, sir, for the following couple of hours anyway. Would you like me to reserve it for you?"

"Yes, please, do so. Thank you, Jen," Daniel nodded to her and then he showed them to the elevator.

Leah sensed that he'd have liked to ask questions and tried hard to restrain himself. She also detected that he was somewhat terrified of the answers he'd receive from them. She felt sorry for him but she couldn't alleviate his fears.

After a brief trip in the elevator, Daniel chose to take a right on the corridor. He led them through a maze of cubicles and Leah was convinced that she wouldn't be able to find her way back to the elevator, had he chosen not to show them the way. Even Mark gave signs of confusion and apprehension.

The lively sound of games came from everywhere and all sorts of exclamations enveloped the three people who were advancing across the open floor. Leah's eyebrows shot up at some of the most colored interjections.

"This is one of the testing floors," Daniel explained apologetically. "Don't worry, though, detectives. We won't hear anything from the meeting room. They're soundproof. I mean all meeting rooms are soundproof," he explained further, and Leah could discern the increased tautness in his voice.

It wasn't something they wouldn't encounter on a daily basis when meeting with people the first time. The word *'police'* had that effect on almost everyone. Few kept their composure in such situations.

Both detectives nodded their understanding and continued to follow him closely. None of them wanted to be left behind.

Finally, Daniel Alekseyev stopped in front of a massive door and input a code on the pad mounted on the wall. The door opened with a resonant click and he invited them to enter the room.

Once the door closed behind them, they found themselves in an oasis of tranquility. No sound came from the cubicles shut out beyond that door or from the street that gleamed behind the window panels that covered the entire far wall.

"Nice setting," Mark murmured, and then, glanced quickly at Leah.

Leah guessed that he wanted to check if she'd heard him. He wasn't supposed to be impressed with the layout of the room, but to pay attention to the people involved in the case.

She chose to let it pass though. It seemed quite petty to reproach him such a slight error. It wasn't like she hadn't had enough opportunities to pick on him if she wished.

Daniel invited them to sit in the armchairs framing a conference table. Leah chose a chair across from Daniel and allowed herself a moment to enjoy the feel of the plushy armchairs.

All the way there, she'd feared that she would have to sit in a leather chair and she hated those types of chair in summer, even if there was air-conditioning in the room. They made her think of sweat and she doubted they were hygienic enough. In theory, the cleaning staff should have cleaned them every day, but somehow she doubted they did it.

After they sat down, Daniel looked from a detective to the other and finally found the courage to ask, "What happened?"

His eyes showed genuine distress and Leah sympathized with him. The waves coming from him revealed that he wondered if something was wrong with his wife and she decided to let him know everything at once. She didn't believe in tormenting someone without a good cause.

She knew it wouldn't be easy for him to hear what she had to say. She leaned on the table and braced herself on her elbows.

In her best soothing voice, Leah said, "I'm very sorry, Mr. Alekseyev, but I have to inform you that your mother passed away."

Daniel's distressed gasp filled the quietness of the room. Both Leah and Mark were watching him closely, although they doubted he had anything to do with his mother's murder.

The way she died had been cruel in the extreme. The woman's body was marred with bruises and cuts everywhere, as if a madman had been at work.

The police officers didn't have any reasons to believe that something so serious had happened between mother and son that could have led to such atrocity.

Leah noted that Daniel was fighting back tears and gave him a few more moments to compose himself and to come to terms with the news. It wasn't every day that someone heard such words and was never easy to come to terms with the death of a loved one.

She saw him unconsciously flex his fists on the smooth surface of the conference table. His eyelashes blinked spasmodically and for a moment she did fear he would start crying.

While she understood why he'd do that, she was afraid that she wouldn't know how to calm him and make him answer her questions afterwards.

That was one of the things she always dreaded in such interviews and Mark was of no help there whatsoever. The maximum extent of his help was to pat someone on the back once or twice and even that without too much conviction.

Finally, Daniel composed himself and looked straight into her eyes when he asked in a gruff voice, "What happened? Was she run over or…"

Leah was about to shake her head when she saw Mark do that and she controlled herself. She chose to reply quietly, "No, Mr. Alekseyev. She was murdered last night."

Her words startled him. His eyes widen in shock and his teeth bit into his upper lip. His fingers grabbed the edge of the table with such force that his knuckles turned white.

The extent of distress vibes coming from him made Leah fear that the shock would overwhelm him and he wouldn't be able to help them with anything.

She looked around searching for a solution frantically when she noticed the water cooler in the corner of the room. She nudged Mark discretely.

"Bring him a glass of water," she whispered to him and Mark glanced at Daniel with blank eyes.

Mark needed about a few seconds to understand the lieutenant's request and her reasons. Only then he went to the cooler and filled a glass with water. He brought it back to the table and handed it to Daniel who thanked him in a hushed voice.

The man drank the water in one gulp and then he turned his misty eyes to Leah.

"Who killed my mother?" he asked and Leah noted with satisfaction that his voice sounded stronger. The man had pulled himself together and now they might get somewhere.

"That's what we're trying to find out," she replied and her eyes remained steady on Daniel.

As if he'd felt some kind of blame in her words, he straightened up. "I didn't kill my mother, detective," he retorted in a cold voice and his Russian accent, which had been barely perceptible when the detectives made his acquaintance, became heavier. "I hope you do have other suspects besides me," he added sharply and the implication of his words was clear.

Leah perceived a hint of sarcasm in the man's voice and wasn't sure how to take it.

"Right now, everyone is a suspect," she replied always calm. "I know that the law says that everyone is innocent until proven guilty, but I have to shift the wheat from the chaff and that's not such an easy task."

Her words seemed to have enough impact on Daniel because he nodded his agreement. "What now?" he asked.

"Now, I will ask you about your relationship with your mother," the detective replied and leaned back in her armchair and laid her hands in her lap as if she'd been getting ready to hear a bedtime story.

Daniel took a few moments to answer and then he began, his eyes fixed on a point in a distance, "We used to have a good relationship… Always… She wasn't a very strict mother and her rules were easy to follow… She always encouraged me to be independent, responsible…," he reminisced.

"Yet, something happened," Leah intervened.

The man looked at her and nodded hesitantly. He seemed somewhat reluctant to explain, but her dogged expression gave no quarter.

"I met my wife in high-school… Ninth grade… She wasn't Russian…"

"Was that a problem for your mother?" Mark asked but Daniel shook his head.

"No, she wasn't interested in that. She accepted that Biskane[1] was part of the First Nations. She didn't have any qualms over that. She liked her just fine…" he reaffirmed and then he paused.

Leah saw that he struggled with something and nudged him gently, "If you have something to say, you'd better say it… We'll find out anyway…"

"Oh, it's not that," he waved her concern away. "I was just thinking… I don't want you to judge my mother too harsh but… I suppose there's no other way," he continued and rubbed the root of his nose with his thumb and forefinger.

Leah felt Mark's eyes on her and turned to him. He looked like a man wanting to say something but she stopped him with a slight shake of her head.

---

[1] Biskane – Burning fire – traditional name for First Nations (Anishinaabe)

She needed Daniel to continue his ideas at his own pace. Along the time, she found out that sometimes interrupting someone's thoughts didn't necessary bring light in a specific matter.

"Appearances played an important role in my mother's perceptions," he said firmly, glancing from one detective to the other. "If a woman was beautiful, my mother would consider her worthy… It didn't matter if that woman was stupid or greedy or… whatever," he clarified and shrugged his shoulders. "My wife, Biskane, is very beautiful," he stated very matter of fact. "When I laid my eyes on her for the first time, she took my breath away," he confessed with a whimsical smile and gesticulated with both hands.

Leah sensed that he felt a little embarrassed but she started to like the man. He seemed real and grounded enough, which was astounding for such a young fellow.

"My mother simply beamed when I brought Biskane at home and introduced her. She was proud that people would see me hand in hand with such a beautiful girl… We were in the ninth grade as I said before…" he tried to gather his thoughts and focused on the wall behind Leah for a few moments.

"My wife is not very tall, detectives," he felt compelled to say, "but she's been blessed with a perfect body and that from early adolescence. Round where it was meant to be round, narrow waist, long legs… Her hair is ink-black, long and shiny. Her cheekbones are high and slightly wide. She is very easy going and in general, she has a happy disposition… It takes a lot to anger her or to see her sad… At the time, I didn't need anything more, of course," he confessed, his thoughts far away. "I was just a teenager controlled by hormones..."

He kept silent for more than a minute but Leah didn't want to interrupt his process of reasoning. Exactly when she became afraid that Mark might intervene, Daniel turned back to them and continued with his story, "After a while, I also noticed that she was smart and kind... I saw that she worked hard... It became evident to me that she wanted to do something with her life – her parents were poor, you see, and her people had been through rough times... I imagine everyone knows that... But she was determined and... And that is something I appreciate in people... And I appreciated the same thing in my mother as well, although I knew that she was frivolous and stuck on appearances most of the time..."

When Daniel stopped again and closed his eyes, Leah understood that he needed some time to recollect. She glanced at Mark and almost smiled when she saw that he was riveted on the story and couldn't take his eyes from Daniel.

Daniel licked his dry lips and Mark immediately jumped out of the chair and brought him another glass of water without needing to be prompted. The man thanked him profusely and then drank every drop of water before he started talking again.

"I moved in with Biskane when I turned eighteen. I'd been working for three years already and even though I started with a few hours part-time, my boss saw some potential in me and gave me more and then more... He pushed me to go to the Toronto Film School and study video game design and animation. He paid for my school, which spared me from taking loans and I was also able to save money from what he paid, and he paid well. When I turned eighteen, I already had a few thousands in savings and investments. He kept promoting me and in not even six years, I'm leader to a design team and I make more than my mother did after almost twenty years… Anyways, after Biskane and I moved together, she started making plans to continue her education, as well. She wanted to become a paralegal and she found out that she could get a loan from OSAP for that. However, I knew that I would marry her one day. I'd known that for a few years already and I didn't want her to be overwhelmed by debt once she finished school so I paid for her tuition. That made sense to me but that was what set my mom up. She was angry and accused… she was very mean to Biskane… She told me that her parents should pay for her school… I pointed out that she didn't pay for mine and that Biskane and I were living together… She fought back dirty… She said that Biskane lived with me only because I made more money than she did and… to be honest, I didn't like it… I told her to get lost… I loved my mother, detectives, but she'd become vicious and unrelenting at the time and… I thought that… if that was what she thought about me and about the woman I wanted to marry… I didn't see the point to waste my time talking to her…," he concluded and looked down at the table top.

Leah saw the lines formed at the corners of his mouth and understood that the man controlled himself only because of his sheer will.

She glanced at Mark and almost burst out laughing. He was so caught in the story that he didn't even blink. He looked like a baby owl and maybe that was the first time that she'd felt something close to tenderness for him.

"That happened three years ago, I understand," Leah told Daniel when the silence stretched too long and he nodded.

"Have you two been at odds ever since?"

"No," he shook his head. "We didn't talk for a few months but got back to normal afterwards... Well, almost normal. There was a strain in our interactions and I knew that it would always be there... I suppose I couldn't forget what she'd said and she couldn't forgive me because I'd cast her away... Ironic enough," Daniel mused, "Biskane and my mother have been the best friends ever since we made up. The strain was just between the two of us..."

"And that was the extent of the dissension between the two of you?" the lieutenant asked and, at the same time, she leaned forward and opened her handbag quietly. She took her iPad out and put it on the table.

Daniel hesitated a moment but then he decided to be as open as possible. He shook his head and said, "No, it wasn't... As I said, detective, my mother was somewhat trapped in appearances. When I turned sixteen, she decided that her time had just come and that she needed someone. So, she looked around. I didn't say anything at the time because I didn't think it was my place, but she was looking only at men that showed a good front. You know the type, good clothes, stylish haircut, appearance of means..."

Both Leah and Mark approved. They'd seen that type, both female and male, and not only once in their line of work.

"She found one and he moved with us quite fast, in my opinion. It was a matter of a couple of weeks… Then, we understood why. The man owned a few suits and a lot of arrogance. Nothing more. He'd just been fired, although he dressed that up. He explained that he intended to start his own business and that was why he'd left his previous employer. While mother could be infatuated with a good-looking man who knew how to dress, she wasn't willing to pay for his expenses. She intended to find someone who would pay for hers. So, that relationship died fast enough. Within other two weeks he was out of the house and I didn't have to say a thing to move the things along."

"Were there bad feelings on his side?" Leah asked.

"Somewhat, yes, I think," Daniel said reluctantly. "For about a year afterwards, we would have the occasional phone call, especially if the guy drank something before. He would shout and swear. In the end, my mother changed the phone number and the calls ended."

"I think I'd like his full name," Leah observed and turned on her iPad.

"I think his name was Iuri Grigoriev," he answered pensively. "Yes, that was… Russian, of course… For a while we were afraid he was involved with Russian mafia… You know, with all the movies and the press…," he gestured and a sad smile appeared on his lips.

Both Leah and Mark smiled back. Sometimes, imagination got the best in people. Yet, they had to check that Iuri and Leah made a note in her iPad.

"Did she give up finding someone?" Mark intervened.

"No, she didn't, but she didn't find a suitable man until about a year ago... Maybe a little more... Or that was what she thought at the time. This one matched her requirements to the *'t'*, with one exception," Daniel explained and rubbed his hands, a sign of anguish in Leah's book.

"What was the exception?" Mark asked again.

"He had a good job and had inherited a lot of money. He was a snap dresser. Yet, he was very stingy. When they moved together, my mother expected him to pay for everything and pamper her. That didn't happen. She had to cajole every cent out of his pocket. Still, she hoped he would marry her and then she would have access to his money..."

Daniel stood up and went to the cooler and poured himself another glass of water. He drank it there, right next to the cooler and after he sipped the last drop, he quashed the plastic cup in his fist and threw it into the bin next to the cooler. He seemed to hesitate a moment and smoothed his hair slowly to buy some time.

Leah sensed that he didn't feel comfortable with the part that followed and that was why she allowed him to take his time and find the most appropriate words. She didn't see that she would gain anything by rushing him.

The man had been open enough and she read him like an open book. He was very straightforward, although he had some remorse now and then whenever he revealed unpleasant things about his mother.

Daniel returned to the table with heavy steps and sat down. That agile gait of his was long forgotten.

He rubbed his hands together and then looked directly into the lieutenant's eyes and said, "I want you to understand and not judge my mother harshly...

Believe me, she doesn't deserve it. If circumstances had been different...," he shrugged helplessly.

He reflected with his eyes on the wall behind Leah and then continued, "I want you to have a clear picture, detectives. My father swept her off her feet in a whirlwind courtship during the summer when she graduated from high-school. Before that time, my grandparents had restricted her outings severely and she hadn't been allowed to have a boyfriend... She knew nothing of the outside world... She was like a ripe fruit ready to pluck... My father did the plucking," he observed and grimaced with dismay. "They were married in less than a month, despite my grandparents' opposition. My mother was extremely passionate and dramatic about her love and she wouldn't be deterred... They had to relent and let her marry because they were afraid that she would harm herself. Anyway, she was already at age and they couldn't do much... My parents lived together for about five years until she found out he had been cheating on her with every single woman in their circle. He'd slept with her best friends and even with two of her cousins... And the cheating part had started right after the '*I dos*' were spoken... You can imagine that she was... devastated... The cheating was bad enough, you see," he said and gesticulated widely, a sign of his agitation. "Worse was how she found out... They were having a party... My mother had worked hard in the kitchen and on decorations... She had wanted him to be proud of her... One of the women got drunk, very drunk. Almost out of her mind... Too much vodka, I suppose... She was mad at my father. He'd just replaced her with a new conquest and she revealed everything in front of everybody and pointed her finger to all the women present at the party and who'd slept with my father… My mother was livid. She was ashamed and hurt and humiliated. She asked my father to leave that very evening… Actually she asked him after a huge show with lots of broken dishes, yelling and name-calling, head-bashing and hair-pulling… It was a big bash as there were many people involved… Women that passed through my father's bed… Men that found out that they'd been cuckolded… They had about thirty guests, I think. Anyway, the neighbors called the police to settle things down… All their friends abandoned her afterwards… Although I don't know if she could call those people friends… Anyway, he got the friends in the divorce, but she took her revenge. She asked for every single piece of common property and managed to get everything. She didn't leave a spoon behind."

"That's what your mother told you?" Mark asked curious. He knew that divorced parents never told the entire truth.

"No," Daniel shook his head. "I heard a few things at the time. They registered in my mind even though I didn't understand them. I asked my grandmother and she told me everything. Her story was darker than what I've just told you but it's understandable, I think… Of course, later on, I confronted my father during one of the vacations I spent back home, and he confessed… he was older and more mature at the time, although he still found it appropriate to cheat on his new wife…," Daniel shook his head in incomprehension. "Anyway, my point is that my mother worked hard to raise me… She was a good mother… A very good mother… She understood me, taught me to take care of myself, boosted my ambition… Actually, I'm here today because she pushed me to do something with my life… But she was alone. For almost two decades… Not easy for a young woman… Now she wanted companionship, someone who would care for her…"

"And that man you were talking about, didn't offer that to your mother?"

"From what I heard – my mother confessed a lot of things to Biskane, you see, he offered some companionship and was a good lover," Daniel said and blushed.

Leah imagined that it wasn't easy for a man to talk about his mother in that specific context.

"Yet, he cared only about himself and his money. If she'd pushed and made him go shopping with her, she'd have found herself in the situation of paying for everything at the cash register. He would say that he didn't need more than a tomato that evening, for instance. Once, he took her to a restaurant… I remember that she called me excited. She thought he'd changed…," he said and a painful smile flourished on his lips. "At the end of the meal he asked the waiter to bring two bills at the table and instructed her to pay for her dinner… She avoided going out to a restaurant with him afterwards… And they were living together, in her house, for which she paid the rent and all the other expenses…" he explained bitterly.

Yes, Leah thought, that guy sounded like an angel. Just the kind of man to bring home and introduce to your mamma and plan a huge wedding with.

"Anyways, she was alone and he provided some companionship," he concluded. "He didn't mind her shouting and reproaches… He even introduced her to his family and his mother, father and three sisters seemed to adore her… Sometimes she thought that they pushed so much for the continuation of that relationship because George, that was his name, George Alder, didn't have a good track with his relationships. He'd been married for half a year when he was young and all his love affairs lasted less than a month…"

Daniel stopped and looked down at his hands. The silence stretched and the tension in the room itched on Leah's skin.

It touched all of them but Mark was the first to break the quietness, "And what happened next?"

Daniel glanced at him, shrugged and only then replied, "They were together for several months. She was involved in all the Alders' gatherings… That was how everything started, in fact…," he added pensively.

"What started?" Mark inquired again.

"She attended a few picnics, parties, Christmas… You name it… She began to have feelings for George's elder sister's spouse… He courted her secretly… They would meet for a chat in a coffee shop or for a walk in a park. Of course, he skillfully avoided the places where they would meet an acquaintance… He would tell her how unhappy he was and how domineering Lydia turned out to be. She had the control of the money – well, it was hers, so…," Daniel gesticulated to drive his point home.

Mark nodded his agreement and Leah grinned.

Daniel resumed his story, "Anyways, after a while, he came forward and told her that he'd decided to leave Lydia, George's sister, because he loved my mother and couldn't live without her… By that time, mom had thoroughly fallen in love. He lacked money and she didn't care. She believed that their paychecks would make a good living for both of them... That was... astonishing to say the least. I'd never thought I would hear my mother say something like that, detectives...," he shook his head.

He still couldn't believe that radical change in his mother's opinions.

"Anyway, she believed him when he said that he wanted to be with her, and she went straight home and asked George to leave. She told him that their relationship ended."

"How did George take the separation?" Leah asked beating Mark to the punch line. She had the satisfaction to see his mouth tighten in a line.

"Not very well, at first," Daniel admitted. "He didn't believe her and refused to budge. I understand that he merely sprawled on the sofa and started watching TV. Mother got ballistic... She had a temper if someone got on her nerves... She stormed into the bedroom and within half an hour she had all his things packed in bags. She dragged everything outside the apartment and left the bags in the hall of the building. All the while, George watched her with wide and incredulous eyes. Then, he started shouting and pleading, but she wouldn't budge... She told Biskane that she'd finally fallen in love again. It took her over twenty years but she did... She was so infatuated that she didn't even stop to consider the consequences of her decisions...," Daniel shook his head in disbelief.

Leah could feel that his mother's behavior still shocked him and she deduced that there must have been something more to the story.

"It didn't stop there, did it?" she inquired.

"No, it didn't," the man admitted in a tired voice. He rubbed his forehead and continued, "Gareth, that's the guy's name, started visiting mom. He would bring flowers and small gifts. He would take her shopping…"

Daniel stopped and shook his head again. He closed his eyes for a few seconds, and then, he trained his eyes on Leah. His eyes seemed suddenly older and tired.

"He bought her everything she wanted. Yet, for that, he used Lydia's money. He didn't have too much on his own name. He had a job, but that was all… He kept saying that he would leave Lydia, but something intervened all the time. Mom knew that Lydia was bipolar and went off the tangent if things didn't happen the way she wanted, and in a way, she understood Gareth's reluctance in telling her the truth. At the same time, she wanted him with her… Biskane tried to reason with mother and asked her what would happen if Gareth indeed left Lydia because he wouldn't have the same financial means. That would mean that all the gifts and the shopping and their outings would cease… Mother didn't care. He was like a poison for her, and I couldn't stop thinking that it wasn't moral. She was doing to that woman what others had done to her… And that woman was close to a sister-in-law somehow," he concluded and took a break. He stared at the far wall and licked his cracked and dry lips.

"Would you like some more water, sir?" Mark asked solicitously.

"Yes, thank you," Daniel replied and rubbed his face with his palms.

Mark returned to the table with another paper cup full with water and handed it to Daniel. The man had scarcely sipped from the cup when his cell phone, which she kept in his pocket, rang. He took it out and glanced at the name on the screen.

"It's my wife," he told the detectives. "May I answer?"

"Yes, of course," Leah approved with a wave of her hand.

"Hey, sweetie," Daniel said and his voice sounded very tired in Leah's ears.

She wondered what Biskane thought of that.

"I think we could meet for lunch then, yes," he responded to something his wife said. "All right, then. See you in an hour," he ended the conversation and then glanced at Leah. "I know I reacted presumptuously, but I don't think we need more than an hour to finish this discussion," he said gesticulating suddenly unsure of himself.

"Probably not," Leah admitted. "What happened next?"

"Well, my mother started saying that she couldn't live without him, which she maintained even two days ago… She would have days when she couldn't think of anyone or anything else but Gareth… Gareth kept promising he would tell the truth to Lydia and move in with mom. It never happened… Though Lydia found out. How, I don't know, but a month ago she came to my mother's building and put on a… let's say, interesting show. No one will forget her soon, I guarantee. The police were called… She attacked the front desk guy… She repeatedly clobbered him over the head with her handbag… I heard that she had so many things inside that bag that it felt like bricks… And then she waited for my mother… Mom hadn't come from work yet… When she arrived, Lydia screeched like a lunatic and hit my mother, as well. She tried to scratch her eyes out… She called her names… She even warned her to stay away from her spouse… You know, it's ironic. Gareth had already told my mother that he had to move on and that he couldn't be with her. He'd decided to go back to Lydia exactly that morning. … Biskane and I expected that…He wasn't the type of man who could live without Lydia's money…. She pampered him… The woman would have bought the moon in the sky for him if he'd wanted to."

"Was that the end of the affair?" Leah asked.

"Yes, it was, as far as I know… I know she pinned on him and had days when she couldn't get out of bed… We worried because she showed signs of deep depression… Suddenly, two days ago she told Biskane that she would go to a party with a guy she'd met at the beginning of the week. My wife implored her to be careful because mom didn't know too much about the man. They'd seen each other only twice before his invitation but mom shushed her concerns and assured her that everything would be fine. She said… something on the lines that her life was back on track again…"

"Did you hear anything from her yesterday?" Mark asked.

He shook his head. "We celebrated our one-month anniversary this weekend. We left for Niagara Falls on Friday and returned early this morning. None of us was in contact with anyone before this morning… It was something we decided some time ago… At least once a month to take the time to be just the two of us…," he explained with a nostalgic smile and the detectives smiled back.

The idea of spending some time in isolation in order to reconnect seemed perfect to Leah. She began to reconsider her initial opinion about the couple's marriage.

"Well," she said, "if you give us Gareth's name as well, we can leave you alone," she concluded.

She noted the name down, next to Lydia's and gathered her things. Mark stood up and started towards the door. When he put his hand on the door handle, he frowned and turned back.

"Would you show us the way to the elevator, Mr. Alekseyev?" he asked while Leah pretended to look for something in her bag. She didn't want him to see her grin.

"Of course," Daniel rushed forward and opened the door for them. "It is the company's policy, anyway," he smiled at them but his smile didn't reach his eyes. "No visitors are allowed on the floors without an employee in tow."

"They would get lost probably," Mark mumbled and Daniel glanced at him.

"I think you're right," he replied but didn't continue on that line.

He led the way to the elevator and once he pushed the ground floor button, he asked, "When can I see my mother?"

"Whenever you want," Leah replied softly and touched his arm. "Although, maybe it's better if you called beforehand," she added. "You understand that we have to do an autopsy," she tried to ease him to the idea.

Daniel glanced away but replied in a harsh voice, "I understand, detective, and I support anything that's necessary to catch my mother's killer."

CHAPTER 5 – COFFEE, COOKIES AND AN AUTOPSY REPORT

That morning, Leah opened the door to her office in a huff and threw her blasted handbag on the desk with dismay. God, she hated plodding around with that bag but she couldn't do without.

The small pockets of her cotton pants wouldn't hold many things and the heat wave which stubbornly baked Toronto for the third day in a row didn't allow her to wear anything but a flimsy blouse and cotton pants. Wearing a jacket was out of question.

She plopped into her chair and turned her computer on. She rubbed her eyes to dislodge the sand that grazed her eyeballs. Her morning cold shower had done little to wipe the cobwebs from her eyes and brain.

She knew that she was testy that morning but she couldn't help it. Three days had already passed since they found the victim and they'd put in a lot of overtime.

And yet, she didn't have any positive results to show for all the efforts they'd made so far.

Leah pulled up the coroner's report on the screen and started to read it again. She had enough time to review it once more as her team wasn't there yet. They weren't supposed to come until eight and she had forty-five minutes until then.

The coroner had turned the autopsy report in the day before, and Leah's mind was still baffled by what she'd read. Besides, she was very dissatisfied with herself and her empathic perceptions.

It would have been easier if she had found out the name of the killer when she touched a corpse but it didn't work that way. She would catch only a glimpse of the victim's more persistent thoughts and feelings. She would read the vibes that defined that person, but nothing more. Only rarely could she sense something more.

Maybe if she'd refined her gift, she would have been able to sense more, she thought bitterly, her lips pursed. A frown formed between her eyebrows.

Absent-mindedly, she snatched a cookie from one of the baskets she'd restocked the day before. She munched on it and reflected that anyway, she'd been too intent on leaving her family's legacy behind and that was why she hadn't thought clearly at the time.

When she finally realized that her gift would help her even in the profession she'd chosen, it was too late. She didn't have the time to undergo all the training and conditioning she'd been supposed to do when she was younger.

Worse yet, this time around, she hadn't even succeeded to catch important things, she admonished herself with annoyance while she skimmed through the report. Like the fact that Klavdiya had been three-months pregnant at the time of the murder or that the police should look for at least three men.

The DNA tests revealed that three men had been at the scene, although the profiles were not complete. The three men had left behind minute traces of their genetic code but, at least, they did leave something. If they found them, they'd have some forensic evidence to nail them.

The victim had been raped repeatedly and yet the coroner couldn't find any semen inside her. The men hadn't had the courtesy to leave their genetic material behind, she grimaced with disgust.

Leah didn't like the killers that thought ahead and made her job more difficult. She had a strong animosity towards the ones she had to apprehend now. Their brutality had shocked even the coroner's assistant.

The traces that the technicians managed to analyze came from the skin retrieved from underneath Klavdiya's nails and from the residual trace of saliva recovered from one of the bites on her right breast. The culprit had taken care to wipe his saliva afterwards, but his teeth had burrowed deep enough into the skin and some traces of saliva remained lodged inside the wound.

Besides the DNA traces proving the presences of at least three males at the crime scene, the doctor also indicated that three blades had been involved in the systematic stabbing of the victim.

He'd analyzed the depth and shape of the wounds, as well as the angles at which the blades had penetrated the body and proved that three different types of knives contributed to the mosaic of cuts scattered all over Klavdiya's body. He even provided some sketches in case that the police officers had the opportunity to seize the knives.

The depth of the stabbings also showed different strengths, as well as some hesitation in inflicting the wound in some cases. The doctor's report explained how he had reached the conclusion that one of the attackers was left-handed and definitely reluctant to inflict pain.

Perusing the report, Leah appreciated again that the coroner's report was succinct and to the point. Leah had expected as much from Dr. Connelly. He never strayed from the facts and rarely offered any kind of suggestions.

The coroner preferred the cold and precise narrative of science and didn't think it was his place to tell the police officers what to do. That was always a nice change from the other coroners.

Satisfied that she hadn't forgotten any details, Leah closed the file and opened the list with Mr. Papadopoulos' guests, but then she glanced at her watch and saw that it was 7:30. Now she could find some coffee in the squad kitchenette.

Nimbly she stood up and snatched her cup off the desk. She rushed out the door and hurried to the kitchenette.

Sure enough, Nadine, the cleaning lady, had already started making a pot of coffee. She wasn't anywhere in sight but the smell of the Colombian coffee filled Leah's nostrils and her step became livelier.

She camped next to the coffee maker and waited for the last drop to drip into the carafe. At the same time, her foot tapped on the floor and her fingers drummed the rim of the cup.

Her mornings were coffee-fueled and her neuropaths needed their periodical charge of caffeine if she wanted to get results.

The brown liquid seemed to drip forever. Leah tapped her foot some more, whistled a merry tune, and even counted the chocolate bars lined on one of the officers' desk, which she could see through the glass panel of the kitchenette. For a tiny second, she thought of going and grabbing a chocolate bar, but her common sense prevailed.

Through the chocolate-hazed cloud which fogged her mind, she heard the hiss announcing the end of the coffee-making cycle.

That beloved sound almost brought tears in her eyes. Leah was a big girl though and had some self-restraint. She was content to fill her cup to the rim and turned back to her office. Now her step was subdued because she kept taking a sip now and then from the hot liquid.

The list with Mr. Papadopoulos' guests was always on the screen and she dropped into the chair with a groan.

They'd sifted through the people on that damn list for hours and they still had a few more to investigate.

Until then they hadn't uncovered anything useful and their investigation advanced at a snail's pace. They'd encountered lots of faces and haughty glances but nothing to steer them in the right direction.

The only thing that shed some light on the case was the vague description of the man who had led Klavdiya into the garden.

Two matrons had seen them leaving together but they hadn't recognized him. They said that he definitely wasn't from their circle. They described him but their description was sketchy at best. It could have been any tall well-dressed man with a bulky frame. The officers asked the others if they were acquainted with a man corresponding to that portrayal but no one seemed to be sure.

Leah helped herself to another cookie and sipped from her coffee pensively. She was positive that they hadn't encountered any of the suspects.

She might not have been as expert in reading the people as her mother for instance, still she'd have caught a vibe to put her on the right track. She hadn't sensed anything like that.

She nibbled on her cookie and started on a new list. There were only ten people left on the original list and she put five down for Anna and Josh and the others for Mark and herself. She kept on her list the two that hadn't gone to the party and hadn't even bothered to excuse themselves from their host.

CHAPTER 6 – AXEL IS CAUGHT IN THE LINE OF FIRE

Leah balanced her bag on her shoulder and muttered under her breath. She wiped the sweat off her forehead and glanced at the sky. Still no cloud, damn it.

Everybody had been praying for rain for some time now but the weather didn't give any sign of cooperation. One step out of the car and her skin would feel sticky.

Her blouse stuck to her back and she made efforts to ignore it. Gingerly, she crossed the street towards the coffee shop where she'd sent Mark earlier to order coffee and a light lunch for them while she ran across the street to leave a small gift for her mother. It was her mother's birthday the following day and she didn't know if she would have the time for a quick visit.

Leah attempted to push back the thought that she didn't feel like seeing her mother right then but obstinately it kept coming back and bothering her.

Fed up with her parents' constant nagging about her age and life's opportunities passing her by, she grasped at straws when it came to visiting them. Any kind of pretext worked for her.

Anyway, her exhaustion and bad mood didn't go hand in hand with an evening in their company. Sparks were bound to ignite and she had enough tension in her life right then.

Luck had smiled on the lieutenant. The receptionist had informed her that her mother still had twenty minutes left from her counselling session with a patient and invited her to wait.

Leah had seized the opportunity. She'd declined the invitation and hastily, left the gift at the front desk. She'd asked the woman to present her apologies to her mother.

Faced with the baffled expression of the receptionist, she'd explained that she couldn't stay as she was on duty. She hadn't given her a chance to reply and she'd left the office as fast as she could.

She opened the door to the coffee shop and the cool air inside caressed her heated skin. She breathed deeply. Now, that was a nice change after the stuffy air clinging on people outside and her lungs danced with bliss.

Leah looked around and noticed that Mark had commandeered a corner table where no one would disturb them. She mutely gave him the thumbs up and went to join him.

Mark was woolgathering when she reached the table and he didn't see her. She mischievously waved her hand before his eyes and startled him.

A faint blush powdered the man's cheeks and neck and he sprang to his feet. Leah grinned at him and gestured for him to sit down.

"So, what will I have for lunch?" she asked him merrily and that prompted him to watch her with circumspection.

A merry Leah was a contradiction in terms, especially when she was obsessed with a case and she didn't have a solution. And right then, that was the case and, unfortunately, his reality.

He handed her the sandwich he'd bought and said, "It's salmon. That's what you usually order…"

"Awesome, Mark," she interrupted his explanation with exuberance. "Is this my coffee?" she inquired pointing to one of the cups on the table.

"Yes…," he hesitated waiting for the other shoe to drop. He didn't trust her when she acted so out of character. Leah was stingy with her praises. "Black, no sugar," he thought to add.

Leah thanked him and sipped from her cup, her eyes closing with pleasure. Then she unwrapped her sandwich and inquired, "Have you already eaten?"

Mark nodded. He'd been starving when he got to the shop so he'd already gulped down an entire sandwich in under two minutes. He had to admit that that was a record even for him.

He'd been so famished that he hadn't even thought to wait for Leah. He excused his attitude though. After all, she was the one who'd pushed their lunch break so late.

Leah shrugged and bit daintily into her sandwich. Chewing quietly, she glanced around. The lunch crowd had already disappeared and the noise in the shop had dropped a few decibels.

It worked for her. They still had work to do and they could start discussing the next step right there in the coffee shop.

"So," she said between chews, "we have only one name left on our list and then we have to take a closer look at those Alders and that Grigoriev."

Mark started nodding his agreement, but then stopped. "Grigoriev's dead," he thought to inform her.

Leah sat straighter, wiped her mouth with a napkin and asked, "How do you know that?"

Mark fidgeted in his chair under her inquisitive look but mumbled, "I checked him out."

"Good…What made you do that? Usually I have to push you hard to do something. It's not like you to take the initiative," she observed and thought that probably that was the reason that she'd been promoted before him. The man had a couple of years more than her in the force and logically he should have been promoted.

"That mafia thing," he replied his eyes steady on the table. He didn't feel like facing Leah's sarcasm.

A smile lit Leah's face. That made sense, at least. That mafia reference must have piqued his curiosity and Mark couldn't resist something like that.

"All right, Mark, well done," she shocked him with her words as her praises were few and far between. "How did he die?" she asked.

Mark didn't react to her question immediately. Her approval had caught him unaware and he was still mulling over her words.

She lifted her right brow and that made him answer in a haste, "He was killed six months ago."

Leah waited for more forthcoming information and then sighed. She had to pull it out of him.

"How was he killed, Mark?" she asked patiently.

Her tone showered Mark with cold water and he finally understood that he was supposed to give her more details.

"He was stabbed one night, on the Harbour Front. No witnesses, no clues… The case is still unsolved."

"Where exactly on the Harbour Front?" Leash asked in an edgy voice.

She was close to slapping him silly. Patience wasn't her strong suit.

"Behind that building with the dog's exhibition… I don't remember the name," he shook his head.

"So, he was stabbed less than forty meters from Klavdiya's apartment and you didn't bother to mention it," Leah observed in a voice that chilled Mark to the bone.

"I… I hadn't made the connection," he confessed. "But she couldn't have killed him, could she?" he asked and his eyes bulged, ready to pop out of his head. Mark was smart enough to understand how some things occured and why.

Leah pierced him with her eyes. No, she didn't think that Klavdiya would have bothered to kill the man. The detective imagined that the woman had forgotten about Iuri immediately after she'd discarded him like yesterday's news.

However, the location of the crime made it a too flagrant coincidence and she was compelled to check it further.

"All right, Mark, listen here. Until I finish my lunch and drink my coffee, you call the office and ask that the file related to Iuri's murder is sent to me. I want it in my office this afternoon. You'll also call Anna or Josh and ask them to gather all possible information about Lydia Alder and that spouse of hers, Gareth, but also about George Alder and his father. Have you got that?" she asked icily.

Mark nodded and started making the calls under her glacial eyes. He tried to keep his composure but the slight trembling of his fingers gave him away. Leah's heart tightened noticing his distress but unfortunately, Mark needed a good nudge now and then.

The lieutenant continued munching on her sandwich and, at the same time, she surveyed the detective following her orders. When she finished the last morsel, she wiped her mouth with the napkin that Mark had left on her side of the table and sipping from her coffee, she checked the notes she'd made on her pad.

The last name on their list was Axel Arnett, one of the two people who hadn't bothered to honor Mr. Dimitri Papadopoulos' party with their presence or to excuse themselves.

The first one, a Mr. Tremblay, had been called back to Montreal where he had business and he'd been in such a rush to get there that he didn't have the time to let Mr. Papadopoulos know about his departure. They'd verified and indeed the man had left two days before the crime and never returned.

Arnett lived in one of the exclusive condos on the waterfront. Whether irony, coincidence or fate, his building was not far from Klavdiya's or from the spot where Iuri Grigoriev's torso made the acquaintance of the sharp end of a blade.

The lieutenant's fingers itched with impatience when she read Arnett's name. She sensed that she needed to meet him and as soon as possible. Her anxiety increased a notch, as well as her wish to leave immediately.

She waited for Mark to end his phone conversations and then she signaled him that it was time to go.

When they walked out of the shop they had the feeling that they'd stepped directly into an oven. It was a short distance to Leah's car but the heat almost liquefied their cells. Leah expected to melt any moment now.

Worse, her restlessness amplified and rushed through her veins. She felt compelled to become acquainted with that Mr. Arnett as soon as possible and she disliked the sensation.

Their drive to the waterfront was uneventful, but tedious, and the lieutenant's patience was frayed. Mark kept stealing glances at her trying to assess her mood and that got on her nerves. Still, she couldn't just ask him not to look at her or to control fretting like a scared chicken.

Leah found a spot to park her car at a short distance from the building and braved the heat and humidity with a determined stride.

She didn't look at Mark as she was still upset with him. His indolence rarely jeopardized a case, but chafed at her all the same.

Mark quietly followed her, his eyes on a sail that flirted with the horizon. The knowledge that he'd screwed up big time nudged at him and made him feel uncomfortable in the lieutenant's company.

***

Sleep was like a love affair for Axel. There were days when he couldn't get enough of it and days when he couldn't run away fast enough.

That day, he'd succumbed to slumber in the wee hours of the morning and he was still blissfully asleep when the front desk called and told him that some police officers were there asking for him.

He scowled and rubbed his eyes. He slid his tongue over his teeth and grimaced.

He pictured the round face of the woman with catlike eyes. He felt threatened somewhat and knew that he had strong reasons for that.

He'd sensed something from her that morning when the police were at the crime scene. Her abilities hadn't been very clear at the time, yet he'd known that he had to remove himself from her proximity.

Apparently, he hadn't removed himself fast enough because she was there now, in his lair, he scowled again. Few people stepped inside his personal space. With a sigh, he asked the reception guy to let them come upstairs.

He couldn't refuse to see them. Their suspicions would have increased tenfold and he would have been called to the police station anyway. Delaying the inevitable wasn't in his nature.

Axel knew that they needed a few minutes to get to his condo and took the time to brush his teeth and pull a pair of pants on.

He'd just grabbed a shirt when he heard the knock on the door and frowned. He'd have liked to be more suitably dressed when they arrived. Clothes were a good armor sometimes. With his shirt in hand, he went to the door and opened it.

Leah's eyes fell on the chest displayed before her eyes and for a few seconds, she just stared. The detective wasn't fond of men that built their body religiously in the gym, but this specimen was something else, and she had a hard time taking her eyes off him.

With effort, she pulled herself together and looked up into the charcoal eyes that burnt on the angular face framed by raven thick hair.

She didn't fail to notice the ironic smile that claimed the corner of the man's mouth. His smile was crooked and gave her the impression that he was mocking her. She narrowed her eyes and her lips pursed.

The man didn't say anything and averted his eyes from hers carefully. He bowed his head in greeting and then stepped aside and waved them inside the apartment.

He closed the door behind them and, like an afterthought, he put his shirt on, but didn't bother to button it. It wasn't as if he hadn't already offered them a show for free and he wasn't very modest.

Axel showed them into his living room, which was almost Spartan. Besides a leather sofa, an armchair and an uncluttered coffee table, nothing else was in plain sight. Even the TV-set was unceremoniously mounted on the wall opposite the sofa but if one didn't look specifically for it, they wouldn't have noticed it.

Apparently, the man didn't care for showing off his means. Leah knew that he had a sizable bank account and several other assets.

The detectives sat down on the black leather sofa although Leah wasn't very comfortable with the idea of sitting there.

The entire scene seemed somewhat unreal. No one had said anything since the moment Axel opened the door. Everything unfolded in complete silence. Mark felt like he was part of the cast in a mute black and white movie and the feeling was unsettling to say the least.

After the officers sat down, Axel headed to the kitchen and, on his way there, he spoke for the first time and asked, "What would you like to drink detectives? I imagine you wouldn't want a beer or a whiskey, as you're on duty, but maybe you'd like a pop."

The sound of his voice startled Leah. She'd listened to the emergency call which the police received in relation to Klavdiya's death. She'd done so repeatedly and she would recognize that voice anywhere and anytime. She had no doubt that it belonged to Axel.

She jumped up ready to go after him and saw his retreating back. From that angle she also recognized the silhouette of the man she'd seen in Mr. Papadopoulos' garden.

Now she understood why she couldn't sense anything from him when he opened the door. She hadn't sensed anything back there in the garden either.

"I'd like you to come back here," she said loudly to his back. "We don't need refreshments. We only need to talk to you," she added and cringed when she heard the edge in her own voice.

"I'm sure you do," his voice came from the kitchen, and then they heard the noise of glasses clattering on a tray and the refrigerator door open. "That's why you're here, I think," he replied loudly.

Mark might have missed a cue now and then, but this time he knew that something was amiss. He also left his seat and came next to Leah taking a defensive position aside her, and that made her smile. The officer seemed ready to protect her and her heart softened towards him.

Leah remembered that there were moments like that that made her like him and even care for him. Mark might have had his weaknesses but he was loyal and dependable when push came to shove.

Axel returned with a big tray piled up with glasses and pop drinks. He stopped just inside the room surprised to see both standing there ready to jump him.

He glanced from one officer to another. His lips twitched, but after a few seconds, he burst into an explosive laughter.

That puzzled the officers and Mark threw out his chest and asked in a belligerent voice, "What's so funny? I don't get it."

Axel stopped, moved the tray to one hand and wiped his eyes with the other. He hadn't laughed like that in a while.

He shook his head and then went to the coffee table and laid the tray there. Turning to them, he said, "You are… I'm just surprised that you didn't have your pistols in hand. That was what was missing," he added snapping his fingers. "Do I really look like the big bad wolf?" he inquired looking at Leah and not without sarcasm.

"Let's sit down," she said softly. "We do have questions for you and you have to explain a few things, mister," she added with a stony face.

"I'm at your disposal, detective," he replied mockingly. "Of course, I'll answer if I can," he thought to make it clear, and after he took a can with orange juice off the tray, he lounged in the armchair. He didn't bother with a glass but drank directly from it.

The detectives stared at him but that didn't disturb him. To her dismay, Leah didn't sense any kind of tension in him, but she couldn't sense anything anyway. The man was like a blank page. There were no thoughts or feelings into which she could delve and that worried her.

Reluctantly, the detectives sat down on the sofa again. The lieutenant grabbed a cold cola off the tray and followed Axel's example. She chose not to use a glass either and she drank directly from the can.

The cold liquid soothed her parched mouth and throat and she sighed contentedly, closing her eyes for a few seconds. After that she glanced swiftly at the two men afraid that they'd heard her.

Mark was drinking a cola as well and seemed in total bliss, as well. Axel's expression was impenetrable.

"Why did you run away when I saw you at the Papadopoulos' house?" she attacked directly.

"I didn't know you wanted to talk to me, detective," Axel answered unconcerned with her directness. "And I didn't run," he pointed out. "If I remember correctly, and, believe me, I do, I just strolled away. If you wanted to talk to me, you could," he observed and sipped from his can again, but he kept his eyes always trained on Leah.

He'd already dismissed Mark. The guy might have been intelligent and might have known his job, but he didn't represent a danger for Axel. Mark had no ESP gift whatsoever and he didn't have a clue about what Axel could do.

Leah, on the other hand, had danger written all over her. Axel guessed that she had a strong gift. She might not have refined it yet, but she knew to use it. He'd felt that in that garden when she tried to probe his mind and he'd also felt it a few minutes earlier when he invited the police officers into his home.

"That's convenient," she remarked tartly.

"What's convenient, detective?" he asked nonplussed.

If she had a hard time to read his mind, so did he with hers. He admitted that he rather liked that, as he'd never met a woman that he couldn't read.

To know every single thought that passed through someone's head got annoying after a while. There was nothing new to discover and he'd found that the unknown held a certain appeal to him.

Axel had enjoyed many women in his lifetime, but lately, he had become increasingly dissatisfied with his romantic life. In the past, he couldn't put his finger on what displeased him, but now, when he became aware that Leah wasn't an open book for him, he understood that he'd been craving for that. He'd longed for something that everybody had but him: the possibility to unwrap layer after layer of a woman's personality and enjoy every new nuance. That was appealing.

"You're the one who called the emergency line," Leah brought him back from his musing. "I recognized your voice, Mr. Arnett," she thought to mention when she noticed his right eyebrow riding up. "If you insist, we can have your voice compared to the recording," she added with nonchalance.

Axel merely shrugged her suggestion away. He knew it was pointless to deny that he'd made that call. Any test would show a one hundred percent match between his voice and the recording that the police had.

He'd thought of that before calling the police to tell them about the murder, but he couldn't just leave that woman there in that garden and not announce her death. It was a matter of conscience.

"So you don't deny," Leah noted and his nonchalant shrug angered her. "All right, explain," she said sharply.

"I can't explain," Axel replied quietly.

"Oh, yes, you can," she answered back with a tough expression on her face.

Axel considered his options and glanced at Mark for a second. He noticed that the man was baffled by the exchange of replies. He didn't understand what was going on and had the feeling that he was missing something important.

"We haven't been introduced," Axel noted and not without a hint of sarcasm.

Leah felt a pinch of guilt. She'd always observed the correct procedure during interviews and yet, this time, she didn't even tell their names to the man.

"I'm Lieutenant Leah MacKay and this is detective Mark Dion," she pointed to Mark.

Axel nodded politely and observed, "I don't suppose you need my name, though. You already know who I am if you are here."

He didn't get a reply to his assumption. The two detectives were just watching him and the silence grew unnerving.

Axel considered his options and leaned forward, bracing his elbows on his knees and said, "I'll tell you everything, lieutenant. But only to you," he added and threw an apologetic glance to Mark. "I apologize, detective, but this is a conversation I'll have only with your lieutenant. It's not for your ears."

Mark frowned and peeked at Leah. She chewed her lower lip for a few seconds, and then said, "That's highly unorthodox."

Axel merely shrugged and noted, "It might be, I don't care. If you don't accept my condition, I won't say anything. Of course, you could charge me with murder, but you will have a hard time proving it. A phone call can be explained away in a hundred ways anyway, but I suppose you want the truth. You can have it but only if we discuss it alone," he stated his position again in a determined voice and Leah understood that there was no other way to make him talk.

They didn't intimidate him and he had the right to keep silent anyway if he chose to.

She turned to Mark and said, "Mark, why don't you go and have another snack? I think there are several cafes and restaurants around here. Bill me afterwards," she added with a smile. "I'll call you when I finish here."

"But, Lieutenant…," the detective started to protest but Leah stopped him with a gesture.

"It'll be fine, Mark. Now, go…" she steered him out of the apartment.

Axel watched him leave and grinned. The detective seemed very reluctant to leave his colleague behind and his hard eyes promised an ocean of pain to Axel if anything happened to Leah.

CHAPTER 7 – A TEMPORARY ALLIANCE

Once the door closed behind Mark, Leah turned to Axel and barked, "Now talk."

"I see that your empathic skills don't extend to your exterior attitude. Politeness isn't one of your strengths," he remarked.

Leah paled under the masked rebuke but repeated stoically, "Talk."

Axel ran his fingers through his thick hair and standing up walked to the window. He looked at the lake without actually seeing anything and reflected about how to start their discussion. It wasn't an easy choice.

Leah had almost lost her last shred of patience and decided to get mean with him, when he turned back to her and eyed her thoughtfully.

"I don't think we should hedge anymore, lieutenant. I know what you are and you know what I am," he said resolutely and yet, in a quiet voice.

"Yes, you're a psychopath," she replied and his eyes flickered with bewilderment.

"I beg your pardon?" he exploded when he finally found his voice.

Leah shrugged and explained without thinking of how it sounded and the consequences of her admission, "All the signs are there. Lack of emotion, no empathy…"

He stopped her by putting up his hand. He shook his head vehemently but she wasn't sure if he denied her assumption or he couldn't believe she'd accuse him like that. She eyed him suspiciously while he rubbed his forehead and massaged his temples.

"So," he began when he found his words again, "you couldn't read me and that led you to the conclusion that I'm a psychopath," he asked for a clarification.

"I don't know what you mean," she retorted, feigning ignorance and her back tensed.

She wanted to bite her tongue. That bit about psychopathy had just slipped out and she was furious with herself.

His mention about reading him didn't sit very well with her. It frightened her that he could be so accurate about what had happened.

"Leah," he started but now she stopped him by copying his gesture from before.

"Either lieutenant or lieutenant MacKay. We're not friends, Arnett, and I don't fraternize with suspects."

He nodded and grinned sarcastically at her.

"I see, **Lieutenant**," he said. "Well, let me alleviate your fears, then. You have to keep an open mind though or otherwise it won't work," he warned her.

"Just talk, Arnett," she snapped at him and both his eyebrows climbed up his forehead when he heard her tone.

"All right. So, **Lieutenant**, I am aware that you can read people's minds and feelings. I don't know how well you can do that, but you can and don't try to deny it," he stopped her denial when she opened her mouth. "You tried to read me that day in the garden and you couldn't. I left because I was afraid that you'd have been able to if you'd insisted. However, my leaving didn't mean that I was involved in the crime," he admonished her and she scowled at him.

"What's all this crap about reading people's minds? Either you partied too much last night and aren't yourself now or you're not quite all there, Arnett," she observed and not without irony.

Yet, she was scared. She didn't know how he could be so close to the truth. She hadn't done anything until then to lead him to that assumption and he appeared to know everything.

Axel scrutinized her and shook his head in regret. He burrowed his hands in the pockets of his pants and returned to the window.

Leah had the feeling that he'd simply shut her out and bit her lip. She was rattled and didn't know how to react.

It wasn't as if she'd been confronted with such a situation every day. That angered her and she searched for the most biting words she could throw at him.

Yet, she didn't have a chance to do so because he began talking again although his voice sounded tired.

"We are the same, you and I… Or almost the same. You can read minds and feelings, lieutenant. I can read minds but I'm not very attuned to people's feelings," he shrugged as if that lack of his had been insignificant. "But I have visions," he added and turned to face her. "It's not something enjoyable, as you can imagine," he said bitterly.

She opened her mouth to squash his assumption that she had such abilities but he shook his head stubbornly.

"Don't bother," he said. "What's the point?" he opened his arms.

She relented and tilting her head, she observed him attentively.

"You mean to say that you had a vision with the crime and that's why you called," she assumed.

"Yes, that's what I'm saying," he replied harshly. "Actually, everything began while I was sleeping. When I woke up, I wasn't even sure whether I'd had a nightmare or a vision but then I saw the continuation of the events while awake so I had to assume that it was a vision… I know very well my friend's house and garden, so I recognized them and of course, it was easy for me to pinpoint the crime scene," he explained and crossed his arms across his chest.

"Why didn't you go to the party? You were invited," she thought to inquire, as she wasn't very convinced he was telling the truth.

"I didn't feel like it," he shrugged. "Dimitri and I don't care about such niceties, so I didn't bother to excuse myself. Anyways, I knew he'd have enough people there to make up for my absence," he observed with indifference.

Leah stared at him with impassive eyes for a few seconds. She'd have liked to refute his assumptions but she knew very well that skills like his were real. There were a few people in her family who exhibited them and she couldn't deny the validity of his claim. She thought that she'd better put to good use what he'd seen and stopped pretending it was all just balderdash.

"I imagine you saw more than just the body on the ground," she went out on a limb.

He nodded. "Yes, I saw almost everything. I mean I saw the victim flirting with a big man. After some banter, which I couldn't hear but things appeared that way, they went out in the garden. They strolled leisurely until they got to the far end and there he grabbed her and dragged her to the place where you found her. He ripped her blouse – I remember she was thinking about that blouse. It was a symbol for her. It encompassed everything she'd achieved," he explained with large gestures and stopped for a moment.

Axel returned to the armchair and sat down after snatching another can of juice. He tapped the can with practiced efficiency and swallowed all the liquid in short order.

He looked back at Leah and said, "I can't hear what people say in my visions. I see only their lips moving and I have a general feeling about what's what. That's how I know about the flirting, for instance. Yet, I can read their thoughts," he specified. "Like that piece about the blouse… That woman was very fond of it. She really loved that top… At the beginning, she was dismayed because the blouse had been ruined and only afterwards she realized she was in danger…," he shook his head as if he couldn't believe it. "Anyway, the woman was a feisty little thing. She fought that guy and who knows, she might have survived but two more came," he continued with regret.

Axel told her every excruciating detail of the crime he'd witnessed and only when he'd exhausted all the specifics, did he stop talking.

Leah looked at him and saw the signs of tiredness etched on his face. Fine lines had appeared around his eyes and they hadn't been there when they came to see him that afternoon.

"It must have been awful to witness that and feel powerless," she observed quietly.

Axel looked at her and chuckled bitterly, "You have no idea."

He rubbed his face with his palms and continued, "The problem is that I don't know how you can use what I've told you. Yes, you'll have detailed descriptions of the three attackers. At least that much it is true. The problem is that you won't find them in the victim's regular circle. They were hired hands," he pointed out.

"You're sure of that," she asked for confirmation.

"Yes, I am," he restated. "I've told you that I can read thoughts even if I can't hear the words when I have a vision… After they killed her, one of them, the one who brought her to that isolated corner, thought that they had a lot of fun and made 30 k each in the process… One of them, the thin one, didn't seem so exhilarated, though. I know that he hesitated whenever it was his turn to plant the knife in that woman."

Leah reflected upon his words and said, "All right. I have their general descriptions, although I'd like you to work with an artist so that I could get detailed portraits. I also know that someone paid 90 k for her murder. That helps, I think."

"Maybe…," Axel expressed his skepticism. "You know, I've told you about that guy… How he thought about the money and the fun…"

Leah nodded and leaned forward. She had the feeling that he had something important to say but didn't know how.

"The thought read like this: *'She'll be satisfied with what she got in exchange for the 30 k apiece and we had fun in the process',*" Axel remembered. "I don't think the victim would have paid them that amount of money to rape and torture her," he observed. "Another woman must have been involved."

"Right," Leah agreed and frowned. She reflected on the words and said, "It means that another woman paid the money to have Klavdiya murdered. Considering how she asked the murder to be done, she must have hated the victim badly."

Axel nodded and stood up. "I need some food, lieutenant. Would you mind if we move to the kitchen?" he inquired.

Leah hesitated. It was out of the ordinary to conduct an interview in a kitchen while the witness was having a snack but then the entire interview hadn't followed regulations so far. She nodded and followed him.

"Would you care for some bacon and eggs? I'm too famished to think of making something else right now," he explained and opened the fridge door to take out the ingredients for the meal.

"No, thank you," she replied, "I just had lunch before coming here."

"I see," he said softly, and his voice brought a frown on her face.

"I didn't mean anything by that, Arnett. I've just eaten and I won't eat twice just to spare your feelings," she specified.

He laughed and shook his head, "You're the first empath I've ever seen who doesn't spare people's feelings. You're a walking contradiction, lieutenant."

She didn't care for his assumption and retorted testily, "We'll have a working collaboration, Arnett, nothing more. Although I'll have to find a way to use what you saw and what you know without revealing the other stuff. People will say we're crazy and that's a label I could live without," she ended her tirade by poking his chest with her finger repeatedly.

"Ouch, lieutenant. That's one bony finger and it hurts when you do that," he said with amusement in his voice and rubbed the spot she'd poked.

He put a pan on the stove and threw the bacon inside to fry and turned to Leah again.

They assessed each other for a few seconds and then the man said, "Now, don't tell me, detective, that you haven't thought of me at all. You must have been at least somewhat intrigued when you couldn't read my mind."

"I was worried not intrigued," she corrected him. "I was convinced you were a psychopath," she reminded him.

"Oh, yes, so you've said," he whispered. "Nonetheless, now you know the truth," he pointed out.

"So?" she inquired.

"Well, I'm intrigued," he confessed.

"Let me say this again," she said. "So?"

"Considering that I haven't been intrigued in a woman for a long time, you can't think that I'd let this chance just go away," he replied.

"Not interested," she retorted with feigned indifference.

"Do people believe your lies?" he wondered keeping his eyes steady on her.

His question ruffled her feathers and she almost growled. Leah was good at hiding her real feelings and wasn't a bad liar either. His astute observation irritated her because she was interested in him indeed and she disliked the fact that he was aware of that.

She'd been fascinated when she laid her eyes on him for the first time, even though she'd had only a glimpse of the man lying underneath those handsome features. Yet, after talking to him and being in his presence for some time, she found it difficult to dismiss his magnetism.

"I don't know what you're talking about. Cook your… breakfast," she ordered. "We have things to do."

Axel mused and turned to the stove to flip the bacon over. He didn't forget to reply though, "I'm a civilian, Lieutenant, and I don't have to take orders from you, remember?"

Leah's irritation reached a new high and she imagined herself snatching the pan off the stove and slamming it over his head with a resounding bang. That fantasy was satisfactory enough and her tension subsided.

Axel, always with his back at her, grinned. When the fury took the best of her, she couldn't guard her thoughts from him as before and he succeeded in reading what she was thinking.

Her little stint with the pan amused him enough. He also appreciated her gutsy nature.

Leah, on the other hand, wasn't able to penetrate his thoughts. She sensed his amusement and yet, she didn't know why he felt that way. Her inability to read his feelings frustrated her to no end.

The woman didn't like it when her own limitations stopped her from doing something. She needed to do something else so that she could take her mind off that failure.

"I'm going to make some calls until you finish making your… lunch," she supplied, unsure what she could call his meal. "I'll send Mark to the office to check on some things," she continued and he shrugged with indifference.

He didn't care what she did with the information he'd given her. He knew she wouldn't reveal how he'd obtained that information because then she'd have to come forward and admit that she believed in ESP.

He didn't think she'd ever do that. Keeping a reputation in the police force as a woman was not an easy task even though progress had brought new standards around.

However, admitting to something that people either dismissed with ignorance or were attracted to like to a freaky curiosity would have led to the end of her career and she loved her profession. She was far too invested in it not to protect it at all costs.

CHAPTER 8 – BEWARE OF A WOMAN SCORNED AND A MAN'S BRUISED EGO

Axel watched the interview with interest. His eyes were on Leah though.

He wasn't interested in observing the sturdy man who was trying to talk his way out of a murder charge. Leah could do that without his help and anyway, it wasn't like he couldn't hear his thoughts.

He was more interested in Leah's demeanor and in her ability to hide what she thought or felt under a blank mask. Axel couldn't discern if she was frustrated or disappointed.

Everyone had expected to have serious problems making the man who lured Klavdiya into the isolated area of the garden talk, but they'd been wrong. The man was singing away, eager to offer them all possible details. He hoped for some leniency when the case would go to court.

Axel shook his head bewildered. He couldn't believe that that man harbored such expectations. He hadn't only raped and killed a woman for money, but he'd deeply enjoyed every torture he inflicted on her.

Axel considered that it wasn't enough if they locked him up and threw the key away. At times like this, he regretted that Canada didn't have capital punishment.

He knew that Mark was in the other interrogation room and together with Anne, who Axel had just met, questioned another of the trio, the thin man who'd appeared reluctant to do his part of the job during the night of the murder.

Leah didn't have too much difficulty finding the three men. Although they hadn't been on Dimitri's guest list, they'd been the only ones in Toronto who, within the last two weeks, deposited 30 k each in the bank.

Axel shook his head. He couldn't believe that people could be so stupid sometimes. He didn't understand how those men could have thought that depositing such a large amount of money wouldn't raise eyebrows. Moreover, all of them had opened accounts and deposited the money at the same bank and at the same time.

Leah picked them up immediately and, ironically enough, the toughest of all couldn't spill the beans fast enough. The other two showed more restraint, though. They didn't confess to anything until they'd been shown some sort of proof.

Axel's head snapped to the door of the interrogation room where someone had just knocked. Leah closed the file she had open before her on the desk and, taking it with her, she left the room.

Axel hurried from his observation post and joined her outside just in time to hear a policeman in uniform saying, "Yes, he's here and asked to speak to that man," he pointed to the interrogation room with his chin.

Axel frowned and glanced at Leah. She pondered the news and then went back into the interrogation room after she asked the officer to wait for a few moments.

When she returned, Axel was leaning back on the wall, his arms crossed over his chest. She spoke directly to the officer, without sparing a glance at him.

"Please, bring the counsel here. I will let the others know."

The officer went back to the reception area and Leah tapped her foot furiously on the floor. She was beyond mad although her face didn't show it.

"What happened, lieutenant?" Axel approached her.

"They've got counsel," she said succinctly and headed to the interrogation room where Mark was with one of the other suspects.

"How come?" Axel asked. "I haven't heard them asking for one and at least that guy in there with you confessed to a lot of things already," he noticed.

"Don't you think I know that?" she whirled back to him.

Now, he noticed that she was beyond furious. Her catlike eyes threw daggers and her skin was taut over her cheekbones.

"I don't know how someone knew to send a counsel for them, but I'll find out," she said and her tone promised nothing good.

"At least you've found out how they got to Dimitri's party," Axel noticed trying to change her mood. "Dimitri won't be pleased when he finds out that he has such disloyal people on the payroll and he has to change the lot of them."

"Look," Leah stopped and turned to him with blank eyes. "I think you should go home. There's nothing more that you could do here."

Axel tried to say something but she touched his chest and whispered, "Please."

He gnashed his teeth and looked away from her but, after a brief reflection, he decided to respect her decision. He knew she had a lot to deal with right then and he didn't want to add more to her burden.

Axel glanced back at her and said sternly, "I'll go now, lieutenant, but you know where to find me."

Leah nodded and then hurried to Mark's interrogation room to stop his interview as well. She didn't want to think of the implication of Axel's words. She pushed them to the back of her mind to analyze them later.

■ ■

Axel was looking out of the window pensively when he heard the knock on the door. His eyebrows raised. No one ever came upstairs without his agreement and the front desk hadn't called to let him know that he had visitors.

He considered going and unlocking the door but didn't feel like entertaining visitors. Then the knock became insistent and the thought that Leah came to visit him crossed his mind.

That was the only explanation. The front desk guy might have allowed her to come upstairs if she'd showed him her ID and asked him not to call the apartment.

Axel unlocked the door and reached for the handle to open it when the door was slammed into his head with force and he was thrown into the opposite wall. When he hit the wall, his brain suffered a second concussion and he lost consciousness.

Axel came back to reality when cold water was splashed all over his face. He sputtered and opened his eyes. The light coming from the bulb just above him hurt his eyes and he closed them with a hiss.

"Oh, no, you don't," he heard a screech, and a pointy shoe kicked him in his ribs and stole his breath for a few moments.

He tried to see who was in the apartment with him and half-opened his eyes. His mind was muddled and he couldn't focus enough to read his attacker's mind.

When he tried to brace his hand on the floor so that he could stand, he realized that he was trussed like a turkey. The rope around his hands and legs was tight and didn't give way to his efforts.

When Axel swore viciously, a maniacal laugh joined his words and two small hands sealed his mouth with adhesive tape.

***

"Bring him here," Leah asked Josh and crossed her hands on the desk.

Her blue-green eyes shot lightning bolts and Mark didn't dare to interrupt her thoughts.

Since the legal counsel showed for the three suspects, Leah had hurled them all into a whirlwind of activity. She wanted to know how the counselor received word to come because the three men had declined counsel from the beginning.

As they'd arrested them in the apartment they shared and no one was the wiser, the only explanation Leah could accept was that someone in the squad room had leaked the word outside. She asked them to check all the calls made on the floor and cross-reference them with all the people they had on the suspect list.

It wasn't easy or fast to check so many calls and Leah's frustration increased with every minute that passed. Everyone walked on eggshells around the lieutenant and avoided making eye contact with her.

They knew that Leah was afraid that the call might have been made from a cell phone or from outside the building. In that situation, they couldn't trace it and couldn't find the leak. More than one case could be in jeopardy.

Josh was the lucky one. He tracked a call made at exactly five minutes after they started the interrogations. The phone number that was dialed matched the cell phone number they had for Gareth.

Now Leah wanted to have a word with him. The last time she talked to him, he seemed very open and expressed sadness and shock when he heard that Klavdiya had been killed. At the time, she sensed that regret and sorrow, but she also sensed a bruised ego.

At the same time, she wanted to chat with the officer that had betrayed his uniform and that before sending his file to the internal affairs commission. The Chief had approved the interview because he knew that she had a murder case to solve.

As Josh went to bring Gareth in and she knew that it might take a while before he came back, Leah decided to begin with the officer who had made the call.

Leah thought that she should interview him in an interrogation room to show him that the situation was serious. She also wanted the interview to take place in the presence of two other officers so that no complains could be raised later. Hence, she invited Mark and a Sargent from the Squad to assist her in the interview.

■■■

When she entered the interrogation room, the young officer who was waiting for the interview to begin stood up. His hands were shaking and the pastiness of his face showed that he was terrified.

Leah waved him to sit down and Mark and the Sargent sat next to her. She recited the date and the names of the people in the room for the video tape and then, she leaned forward.

"Do you know why you're in this room?" she asked the officer.

The young man shook his head and licked his lips. He hid his hands in his lap.

Leah had already noticed that his fingers were shaking visibly but didn't feel any compassion for him.

"Do you remember that you called Gareth Black three hours ago?"

The man glanced from one interrogator to another. He muttered something under his breath, but the officers couldn't make out the words.

Leah sensed his fear. The man couldn't gather his thoughts and was instinctively looking for a way out.

"Paul," she called him by his first name.

Her quiet voice penetrated the haze of his panic and he looked up at her.

"Calm down now, all right. You've made a serious mistake. That's true. Don't compound your mistake with another," she pleaded looking straight into his eyes.

Her voice soothed the young man and his anxiety subdued. He wiped his face and breathed deeply.

"I'll tell you everything," he suddenly decided. "Lydia, Gareth's wife, is my cousin... She's... special... She's always had a strange look upon the world... She thinks that she deserves everything and no one has the right to refuse her what she wants... Her parents encouraged that streak... Probably because they were afraid... I don't know... Anyways, if she perceives something like an attack against her... no matter how insignificant, she reacts... Detective," he said turning to Leah and addressing her directly, "to be honest, I'm afraid of her. I know how mean she could get when we were children... My parents asked my uncle to have her seen by a doctor if not committed, but he refused... Now, two days ago, Gareth came and told me that she'd hired three guys to beat up a woman who tried to lure him into her bed... Just to beat her... But they went overboard and killed that woman... I believed him... or I wanted to believe him," he chose to be honest. "I wanted to believe him because I was afraid. When he asked me to let him know if there was any arrest in this specific case, he also told me that Lydia would be grateful to me if I helped her. If not... He didn't say what

Lydia would do but everyone in the family knows what she can do… She's sneaky and got away with a lot of things along the time… I have a baby, lieutenant…," the officer said and his eyes shimmered. "Gareth told me to think of my baby girl… I know Lydia and I didn't want her to hurt my child. She wouldn't do it right now, but maybe tomorrow or the day after tomorrow… She once waited for five years to take her revenge…"

"All right, Paul, I understand that," Leah said.

She did understand him and she sensed that his distress and fear were genuine. She didn't understand why he hadn't come to her when Gareth asked him to snitch for him, but that was another matter altogether.

"Tell me what information you gave to Gareth," she asked him quietly.

***

Leah, Anne and Mark drove as fast as possible to Axel's address. An intervention car accompanied them. They wanted to be ready for anything.

When Leah heard that Gareth had been informed about Axel's involvement, she knew that Axel would be on Lydia's revenge list. She'd had one for the last thirty years, apparently.

As far as everybody knew, Axel had stumbled onto the crime scene that night, seen the three attackers right after they killed the woman, and had run away to call the police.

Leah explained to the Chief that he hadn't waited near the crime scene because the men were still there. He was alone and couldn't fight three men armed with knives.

The Chief accepted the explanation and Axel's written testimony, which would throw the three men in prison for the remainder of their life.

They couldn't be sure that Lydia would act so quickly after finding out his name and address but they couldn't leave anything to chance. The young officer had given every piece of information to Gareth and when they spoke to him, Gareth confessed that he'd already passed it on to Lydia.

He'd also told them that she had a way inside Axel's building. She had a friend who lived there and she could pretend to visit her at any time. The front desk people knew her and wouldn't ask her where she was going.

Gareth had been very talkative once he realized that he had no chance to go back to his luxurious life. He had a lot of things to say but Leah didn't bother to wait around. She left Josh in charge of the interview and assembled a team to go to Axel's house immediately.

They didn't park the cars when they got to the building but left them in the street. They rushed inside and the man from the front desk immediately opened the door to the elevator when he saw policemen in uniform. He didn't even ask them where they wanted to go.

When they exited the elevator, Leah signaled them to be quiet and they tiptoed to Axel's door. She led the way and leaned on the wall on the side of the door when she saw that Axel's door was open.

Leah waved the officers to stand down and she took her pistol out of the holster. She checked to see that it was working properly and then she entered the apartment.

Her mind was assaulted by a turbulence of emotions. She could read anger, frustration, hate, anguish and triumph. It was a cacophony of feelings that pointed to emotional disequilibrium and that made her believe that Lydia wouldn't stop just because she saw the police.

When Paul told them about Lydia's special emotional state, she'd thought that he exaggerated because he wanted to explain his actions. Now, she understood that she'd been wrong. That was a woman capable of anything.

Leah breathed deeply and entered the apartment. She heard a muffled shout from the living room and headed towards the sound.

When she reached the living room, she saw Axel thoroughly bound on the floor and Lydia leaning over him. She had a knife in her right hand and, apparently, she'd used it a couple of times on Axel's body.

Leah wasn't able to assess Axel's condition from that distance. She could see blood stains on his arms, legs and chest but she had no means of determining how serious his wounds were.

"Lydia," she called out to the woman who'd just raised the knife to stab Axel again.

Lydia turned around with a yelp. Her beautiful features were contorted from rage and the dilation of her pupils showed that she was beyond normal comprehension.

"Step back," Leah ordered her.

Lydia looked at her and then at Axel. With a snicker, she prepared to plunge the blade of the knife into Axel again.

"Put the knife down," Leah repeated with more authority but Lydia didn't heed her warning and raised her arm to drive the blade with more force in the body lying at her feet.

Leah didn't repeat the warning. She shot Lydia's hand and the bullet went through one side of her palm into the other.

A howl of pain erupted from the woman's lips and she curled on the floor whimpering.

She didn't seem to understand what had happened and Leah read her frantic thoughts with clarity. Lydia had no memory of what she'd been doing there. She knew only that she was hurt and in pain.

Leah called Mark to take her away and she rushed to Axel's side.

EPILOGUE

When Leah entered his apartment, she heard the noise of a football game on the TV and she shook her head. Axel should have been in bed.

She'd had to fight him to make him remain in the hospital for two days and she relented afterwards only because he'd promised to rest.

"That's not resting," she said in a dry voice.

Axel turned his head from the screen and grinned at her, "Football is always relaxing for a man, Leah, didn't you know?"

Leah pursed her lips but she couldn't be upset with him. After he'd been stabbed five times and survived, he had the right to spend his time with the things he loved.

She came to the sofa where he lounged and put the bag with Chinese food on the coffee table.

"Brought you some lunch," she said and without realizing it, her fingers brushed a lock of raven hair off his face.

Axel watched her with serious eyes and then he took her hand in his. He looked at the hand that had saved his life and then, he leaned his cheek in her palm.

Leah felt strange. She stared at his face and closed her eyes and tried to read his mind to see what he was thinking but she couldn't. She saw contentment on his face and that was the only thing she could be sure about.

"Would you like to eat, stranger?" she asked him softly.

He nodded, at the same time nuzzling her palm, and electrical shocks ran up her arm. She tried to stand up and they played a game of tug of war with her hand.

Leah couldn't stop a merry laugh and she pushed him gently back. He fell on his back and said, "You'll come back, you know."

She nodded and smiling went to the kitchen to bring what they needed to share the food.

***

"So, did you close the case?" Axel asked and forked some more chicken into his mouth.

Leah nodded, chewed and then she said, "Actually, I closed two cases."

"Do tell," Axel said and sat straighter.

"That Iuri Gregoriev… You heard about him…," she looked at him inquiringly and Axel bobbed his head in agreement. "Well, Lydia killed him too. She wanted us to arrest Klavdiya and she tried to plant some evidence, but the officer in charge of the investigation didn't even look in Klavdiya's direction. That was why Lydia decided that she had to make her pay in another way."

"I understand that the killers got into Dimitri's house because they paid some guards. What I don't understand is how they knew she'd be there," Axel frowned.

"Simple. The guy that Klavdiya had just met… George Adler paid him to pick her up, charm her and invite her to the party. The man was in dire financial straits and needed every cent he could make," she explained.

Axel shook his head in puzzlement. He knew that guy. Not very well, but well enough. He'd never have expected him to approve of such a scheme.

"So, you closed the files," he murmured watching her carefully.

"Yep," she said and picked up her can of cola and sipped.

"Then, you don't need me anymore," he observed.

She shook her head and something fluttered in his heart. It tasted like regret.

"I see," he said and left the food on the table. "Excuse me a moment," he said and stood up with difficult to go onto the balcony. He needed some fresh air because his throat hurt.

"I'll come with you," she said. "You owe me your life, remember," she joked. "I have to keep a close eye on you from now on," she added.

He turned to her and for the first time since they met she saw emotion in his eyes. He slid his good arm around her back and crushed her to his chest. Leah didn't imagine he'd have so much strength after all that stabbing and bleeding.

AN IMMIGRANT

CHAPTER 1 – CARVED LIKE A THANKSGIVING TURKEY

'Bad move, Victor boy,' Victor thought, glancing around him with his blue, sharp eyes, searching the surrounding shadows.

Unease whirled inside his chest, and he rubbed his fingers unconsciously. He was itching for a cigarette and in a bad way. He had decided to quit, but his resolve was challenged once more. His job didn't make quitting easy.

He had a bad feeling. It had been bothering him since he accepted the rendezvous with the so-called informant in the Music Garden. His eyes swept the grove again.

'Not a smart spot for a clandestine meeting,' he mused, looking around with apprehension. *'Especially not so close to midnight and at the Sarabande,'* Victor shook his head, displeased with his lack of foresight. *'I should have*

insisted to meet at the Prelude or Minuets,' he repeated for the tenth time that day.

The Sarabande, majestic in daylight, looked gloomy at night. The anemic moonlight, barely penetrating the thick and heavy clouds, didn't help at all.

The weather man had announced rain, but Victor had stopped counting on his accuracy for a long time. The weather channel had been announcing thunderstorms for the last three days.

Victor still had to see a rain drop or hear the thunder. Following one of the hottest summers on record, that late September was scorching, and he would have welcomed a little rain.

Victor leaned on the closest tree and patted his pocket, where he had stashed a recorder. He knew his source wouldn't have liked to know he intended to record his accounting, but Victor couldn't care less. He paid for that information, and if he paid, he understood to take full advantage and use it as he found fit.

Restless, he kept his eyes and ears open. He knew his impatience to solve the case had made him overlook some elementary cautious measures. Now, he had to compensate, if he wanted to keep his hide intact.

'One mistake, one step closer to the grave. Things won't always go your way, Victor boy,' he thought. *'I'm far too old for taking such stupid risks. Heck, I'm far too old for this crap,'* he chided himself, just one second before he heard a crack somewhere on the right.

He had just turned his head toward the noise when a strong arm shoved a knife into his back. Victor groaned and fell to the ground like a log. A strapping man, over six feet tall, and around 220 pounds, his fall felt like a small earthquake.

'*Now, I'm done,*' he thought, his brain on fire, pain churning in his belly and chest. '*Carved, just like a Thanksgiving turkey,*' he observed with bitterness.

His fingers knotted in the leaves on the ground. He felt grateful when the sound of receding steps reached his ears. At least no one was pressed to finish him off on the spot. Then, he passed out.

***

Leah burrowed more into Axel, as if she wanted to steal his heat, although it was warm enough, even with the balcony door open. His arms surrounded her, and his head rested on top of hers. Axel's lips brushed absently over her hair now and then.

She felt comfortable, cherished and, quite strangely, protected. '*What the heck! I don't need protection, do I?*' she wondered, a slight feminist streak showing its head.

Leah had lost count of the evenings and nights she had spent with Axel. Days had turned into weeks and weeks into months. Well, about two or three months, give or take a week or two.

The movie on TV didn't hold Leah's interest, but Axel's scent and heat did. She closed her eyes, breathed him in, just content to be in his arms.

Axel's thoughts didn't overwhelm her mind. Now, she found that restful. In the beginning, that bothered her, but not for long.

It was quite a change of pace not to pick on random thoughts from someone she dated. More often than not, those thoughts had had the gift to sour her mood.

With Axel, the unknown exhilarated her. She had to guess what he wanted. She didn't know what he thought when he looked at her. That kept her on her toes, and she became more attuned to him.

Despite the action on the TV screen and the explosions blazing through the speakers, Leah fell asleep in Axel's arms, her head on his chest. Her fingers burrowed beneath his shirt, as if she wanted to get closer, and Axel grinned, leaning back to see her face.

One by one, Axel had broken down all Leah's defense walls. It hadn't been easy. Not for the first time, he wondered if he shouldn't thank that wacko woman who had stabbed him. Leah had cared for him afterward, and that counted for something.

Axel leaned his chin on the top of Leah's head once more, and returned his eyes to the movie. Leah amused him. She had chosen a very bloody and noisy film, and yet, she had fallen asleep.

Her even breathing relaxed him and Axel stroked her arm and shoulder with tender touches. His mind wandered away, lulled by the lack of tension.

Suddenly, he gasped and his arms tightened around Leah's body. She woke up wincing.

"What's wrong, Axel?" she asked when her eyes met his fixed gaze.

Axel appeared to stare into space.

"What's wrong?" she asked again, and this time, she also shook him for good measure.

Axel blinked and glanced at her. He brushed his fingers on the side of her face.

"We have to go now, Leah," he said with sadness.

"Go where?" she asked, her eyes showing her confusion. "What happened?"

"Someone might die," Axel replied very matter-of-factly.

Leah's eyes widened and her lips parted in surprise.
"Now?" she asked in a loud whisper.
Axel just nodded.

CHAPTER 2 – FATE LOVES A GOOD JOKE

The weather man hadn't been wrong this time. The sky lit with lightning and the downpour belted Victor's face, half buried in the leaves scattered on the grove's floor.

With a groan, Victor stirred under the cold rain, and opened his eyes with effort. Aches assaulted him from everywhere. Strange enough, his back felt numb.

'How accurate. I'll die under the rain,' he groused with cynicism, his sight blurry. *'Full circle, huh?'*

Victor remembered his mother's stories about his birth. He had laid eyes on the world in a small village in Transylvania in late September.

'Yep, five more days and I'd have celebrated my birthday,' he scoffed.

It had rained heavily the night he was born. His mother almost hadn't made it to the new communal hospital. At that time, hospitals were set up in cities, metropolis and counties. The small communal hospital was just a pilot project, and not one very well thought.

The way she said it, Victor hadn't seemed happy with the surroundings. With intrinsic determination — the same determination that would see him through a lot in his lifetime, the baby had bellowed his discontent.

His wailing had travelled beyond the improvised maternity ward and made the two other nurses on duty wince. He had good lungs.

Little did he know at the time that his name would go down in the history book of the small cluster of villages. He became a celebrity on his own — the first baby born in the new hospital, built at the foot of the mountain.

'Is this the crap, people think about when they conk out?' Victor wondered, flexing his fingers, just to make sure he was still alive.

Then, Victor shook his head. It wasn't like him just to give up. He was a man of action.

He tried to move and fire blazed through his entire body. He tightened his teeth, and a long hiss escaped through his lips.

'I need a moment only,' he surmised, when the pain subsided. *'Then, I will surely move,'* he groused with determination.

If he wasn't anything else, Victor was a determined man. When he made a decision, he followed through to the bitter end. He decided he would live, so he would.

He closed his eyes and fisted his hands. He would take a moment to rest and try again later. Meanwhile, he had time to ponder on his life.

He hadn't had the time for that for the last twenty-two years. What, with the university, and then, immigration... A lifetime...

He was due a serious thinking. It wasn't as if he could move and do something else right then.

Victor's life had followed a predictable path for the first eighteen years. Victor wasn't very studious, but he had street smarts, and a good memory to go with that.

He would talk his way out of anything. If he had to lie, he didn't shy away, but lied with such a serene face and conviction that people believed everything he said.

In class, teachers avoided asking him questions. They did ask him questions at first, but they learned their lesson.

He had a special gift — he talked fast and in circles. He would confuse everyone, including the teachers. No one knew the correct answer afterward.

Not few teachers found themselves looking into text books after discussing a topic with him. They doubted their own knowledge.

Anyway, it wasn't like they could make him repeat the year. The policy was clear — no child left behind.

So, Victor graduated year after year and most of the time, with good marks. Not because he worked hard. Yet, if he came to class, he soaked up information like a sponge. That helped him to get admitted into high-school, as well.

During the winter of his thirteenth year, things changed, at least at the surface. The change came with the boom of the revolution. New possibilities arose.

The shift between socialism and capitalism began, and Victor sensed that the latter could make or burry a man. He had seen enough movies on that fantastic invention that populated his last two years — the video player. He had a clear idea about what was going on in the world.

He had his eyes and heart on possible businesses, but he had forgotten one thing — he also had a very strong-minded mother. He had taken after her, above all.

As most people living in the country and farming the land, Maria Dobrota dreamed of having her son graduate from university. She desired a diploma for him.

In the words of her fellows, she wanted him to become a *gentleman*. Not because she was ashamed of her work, but because it was hard and back-breaking work and she wanted better for her only son.

She refused to listen to any of his teachers' words, who advised her to send him to a trade school because high-school was expensive. The boy would have had to go and live in the county capital, and that meant a lot of money for residence and meals.

She fought them when her Victor finished grade school and went to junior high-school, and she fought them when he passed his admission exams for superior high-school.

She was more than ready to fight them again now, and she decided to pay for private tutoring, just to have her son become an engineer. The sound of the word made her giddy with pride.

'*Oh, mother, mother,*' Victor thought with tenderness. She had always seen the best in him and nudged him to be someone.

Victor had tried to change her mind. He explained to her that times had changed and an engineer wouldn't have had the same prestige as a businessman, but his mother was unmovable.

Maria Dobrota knew nothing of that businessman stuff. What she knew was that her cousin's son was an engineer and everyone respected him, even though they didn't know what exactly he was doing.

She wanted her son to enjoy the same respect. She daydreamed about talking to people about her son, the engineer, with pride.

Victor didn't stand a chance. He was saddled with a university professor who tutored him in exchange for a good chunk of his parents' income and their farming goods.

Victor's father would grumble now and then, but, in their household, his mother was reigning with an iron fist and that was that. The man had hung his pants the day he married her, although he towered a good foot over his wife.

Victor cursed the lessons, and the professor gritted his teeth. Yet, he did his best to make Victor learn the principles of calculus, algebra and geometry. Luckily, Victor liked mathematics.

Two months into the grueling schedule, Victor was introduced to yet another university professor who accepted to tutor him in Physics, one of the subjects Victor abhorred the most. Give him a subject in history or literature, he knew everything about.

In his defense, that poor man didn't know what he was getting into. He had miscalculated. He didn't think of what came with the advantage of having a student from the country, who would provide him with things he couldn't find at a reasonable price in town.

He hadn't foreseen that he would have to cover a good chunk of the subject. His pupil had spent years playing hooky and driving his Physics teachers up the wall. Victor had probably spent a total of a few minutes with the Physics text books.

Ironic enough, Victor passed the entrance examination in the Polytechnic University and became a student. He found his name somewhere at the middle of the admission list, but it was there.

Everybody, but his mother, shook their heads when they heard the news. Not even Victor had thought it was possible for him to master Geometry and Physics enough to be admitted in the university.

His tutors added his performance to their portfolio. If they succeeded in teaching him so he got admitted, then they could teach anyone.

'Of course, they intended to bank on that,' Victor thought. *'I'd have done the same,'* he reckoned.

He tried to shrug, but the fire flashed back through his body, awakening nerve endings he would have preferred to remain asleep. He gritted his teeth once more.

To forget about the pain, Victor returned to the past. It wasn't like he could stand and go anywhere. Or crawl, for that matter. He was stuck there in the grove, anyways.

Revolution aside, hard times were bound to come. Everything changed, seemingly overnight. Values turned upside down and politics showed its ugly face. A guy had even said on TV that it would take twenty-five years for the things to get better. Not that Victor believed in such ad-hoc prophecies. It always depended on people.

The prices showed the tendency of going up and up. They had forgotten their way back down. Every morning would come with a few more cents added to the price for bread or milk. Many people lost sleep over that.

'*Not my mother,*' he smiled, recalling that year.

His mother was in the seventh heaven and couldn't care less about prices. She would strut full of pride on the main street and accost people at the drop of a hat. She was full of stories about her son's success.

Soon enough, sick and tired of hearing about Victor's genius, people learned to avoid her. Whenever they ran into her, they would sprint to the corner of the street or remembered about visits they had to make right that moment.

However, some weren't fast enough and had to hear again and again about Victor's great achievement. They would nod and smile, and their mind would brush up their curse repertoire.

Breathing in the smell of wet leaves, Victor remembered he had had no care in the world at that time. He spent a beautiful summer before his first year in university.

His mother decreed that the boy had worked hard enough. He deserved the best vacation ever before he went to university and prepared for a career that would last a lifetime. It was his last summer when he could enjoy his days without a worry in the world.

She was also all over the moon that the revolution had put an end to the draft. Victor wouldn't have to sacrifice a year of his life to the army.

Despite the pain, Victor's lips arched into a smile. He still remembered that summer.

Her mother efforts had led to a wonderful and expensive vacation at the seaside for an entire month. That year, it was the first time he had seen the sea and it fascinated him. Not enough to forget about his mountains, but enough to make him dream about it once in a while.

At the time, Victor's father tried to make his wife understand that it was too much for them. They didn't make much money and they had already spent most of their savings on Victor's tutoring.

In the fall, they would have to pay for the boy's residence and food and books... There were lots of things to take care of.

Victor wouldn't have qualified for a social scholarship, and with his academic track, no one would give him another type of scholarship. The boy had never chased good marks.

Now, nearing forty, Victor understood his father's worries. Then, he had been happy to have his mother in his corner.

She turned a deaf ear to anything his father had to say. She knew her son needed relaxation and a suitable reward. She gave Victor enough money to last him for an entire month.

She was happy. Now, she considered herself an engineer's mother, as if Victor had already had the five years of university and final exam in his pocket.

That vacation opened his horizons. For the first time, out from under his mother's wing, Victor saw what life was really about. The years spent in residence during high-school hadn't prepared him as much as that vacation.

Victor lost a quarter of his vacation money during the first night on the beach. He joined a group of older guys who introduced him to the beauty of a card game he had never played before — poker. He was hooked.

Two more nights of losses came along, but he gritted his teeth, and his street smarts and sharp mind helped him to soak every rule and every move. The fourth night brought him the jackpot and he never looked back.

He had learned a skill which would help him put food on the table and a roof over his head whenever life hammered him down.

Victor's fingers brushed the leaves away. He put his head on his folded arms, a smile tucked in the corner of his mouth.

He remembered well his parents' surprise when he had stopped asking them to send him money. When he also started sending money back home, they were baffled.

Victor recalled his father's pride when he told him he had got a job. Little did the man know that Victor's job was cleaning rich people's pockets playing poker.

At least he had ensured he could pay for the five years of residence, for his meals and his books. He loved to read and with his gains, he could buy all the books he had always dreamed about.

Victor sighed, staring into the night. Contentment glimmered in his eyes. At least he had made the old man happy once in his lifetime.

The echo of hasty steps coming from the direction of the Gigue reached his ears. With trepidation, Victor lifted his head and stared unblinkingly into the night.

Anxiety and fear nudged at him and he pushed hard with his palms into the ground to move. Pain instantly radiated everywhere in his back, but resolute, gritting his teeth, he tried to crawl under a tree. It felt as if he had moved through molasses. Each inch he covered brought more sweat and aches.

'*At least I'm alive,*' Victor thought. '*But not for long, if I don't move out of this darn trail,*' he groused and pushed harder, gritting his teeth to contain his grunts.

"He fell somewhere here," a strong male voice shredded the silence.

"Are you sure? I can't see anyone," a throaty female voice replied with evident doubt.

Victor stopped any movement and tried to become one with the ground. He knew he was in the shadow and they couldn't see him.

"I can hear him," the woman said with enthusiasm, and Victor grimaced.

'*How the heck can you hear me?*' he wondered and his eyes widened. His fingers dug into the floor of the grove, as if he wanted to anchor himself.

'*I'm not saying jack,*' he thought. '*I'm not so out of my mind that I'm talking without being aware of that, aren't I?*'

"Yeah, I hear him too," the man's voice replied. "He's kept his humor so he mustn't be in a very bad shape," he noticed drily.

Victor's eyebrows shot up his forehead. '*Who the heck are these people? More important, what the heck do they want with me?*'

"I don't hear anyone around," the woman said. "Take out your flashlight," she ordered.

'*She's like a drill sergeant,*' Victor mused, listening intently to every sound they made.

CHAPTER 3 – SOMETIMES GOD SMILES UPON YOU

Victor gave up any pretense when the light swept over him. He didn't know those people but there were only two options —either they came to save him or finish him. There wasn't any way around that.

He lifted his head, and gnashing his teeth, he turned to the light. The flashlight blinded him, and this time, he couldn't hold a groan.

"He's there," the man said, and rushed to kneel next to Victor. "Hey, buddy, are you still with us?" he asked, and Victor sensed the smile in his voice.

Victor grunted and nodded once. He didn't know whether he still had his voice. His eyes searched the man's face. Satisfied he had never seen him before, he laid his head on his folded arms again, and closed his eyes.

"Is he still alive?" the woman's voice asked.

"Yes, he is. What should we do now?" the man inquired, rousing Victor's curiosity.

'Why would he ask for her advice?' he thought, and the next moment, the man's laughter filled the air.

"Because she's the boss now," the man replied with good humor.

His words shocked Victor, and he just froze, his eyes zeroed in on Axel. He couldn't even blink.

"Now look what you've done, Axel," the woman chided her companion. "You scared him."

"He'll survive," Axel answered matter-of-factly, and Victor had the distinct impression that the man shrugged with nonchalance.

"Who are you people?" Victor croaked, unable to keep his mouth shut one second more.

He felt as if he had fallen in a strange dimension. This time, he was sure he hadn't voiced his question.

The woman's cold hand brushed his hair off his forehead, soothing his increasing fever.

"I'm Leah MacKay, a detective, and this is my boyfriend, Axel Arnett," she replied in a kind voice. "I'm going to call an ambulance for you," she continued.

She tried to stand up but the man's fingers closed over her wrist with surprising strength.

"No police," he groused.

He bit his lips. The sudden move had sparked arrows of pain along his spine and lower body.

Arnett burst into a hearty laughter. The sound gritted on Victor's nerves. If he had had the strength, he would have knocked the man down.

"Sorry, pal, the police are already here," Axel explained with cheer, making Victor lock his teeth again.

Leah pried his fingers off her wrist gently and took her cell phone out of her pocket. She dialed 911 and explained to the operator who she was and that she needed an ambulance and her team at the Sarabande.

Defeated, Victor sighed and laid his head on his arms again. He'd seen a commercial once with a small hedgehog coming out of a hole just to be hammered down once more. Now, he was the hedgehog. He had lost control of his life. *'Eh, it's not for the first time,'* he mused.

Axel Arnett leaned over him and whispered, "Everything will be well, don't worry. She's the best."

"That's what I'm afraid of," Victor grumbled, prompting Axel to chuckle.

Axel liked the man and felt satisfaction that they got to him in time. Hopefully, he would survive.

Axel felt the strength in him and counted on his built. He wasn't a man that could be easily taken down.

***

In less than fifteen minutes, the place was crawling with people. Apparently, the detective, Leah MacKay, carried some clout.

Two paramedics kept prodding at him and Victor felt like clubbing them over the head, and repeatedly. He was already battered. They needn't try so hard.

They didn't remove the knife, which was still stuck in his back, and he thanked God for small favors.

He feared he would black out and needed to keep his wits about him. Plus, he didn't think that taking the knife out would have been a good idea.

When the paramedics finished with their prodding, they got ready to carry him out. They loaded him face down on the stretcher, they had brought with them, and secured him as well as they could.

Leah, who had been busy barking orders left and right, strode to them.

"Well, guys, is he fine?"

One of the paramedics nodded, but the other, a woman, just shrugged her shoulders.

"We don't know yet," the woman specified. "They'll have to check him out at the emergency room, but he will survive until he gets there," she explained in a dry voice.

Leah nodded that she understood, and then, she addressed to him, "Before leaving, just give me your name and tell me again which is the precise location where you were attacked."

Victor's dark blue eyes settled on her face. He pondered her questions, but he knew he would have to give her straight answers in the end.

"Victor Dobrota," he introduced himself in a raspy voice.

Leah spelled the name while writing it down, and he approved.

"And where exactly were you when you were stabbed?" she repeated her previous question.

Victor pointed to the edge of the grove.

"Right there, I think. Maybe a few steps in the shadow. I didn't want to be seen. Not that it did me a lot of good," he mumbled, visibly upset, mostly with himself.

Leah smiled at him. She understood his anger and commiserated with him.

"All right, Victor. Now, go to the hospital and I'll see you there after a while, all right?"

Victor nodded briefly and leaned his head on his right arm, closing his eyes. He wasn't a wilting flower, and yet, the events of the night had drained his strength.

***

Victor gritted his teeth when they moved him from the gurney to the CT-scan bed. He gritted his teeth some more when they moved him to the OR.

Once they put him under, the gritting stopped. He welcomed the blackness, even though he had fought hard to keep his consciousness not half an hour before.

Two hours later, Victor slowly opened his eyes to find himself in ICU.

'Yep, it was high time I visited one of these places,' he thought with sarcasm.

He had never been in a hospital before, although his adult endeavors would have guaranteed it a couple of times.

Victor had his scrapes and cuts as a child and later as a teenager. He was the apple in his mother's eye, but she wasn't the coddling type and didn't care for the doctors' help anyway.

Later on, he learned to take everything in stride. He often walked his bruises with resilience, and even a couple of concussions didn't deter him.

Victor looked around with open curiosity and saw that the second bed of the unit was empty. He tried to lift his head to see the room better, and nausea hit him. He gave up and let his head fall with a thud on the pillow, which made his eyes cross.

His mouth felt dry and he slid his tongue over his teeth, but the dryness didn't go away. His throat was sore, and instinctively, he felt like coughing. Yet, he couldn't summon the strength to do so.

When the door opened, he lifted his head to see who came in and groaned. His left hand automatically cradled his forehead. He had tried to move his right arm at first, but something held it in place and a hint of panic raced along his spine.

"Let me help you," a melodic voice came, followed by fast steps, muffled by the rubber sole of the shoes the nurse was wearing.

He almost expected to see an angelic face to go with the voice. When the woman came into his line of sight, he almost flinched. The nurse was ugly like sin, yet her eyes warmed him to his core.

Her cool hand touched his forehead first, and then, she smiled at him.

"I'll raise the bed just a notch, and you won't have to lift your head, all right?" she told him and Victor blinked.

He didn't think he could move his head without being hit by waves of nausea.

"You might feel some nausea and mouth dryness for a while," she explained to him. "It's the anesthesia, but it will go away soon," she assured him.

"Thank you," he felt compelled to say, and his voice sounded hoarse in his ears.

The nurse patted his chest and smiled again.

"Just rest for a spell. The police will be here to talk to you soon enough. If you need anything," she waved her hand, "like water or ice, let me know. You see this button there?" she showed him a button he could reach with his left hand. "Just push it and someone will be here with you."

"Thank you," he said again, and followed her exit with his eyes.

When the door closed behind her, he relaxed and thinking of what would happen next, he decided to get some shut-eye. Weary, he fell asleep in a few seconds, without the time to ponder on anything.

CHAPTER 4 – THE RECKONNING

Victor woke up at 7:30 when another nurse came into his ICU reserve to check his blood pressure and fever. When he laid eyes on her, his pupils dilated, pleased with what he saw.

'*This one's a beauty, all right,*' the man in him smiled, his interest aroused.

Then, she opened her mouth, and he winced. The beauty's voice reached very high notes, and it was grating on his already strained nerves.

"We're all right this morning, eh?" she said cheerfully, and Victor felt like stuffing something into her mouth to shut her up.

She checked his fever and his blood pressure, but her mouth didn't shut up for one second. A headache started pounding in his head with a vengeance.

Happy like a magpie, she chirped, "We don't have so much fever anymore. Blood pressure is almost normal. Yes, we're fine," she continued.

'We… we…' Victor grumbled under his breath and scowled.

The woman talked to him as if he were a simpleton. He couldn't remember when someone had last talked to him like that, but definitely not during the last thirty or thirty-five years.

Impatient to have her leave, he asked abruptly, "When will the doctor be here?"

"Probably in an hour or so," she patted his arm, and then, she fussed with his IV for a couple of minutes. "We'll be good until then, won't we?"

"I don't know about you," he groused in a mean voice, "but I intend to catch up on my sleep."

Her eyes widened at his tone of voice. Baffled for a moment, she remained still, riveted to the same spot.

Then, she shook her head, and said, "I'll leave you then. If you need anything just call me, and I'll be here at once," she tried to smile, but her cheer had wilted.

He nodded curtly, just to see her go. He wondered if she wanted to finish the stabber's job because she definitely was on the right track. His head throbbed and his eyes burned.

'*Too early in the darn morning to listen to your prattle,*' he thought.

Miffed, the nurse left the room stiffly. Her gait and posture reminded him of a broom.

Victor understood he upset her, but he refused to let people treat him differently just because he was hurt. He had been stabbed in his back. His brain still worked.

Besides, Victor had never spent the morning with someone since he had the bad inspiration to take a brief vacation with a woman, a decade or so back. The memory still gave him chills.

Victor was used to his own company before noon, and he didn't need more than that. He didn't even turn on the radio before he had his coffee and breakfast. He abhorred any kind of noise first thing in the morning.

He closed his eyes again. He doubted he would actually sleep, but he needed to gather his thoughts.

Victor remembered the detective who found him at the Sarabande and he knew she would be back with questions soon. He didn't know how much to reveal, especially because he didn't have enough proof to back up his hypothesis.

He prided himself that he always finished his job. He was afraid that if he gave the information he had to the police, they would push him aside.

Yet, he questioned his ability to continue with his investigation in the following few days and even a couple of weeks. He didn't want to hear that anyone else died because he wasn't able to act. The victims' list was extensive enough already.

'This is a conundrum,' he thought, and started drumming his fingers on his chest, unaware of his preoccupation.

Suddenly, Victor remembered the strange conversation he had had with the detective and her boyfriend during the night. He couldn't believe they had heard his thoughts, yet he was confident he hadn't said those things aloud.

His position about ESP had always been equivocal. He had never thought about it much, but he couldn't say that he didn't believe that some people did have special skills.

'Probably, it is a matter of concentration,' he shrugged. *'Anyways, if that detective does read minds, then it doesn't*

matter what I want to tell her. She'll find out everything I want to conceal,' he shrugged.

A grin appeared on his lips when his father's image popped into his mind. Old Dobrota didn't have ESP, but he always guessed what Victor had done or wanted to do.

A pang of longing made him fist his hands. In fifteen years, he had visited his parents only six times. He hadn't succeeded in convincing them to visit him.

At least, they learned to skype. Victor chuckled when he recalled his parents' side conversations during the first talks with them on Skype. At the time, he felt like tearing his hair out, but now, he found those discussions amusing.

Unawarely, Victor fell asleep with a grin on his lips.

***

Leah entered the ICU reserve with Axel in tow. She knew that letting Axel tag along was a breach of protocol somehow, but she intended to clear everything with her chief later.

Anyway, the police were already on the verge to hire Axel as a consultant. His degree as a psychologist had gone a long way to pave for that acceptance, as well as his help in a previous case, when he *'read'* the behavior of the people involved.

Because of his *'help as a psychologist'*, they succeeded in nailing the guilty person and exonerate the innocent and in a very short time.

Little did the chief know that actually Axel had already known the truth. In one of his vision, he had seen the culprit taking the life of the victim. He *'read'* the rest by simply reading the minds of the individuals involved.

'But of course, we couldn't tell him that,' Leah mused. *'The chief would have blown his stack.'*

Leah couldn't take Mark with her at the hospital. She feared that Victor might slip and say something about what had happened when they came to the scene the previous night, and she didn't want any kind of ideas in Mark's head.

He already showed some strange jealousy signs toward Axel. And not because he would have been interested in her.

Barely had they closed the door behind them, when Victor woke up, cautiously staring at them.

'This is a man with good instincts,' Leah thought. *'I wonder how and where he honed them so well.'*

"Good morning," she greeted him, a small smile tugging at the corners of her mouth.

Axel just tipped an imaginary hat and grinned at Victor.

"Good morning," Victor replied, wariness obvious in his voice.

"I know it is early and you still need time to recover," Leah apologized after she glanced at her watch. "We wanted to catch you and the doctor at the same time, and I know your doctor should make his rounds around this hour," she shrugged.

"Why would you talk to my doctor?" Victor asked in a hard voice.

His eyes turned into slits. He had never liked it when people believed they could interfere with his life, but now the detective's intention chafed him even more.

"We need to keep an eye on you," she replied in a calm voice, apparently undaunted by his annoyance. "If you remember, someone sliced a piece of you the other night."

"Of course, I remember," he growled. "I'm stuck in this hospital bed, aren't I? It would be difficult to forget," he grumbled and his eyes flashed with anger.

Axel grinned when he noticed the sparks in the man's blue eyes. Victor wasn't a tame man and he didn't take well to orders.

"You're a lone wolf, aren't you?" Axel's question was out of his mouth before he realized.

Both Leah and Victor stared at him, completely baffled.

"Just ignore me," Axel shrugged. "Sometimes I run my mouth without thinking."

"Anyways," Leah sighed and rolled her eyes, "let's get back to the matter in hand."

Axel's lips twitched, and that prompted Victor's grin as well.

"All right, detective, what do you want to know?" he asked.

"What happened last night, for instance," Leah said, straightening her shoulders.

"You couldn't have missed what happened," Victor replied in a dry voice. "As you said, someone tried to carve me out."

"That was obvious," she replied patiently. "But why? That's the question, eh?"

Victor shrugged and didn't feel anything more than a tinge of pain. *'At least they have good painkillers around here,'* he reflected.

"Don't play coy, Victor," she snapped. "You know why."

Victor narrowed his eyes and reassessed the detective. Not a bad looking woman, Leah MacKay had a back bone of steel. Her gaze penetrated his protective wall and he didn't like it.

'*How much should I reveal*?' he mused, unsure of what he should do.

"Everything, Victor," Axel observed quietly.

Victor's eyes snapped at him, the dark blue stormy now.

"You do read my mind," he accused. "And she does too," he pointed to Leah in a huff.

Unconcerned with Victor's anger, Axel just shrugged, "I thought we had already established that last night."

"Then why bother to ask me questions?" Victor replied, and his voice shook in anger.

"Because it is polite," Leah replied softly. "I'd prefer you tell me what's what. I don't like to pry."

"Huh!" Victor scoffed with disbelief. They hadn't done anything but pry until then.

"No, she's right. She doesn't like to pry," Axel pointed out. "Me, on the other hand, I don't have any compulsion. I want to know something, I do whatever it takes," he shrugged again. "You know how it is. You and I are the same," he explained, waving his hand between the two of them.

"I wouldn't say so," Victor retorted heatedly. "I can't read your darn mind."

"No, you can't. But I was talking about the type of people we are. You are also willing to do whatever it takes to get what you want," Axel elaborated.

"Hmm, you're not wrong," Victor answered pensively. "I am able to do whatever it takes…"

Victor looked down, apparently extremely interested in the lines of his palm. Leah looked at Axel interrogatively, but he signaled her to be patient.

He strode to the corner of the room and brought back the chair he had seen there earlier. He placed it next to Victor's bed and invited Leah to sit. He stood next to her, his hand resting on the back of the chair.

Victor had abandoned his intense palm reading and watched his moves out of the corner of his eye. When Leah took a small book and a pen out of her bag, he decided to talk.

"All right, I'll talk," he announced, but didn't go on. He waited for their questions.

Axel grinned when he understood Victor's intention. He shook his head and invited him to talk with a wave of his hand.

Victor practically growled, but gave in. It wasn't like he could keep anything from the two of them.

"I had a meeting there with a guy. He said he had important information in a case I was working on."

"What kind of work you're doing?" Leah asked.

"I'm a private investigator. I also take cases for insurance companies. Actually, most of the time, I work for them," he amended his answer.

"I see," Leah murmured. "What was the case now?"

"A company had to pay for a number of life insurance policies, whose clause for accident increases the face amount tenfold. They wouldn't have noticed anything because the accidents took place at various intervals, but they had an audit scheduled and the audit guy seemed intrigued."

"Why? People do die in accidents. Were they related or what?" Leah asked.

She didn't understand why all that fuss if the deaths hadn't been related one to the other.

"No, it wasn't that," Victor waved his hand. "The man noticed the policies had been bought through the same broker. The same type of policy, the same provisions. The policy doesn't pay the face amount if the insured dies due to sickness or natural causes during the first two years. It pays only the equivalent of the premiums already paid by the policyholder and ten percent more. However, in case of an accident, the two-year clause doesn't apply. When they called me in, the company had already paid for seven policies, which had been only a few months old, and the audit expert still continued to dig. A guy with OCD, very meticulous. I met him," Victor flapped his hand.

"And what did they want you to do?" Leah asked.

"Well, the situation wasn't very simple," Victor replied. "The audit guy knew another audit guy from another insurance company. We're talking small companies here," Victor specified. "I don't think anyone would dare to play hard with one of the big ones," he shrugged. "Anyway, he asked his friend to check policies issued through the same broker. Sure enough, they found five, paid only during the last year. All the insured people died of accidents, all of them in less than six months after the policy was purchased."

"What kind of accidents are we talking about?" Axel intervened for the first time.

"Various," Victor waved his hand. "From car accidents to electrocution, slip on stairs, drowning, you name it."

"And they asked you to investigate the accidents?" Leah asked for clarifications.

"At least some of them. I am only one and I couldn't possibly verify every single darn accident," he shrugged. "They also wanted me to investigate the broker. I had just found a guy willing to give me some info on the broker and that was why I was in the grove last night."

"Who was the guy? Do you have a name?" Leah asked.

"Yes, it was one of the insurance advisers who works for the broker I told you about. He didn't want to talk to me in daylight or on the phone. He insisted that our discussion couldn't be traceable."

"All right, give me the name," Leah insisted. "And the broker's name."

"My informant's name is Lars Gunther and the broker's name is Paul Smidgen."

"Are you serious?" Axel grinned.

"Axel," Leah chided him, but Victor just nodded.

Leah shook her head and then took her phone out of her bag.

"I'm calling Mark. I will ask him to check out our informant and bring him to the station. I will have Anna and Josh gather info about Mr. Smidgen," Leah told them and left the room.

Axel sprawled in the seat Leah had just vacated and asked Victor, "How did you become an investigator?"

Victor just shrugged, but didn't volunteer any information.

"Come on, don't be petty. Give me something! I'm sure you're a man with an interesting story," Axel remarked.

CHAPTER 5 – AXEL IS CURIOUS

Victor just stared at him. The man reacted as if they had been best friends for ages and he didn't understand why.

Victor knew he couldn't possibly have anything that Axel would need. During the last fifteen years, he had never met someone who would offer their friendship without asking anything in return.

Axel turned his palms up, begging for a story. The light in his eyes made Victor laugh and forget his cynicism for a moment.

"What do you want to know?" Victor asked, glad that at least Axel considered to ask questions instead of prying for answers in his mind.

"What made you become an investigator?"

Victor shrugged, and then replied, "I'm an immigrant, you know."

"At least half the country is," Axel waved the matter as inconsequential.

"Well, some are a second or third generation," Victor mentioned. "It gets easier in time, I suppose. But when I came here, I came with certain expectations and I found myself in a completely different position."

"What do you mean?" Axel frowned.

"A cousin of mine came here about five or six years before I arrived and he boasted at home."

"About what?"

"About his life, work and house," Victor shrugged his shoulders. "My mother is the type of woman who always aims high. She wanted me to have that type of life. I earned my living back home, but I was far from what my cousin said he accomplished here. So, she pushed me to immigrate as well," he explained. "And it wasn't easy for her, mind you."

"So what happened when you came?" Axel's curiosity rushed him to go on.

He leaned forward, braced his elbows on his knees and put his head in his hands.

"Well, when I came, the situation was far from what he had said. They lived in Quebec. My cousin was an engineer back home and his wife was a researcher. And she was a very good one, too. They thought they would work in similar fields here but... Their experience and studies didn't really count, you see... Here, he works in the harbor —physical work, you know. He is a longshoreman. And his wife cleans the rooms in a hotel. The house he told everyone about doesn't belong to him. He just rented a tiny apartment in that house. Everything he had told his parents and friends from home was a lie. In my experience, most people do lie. There are exceptions, of course, but too far and in between."

"But why?" Axel's eyes widened.

"The heck if I know," Victor shrugged. "Probably, they didn't want to confess their failure… Anyway, my cousins could have had a better life if they had gone back to school, but he didn't feel like going through that again and his wife was stuck with the children, as well. Mostly she was too damn tired to care about anything."

"What about you? Did you go back to school?"

Victor's eyes widen in surprise, and then, he burst into laughter. He didn't stop until he had tears in his eyes.

"What's so funny?" Leah asked, coming back into the room.

Axel immediately stood up and offered the chair back to her.

Victor shook his head, wiped his tears and replied, "I didn't want to go to school to begin with. And I was eighteen at the time. Imagine, I wouldn't have gone a second time. I prefer action to sitting in a classroom. Even the private investigator courses tried my patience."

He didn't say anything for a few seconds, just stared in the distance pensively. Leah and Axel watched him with various levels of curiosity.

"I'm a strong man. Work has never been an issue for me, even hard work," his eyes came back at them.

He waved his hand, as if he had wanted to chase away any kind of misconception.

"Would I have had an easier life back home? Maybe, one never knows…"

He brushed his fingers through his coarse black hair, and then he glanced at them inquiringly.

"You know what's difficult in the beginning? Waking up and knowing you had to go out and speak another language. And knowing that you can't hear a vernacular word... You know, like when you're crossing the street and a driver swears at you... It's different in my language — more colorful," he explained pensively. "I miss that. And I often miss the old friendships. It isn't easy to make friends like the ones you've had from childhood," he shook his head. "And then, there's the atmosphere... A different culture, a different rhythm... Of course, different people..."

He took note of the sympathy in Leah's eyes and the interest on Axel's face. He felt embarrassed and decided to push his nostalgia at bay.

"Anyway, I tried a lot of things," he said and shook his head. "I couldn't find my place. I worked in forestry in Quebec, in oil drilling in Alberta, even went fishing in Alaska for a while. Unencumbered by a wife and children, it isn't difficult to make a living and save money at the same time," he shrugged. "I am not keen of material possessions, like clothes and the sort, and I don't get wasted. I saw a lot of men spending all their hard-worked money on booze... Plus, I have a gift," he mentioned, glancing sharply at the detective.

'Which is?" she inquired sweetly, but her eyes sharpened.

Leah had the feeling it wasn't something in the strict letter of the law, but she didn't intend to scare him from the get go.

"Now don't get in a huff, lieutenant," Victor recalled her rank from the night before. "It was quite legal. I played poker in the States. Tournaments, you know," he waved his hand. "I made enough money to send to my parents back home so they could have a comfortable living and hire people to work their land and care for their livestock. I also had enough to buy a house in Toronto and I still have enough savings. Financially, I'm sound," he shrugged his shoulders.

"Really?" Axel asked and his face lit with interest.

"You read minds," Victor noticed dryly, "I read faces and telling signs. That helps a lot in such tournaments."

"And still you're here, in Toronto, working as an investigator," Axel noticed.

"I got bored playing poker. I needed something more stimulating," he shrugged his shoulders.

Axel chuckled. He had felt Victor was an interesting guy when he saw him in his vision the night before.

"Well, last night was stimulating enough," Leah remarked in a dry voice.

"A little too stimulating for my taste," Victor admitted, clenching his fists.

He had had his brushes with death in the past, but this one rattled him. A metallic glint appeared in his eyes.

"Oh, oh," Axel murmured. "Someone thinks of revenge," he whispered in Leah's ear.

"Wouldn't you?" Victor asked, proving his earing was still good.

Axel just shrugged his shoulders. He didn't want to fuel the man's negative emotions.

The ring of Leah's phone startled all of them.

CHAPTER 6 – ONE PLAYER IS KICKED OUT OF THE GAME

Both Axel and Victor listened intently to Leah's monosyllabic answers. She had taken the call, but hadn't left the room. She had just paced to the window and stopped there.

Victor didn't like that he couldn't see her face. The detective had turned her back to the room and faced the window.

Yet, the rigid line of her shoulders showed that she didn't like what she was being told. He could hear only her replies.

"All right, Mark. Call the forensic team and the coroner… I think it's Dr. Connelly on duty, which is good. He's a very methodical man… I don't know if I can come soon enough, but let me know if you finish there so I don't make the trip for nothing."

She listened some more to what Mark said, and then replied, "Got it. Have uniforms ask the people around, maybe someone saw or heard something. Anyway, you don't need me to tell you how to do your job."

Axel sauntered to her, reached out and took her hand when he felt she was upset. Leah squeezed his fingers and without bothering with goodbyes, she hung up.

Leah remained there, her head bowed for a few seconds, and then, she returned to Victor's bed.

She answered to the inquiry in his eyes, "Your informant is dead. He was probably killed after he left the house to meet you last night, so he wasn't your attacker. Of course, this is just Mark's guess," she shrugged. "We'll see what the coroner says."

"Too bad for him," Victor noted with regret. "He was young, much younger than I am," he explained, flapping his hand. "I didn't find him to be a callous individual," he shook his head.

Victor didn't say anything for a few seconds. He just stared in the distance, and Leah didn't rush him. Axel had no compulsion to read Victor's mind and made note of his sorrow.

"He was just stuck in an uncomfortable situation," Victor said, and then stopped again.

He looked up at them and noticed their confusion. He thought he should explain what he meant so they could understand.

"I understand that the broker advanced him the money for his courses and certification exam. In consequence, Gunther had to work for him. He couldn't leave the firm and work for another broker or for himself… From what I saw, Gunther didn't seem very at ease with Smidgen's business. That's why he accepted to talk to me in the first place," he clarified.

Victor's eyes fell on his palm again. Now and then, he was fascinated by the lines in his palm and the map they depicted.

He didn't know what to believe or if indeed there was any science or rationale behind the palm reading. Yet, once, when he was a child and went to a fair with his parents, a gypsy had told him that he would have a long life.

Apparently, the life line on his palm went on and on and didn't fade. It blended with the lines around his wrist.

If he were to believe her, he would survive this time, as well. Everything else she had said, or almost everything, turned out to be true.

She had seen he would be a wanderer and he had moved around quite a bit. She had also foretold that he wouldn't find his peace before late in life. He was still looking for it.

Lost in his thoughts, Victor didn't realize that the silence had stretched in the room, thick with tension. Leah leaned forward and touched his hand, and he came back to the present moment with a jerk.

"I apologize, detective. I just got lost in my thoughts for a moment there," he replied morosely. "It happens now and then. Put it on my heritage," he shrugged his shoulders.

"You've got just a faint accent," Axel noticed. "I wouldn't have pegged you as a Romanian," he said with a shake of his head.

"How do Romanians speak?" Victor asked in a quarrelsome voice.

He was sick and tired of the stereotypes he had heard for the last fifteen years.

"I didn't mean any disparaging," Axel replied, putting up his hands to show he meant no ridicule. "However, most have an accent. I have a Romanian friend and when I met him for the first time, I actually thought he was Russian," he explained, and then noticed the scowl on Victor's face. "I repeat, I mean no disrespect. You're a tad too sensitive to this matter, buddy," Axel shook his head.

"Somewhat," Victor groused, without looking at them.

Then, he shut up unwilling to voice any complaints. Over the time, he had learned it didn't help an iota to do so.

Leah touched his hand with understanding and he looked up at her. He didn't know if he liked what he read in her eyes. He didn't need anyone's compassion or pity. As a matter of fact, he loathed it.

The door opened and he glanced in the door's direction. A doctor came in, a smile on his lips. He didn't seem old enough to be a doctor, but Victor knew appearances misled more often than not.

"Good morning," he said to everyone, in a cheerful voice.

Leah stood up to welcome the doctor, and together with Axel, greeted him.

"I understand your fever subsided," the man said checking the chart. "Yes, and your blood pressure is close to normal. I will want to check your wound now. Probably, you two should leave now and return later," he addressed to Leah and Axel.

Victor shook his head and waved his hand to show he didn't care one way or another.

"They can stay. It's not like they didn't know what happened," he said gruffly.

The doctor shrugged his shoulders. It didn't really matter to him.

"As you wish. Now, flip on your stomach and let me see."

With effort and muffled groans, Victor changed his position in bed. Luckily, Axel also helped him and that made it a little easier.

'What the heck! I'm weaker than a newborn,' Victor reflected with bitterness.

"Give it time," Axel whispered encouragingly in his ear.

"Get out of my head," Victor rebuked him, and Axel chuckled.

The doctor glanced at Victor and then to Axel. He didn't understand what they were talking about. He shook his head and went back to checking Victor's wound.

"It seems fine," he said after redressing the wound. He straightened up and continued, "I'd like to keep you here another night, to make sure everything goes well, all right? Of course, you won't be able to do much for about two or even three weeks. You'll need help, but I'm sure you'll find some," he concluded, looking straight into Victor's eyes.

Victor didn't approve or disapprove his assumption, but replied, "Being discharged out of the hospital would be good."

The doctor took his leave, and after the door closed behind him, Leah asked Victor, "Do you have anyone to help you?"

Victor shrugged, but answered, "I leave alone."

"A girlfriend, something?" Axel asked.

"I have a date here and there, but no, no girlfriend. I haven't found a woman interesting enough to want her as my girlfriend," Victor shrugged. "Probably, I'll never will. I'm a lone wolf, remember?" he replied with a grin for Axel.

A few moments, no one said anything. Then, suddenly, Victor's eyes widened and slapping his forehead, he exclaimed. "Oh, my gosh! I forgot. How could I forget?"

CHAPTER 7 – SURPRISES ABOUND

"What? What is it?" Axel asked, in an excited voice. He was so curious that he forgot about prying into Victor's thoughts.

"Tomorrow, at 3:35 in the afternoon, a woman comes from Romania. I have never met her, but my mother insisted that I offered her a place to stay for a couple of months until she found a job and could rent an apartment," Victor explained in a rush. "She's the youngest daughter of one of my mother's school friends who married and moved to Sibiu. That's why I don't know her."

"That's good," Axel said. "Isn't it?" he asked when Victor scowled. "She could help you during the following few weeks."

"Not really. I don't know her and she doesn't know me. What I know is that she divorced a couple of years back and has got two small children. That's what I was missing," he said with sarcasm. "And how the heck am

I supposed to get to the airport and bring them home? And of course, I can't leave them in the airport, can I?"

He gathered more and more steam along his heated speech.

Leah patted his arm and tried to calm him down, "I'm sure there are solutions."

Victor just scowled at her. *'Where? I can't see one. Mother will have my head.'*

Axel grinned. His curiosity appeased, he didn't have any difficulty in sneaking into Victor's mind once more.

"I'll help, don't worry," he assured Victor.

Victor looked at him as if he were about to sprout horns. In his experience, people didn't offer their help — they just tried to take advantage.

"Don't be so mistrustful," Axel chided him. "Have a little faith. I don't know what kind of people you have met so far, but not everyone is out to get you or take advantage of you. We'll take you home tomorrow, and then, I will go to the airport to welcome your lady friend and bring her home to you," he explained.

"She's not my lady friend," Victor gritted his teeth. "And why would you do that?" he inquired. "What's in it for you?"

Axel shook his head in reprimand, and then, he reiterated what he had said before, "You're one cynical man, Victor. I just want to help you. Don't know why, but I like you."

Victor narrowed his eyes to slits, and now, it was Leah's turn to laugh. He glanced at her inquiringly.

"Don't be so apprehensive. Axel really just wants to help. He can afford the time and everything. I don't suppose you shopped for groceries and other things," she said in an inquiring voice.

At her words, Victor grimaced and slapped his forehead again. Dismay reflected in his dark pupils.

'Another thing to think about. They pop all over the place,' he reflected with acrimony.

"No, I was thinking to do it tomorrow morning, before their arrival," he confessed. "I don't even know how much English the woman knows and if she's able to do the shopping herself," he shook his head with bitterness.

He knew it wouldn't be easy for her anyway, but if she didn't know the language, then the obstacles were higher. The opportunities for the non-English speakers were slim to none.

"I tried to talk her out of coming here, you know… Especially with two small kids… But I didn't have a chance to speak directly to her and mother said she refused to budge. She'd decided to immigrate and that was that," he explained. "Probably, she wanted to escape her past or her ex-husband… I don't know," he continued in a pensive voice.

"Being the single parent of two small children doesn't mean she's helpless," Leah pointed out to him. "She might surprise you. Women are resilient. Sometimes, more resilient than men."

'I doubt,' Victor thought, and then, he glanced at Axel, remembering the man's habit of reading his thoughts.

Indeed, Axel had done just that. The impish glimmer in his eyes told Victor everything he needed to know.

Axel simply chuckled, and then, he assured Victor, "Well, no worries. You will make a list and I will do the shopping for you before going to the airport."

Victor stared at him and said, "You know, I wanted to buy some things from the Romanian store so they didn't feel everything so alien here…"

"I can go there," Axel waved his worries away. "Just make the list and write down the directions so I can get to that store. If they have a website, it's even easier. I can take the directions from the Internet."

When he saw Victor's speculative glance, he felt compelled to explain his reasons. '*The man is a doubting Thomas,*' he thought.

"In a way, I saved your life last night, Victor. As the good detective here once told me, you owe your life to me, and I can't lose you out of my sight. I have to make sure that you are on the mend and my saving you didn't go to waste," he winked at Victor.

Leah laughed, slapping his arm, "You, imp. My meaning was different and you know it."

"Well, I do hope it was different," Axel said dryly, pretended to be vexed. "Of course, I don't have for him the same feelings I have for you," he said in a very matter-of-fact voice.

Then, he leaned over Leah, and touched his lips to hers tenderly. His fingers brushed over a lock of her hair and she sighed softly.

The mushy stuff almost made Victor cross his eyes. Both Leah and Axel felt it, and they turned to him. They burst into laughter at his expense, and Victor practically growled.

CHAPTER 8 – NITTY - GRITTY POLICE WORK

Leah strode with purpose onto the detectives' floor. A few people looked up, hearing the determined cadence of her firm steps.

Their eyes followed the lieutenant's advancement with open curiosity. Her gait showed that she was preoccupied, and her thoughts were involved in complex reasoning.

When she glanced their way, suddenly they became active. Everyone found something to do.

The lieutenant disliked laziness and she had made her opinions well known in the past. No one wanted to be the subject of her wrath.

Leah made a sign to her special team, and Anna, Mark and Josh immediately stood up. They gathered their notes and rushed to follow her into her office.

Leah threw her handbag onto the desk and sat in her chair with a soft groan. Exhaustion had caught up with her. She hadn't slept since the previous evening when she fell asleep in Axel's arms.

She knew Axel hadn't slept at all, and still he didn't go home for a nap. He baffled her. He had said he had his monthly meeting with his accountant and he would catch up with her after a few hours. He didn't even think of rest.

"Tough night, boss?" Mark's mouth ran out without any prompting from his thoughts.

When he realized what he had said, he grimaced. Leah's eyes thundered at him, and his heart fell in his boots. She appeared ready to bite his head off.

Mark knew better than to rile her when she was exhausted. Yet, she chose not to react when she noticed Mark's remorse and apprehension.

"So, what do we know so far?" she asked him.

Mark sighed with relief when he understood that she chose to let him off the hook. Then, he eagerly started to explain what information they had gathered so far.

"Dr. Connelly didn't say anything specific about the body. You know how he is," he said and rose his eyebrows.

The coroner never hazarded to give the COD before completing the post mortem. If someone insisted, he told them off.

"However," Mark continued, "he mentioned that the guy was stabbed, probably around eleven or twelve last night. A stab in the back. The same MO as with Dobrota, but in Gunther's case, the knife had been retrieved, and as result, he bled to death."

"Could he have lived with immediate medical care?" Leah asked with dismay.

She wondered why Axel didn't perceive Lars Gunther's death in his vision. She supposed Axel shared a weird, but deep connection with Victor, although not even Axel could explain why.

Mark shook his head at her question.

"The coroner says he couldn't have survived. The bleeding was excessive and fast. Probably, the knife hit an artery. It took only a few minutes."

"I understand you didn't find him at home," Leah said inquiringly.

"No," he shook his head. "I had just got to his house when Anna called me. The team searching the Music Garden found him behind one of the trees in the circle of Dawn Redwood trees in the Allemande. We think he had been stabbed just before Dobrota was."

"Any forensic evidence?" Leah asked, her eyes glancing at each of them, waiting for answers.

Anna shook her head unsure of what she could say. She glanced at her notes, although she knew what she had written there.

"No footprints, for sure," she began. "It hadn't rained for a while before last night, and the crime took place before the rain started. With the rain, any other traces have been erased."

"No prints on the knife either, although the forensic team said they found a third trace of DNA. The guy surely nicked himself," Josh contributed with information.

"And I suppose no witnesses," Leah noticed with dismay.

"Actually," Mark interjected, leaning forward in his chair, "there is a homeless guy. He took residence near the Community Centre, on Queen's Quay West, right across from Bathurst Street," he explained at length. Large gestures accompanied his words. "The man said it is his usual spot for the night, even though others challenged him in the past. You know, how it is with these spots," he shrugged. "A coveted spot brings the worse in people."

"Is there a conclusion to your rambling?" Leah asked in a dry voice, too tired to listen to his long-winded story.

Mark blushed to the top of his ears. Something was wrong with him that day. He didn't know when to stop talking.

"The homeless guy didn't see Dobrota. Probably, he came from the other side, from the Gigue. But he saw Gunther. He noticed him when he got off the streetcar at Bathurst Street. He described it to me. Gunther was a big man and he couldn't have missed him. He followed him by sight when he entered the garden. He thought the man was crazy to go there at night, especially because he seemed fearful and kept looking back. When Gunther entered the Allemande, he lost him from sight. Not five minutes later, another man came out running from the garden. He crossed the street on a red light, and climbed into a car parked across the street. He didn't have a good view at his face, but he said it was blond, short and stout. He moved fast enough though," Mark didn't forget to mention.

"So the homeless guy didn't notice anything distinctive?" Leah asked to make sure Mark hadn't forgotten anything.

Mark shook his head and turned his palms up to show his disappointment.

"All right," Leah accepted defeat there. "Any kind of information about Smidgen?" she turned to Anna and Josh.

"Not much for the moment," Josh grimaced. "He started his own business five years ago and he's got five other licensed advisors working for him. He paid for their licenses, so they cannot work on their own or for someone else. He doesn't get involved in business with big insurance companies, just small ones. He's also involved in financial brokerage. You know, putting lenders with borrowers together. He's also involved in some financial planning and mortgage stuff…"

"A very busy guy," Leah noticed with sarcasm.

Anna nodded, "Yes, he is, and I think he's got some very shady businesses. I was thinking to ask our forensic accountant expert to take a look."

"All right, but stealthily. I don't want to tip our hand before it is time," Leah warned her.

"And, we do have to note that," Josh intervened, "Smidgen is short, stout and blond. Too bad the homeless guy can't make a definite identification of the man he saw last night," he shook his head.

Leah nodded. She didn't like their lack of luck either. She shrugged and then she turned on her iPad.

"I have a list here with some accidents I want you to check out. You won't be able to verify everything yourself. Get some of the other guys to help. Start with the bottom of the list," she made sure to mention. "Dobrota has already checked the first seven and gathered a lot of data. I will get the information from him tomorrow. It doesn't make sense to duplicate his work," Leah explained.

She sent the list to Anna by email and let her know. Then, she turned to Mark.

"I have here the contact information of a claim auditor. I want you to talk to him. Have him explain everything to you. Let him know that Dobrota is still alive, but considering the situation, we will take over the investigation. He will introduce you to another claim auditor from another company. Discuss with him, as well. Josh, you will go with Mark," she turned to Josh. "Anna will hold the fort here, and you two will take care of this line of investigation," she said and stood up.

"Where to, boss?" Mark asked before he was able to censor himself. He closed his eyes and shook his head.

Leah just burst into laughter, "You aren't having a good day, Mark, are you?"

She gathered her things off the desk and accompanied her people to the door.

"I have to go and see the chief. I need Arnett on this investigation," she said. Then, out of the corner of her eye, she noticed Mark's scowl.

"What's with you and Axel?" she finally decided to ask. Curiosity had been gnawing at her for some time already and she was sick of skirting around that matter. "Why do you dislike him so much?"

"I don't dislike him," Mark mumbled, but didn't dare to look at her. "I just think we can do our job without him. He's a civilian and knows jack about police work," he groused.

"Come on, Mark," Josh intervened, patting his colleague on the shoulder. "Arnett would be a serious asset to the team. Do you remember how he nailed that guy?"

"Yes," Mark said with dismay. "But it's something about him... I don't know."

Leah's brows shot up. She knew Mark was sharp, but not so sharp. She didn't imagine he would catch onto Axel's skills.

"Anyways," Mark shrugged his shoulders, "he *is* a good asset to the team. I shouldn't complain."

A grin in the corner of her mouth, Leah left the office and crossed the floor to the stairs with long and hurried strides.

Behind her, the detectives on the floor relaxed. Four of them gathered together and started gossiping about one of the uniformed police officers, and their chuckles filled the air.

CHAPTER 9 – EVERY BULLET HAS ITS BILLET

Axel rushed into the Arrival terminal at the Pearson Airport, a piece of cardboard in his hand. He didn't need it and he had actually told so to Victor. Yet, Victor had insisted.

Victor knew Axel would have been able to probe the minds of the people coming off the plane until he found the woman he was waiting for.

'Dah, it wouldn't have been any trouble to probe a few minds,' Axel scoffed, recalling his discussion with Victor.

However, Victor had explained to Axel that Liliana would be apprehensive enough, and she didn't need the shock of an unorthodox meeting with Axel. She came into a new country, on the verge of living in the same house with a man she had never encountered. She was probably terrified, not knowing what to expect.

Victor hadn't talked to her at least once. Victor's mother had always had excuses at the ready whenever he asked her to invite Liliana to a Skype conversation.

Victor wasn't sure what to think about that, but he surely didn't like it. He had a bad feeling about the entire arrangement but he couldn't have refused his mother's request. She had framed it in such a way that it sounded as if he had committed a capital crime if he hadn't accepted to help.

When he asked for a photo so he could recognize the woman, his mother told him that he needed just to write her name on a paper and hold it up at the airport. Liliana would find him.

He started to believe the woman was a hag. He shivered whenever he thought he had to look upon her every day for a few months. He knew it would take at least two or three months before she could find a job and move out of his house. He didn't have any illusions.

Anyway, no matter how she looked, Victor didn't think the woman needed the shock of being accosted by an unknown man who knew who she was just by looking at her.

Axel had given in. He understood Victor's reasons well enough, even though he didn't feel comfortable to stand in the airport with the cardboard in his hands.

Axel glanced at the arrival board and sighed with relief. The flight had landed only ten minutes before. Definitely, Liliana still had to go through customs, so he had a few more minutes to wait.

Axel had been afraid he wouldn't arrive in time. He had run a lot of errands that morning, and the traffic hadn't cooperated with him at all. He got stuck in traffic jams twice that day.

In the morning, he headed to the hospital and picked up Victor. He drove him home, as he had promised the day before.

Anyways, Axel didn't have anything else important to do. Leah was still working on finalizing the necessary paper work so he could work with her on the case.

She had told him it might take a couple of days more, but he couldn't wait. He relished every single moment spent in her company and her reasoning processes.

Still, the delay gave him the time to take care of Victor. Not that he wouldn't have done it anyway.

Axel liked the man enough to look for his companionship. He saw himself in Victor, minus the cynicism. Deep down, Axel knew they were kindred brothers.

People started flowing out the gate and the movement stirred him up. He put his reflections aside and lifted the cardboard, feeling silly holding it. A glance around him, showed a few drivers holding similar signs. He scowled.

'Relegated to the role of a driver, eh?'

Soon, he forgot about his misgivings. The random thoughts he picked up here and there were more diverting. Axel never refused to tap in a source of entertainment.

Victor had asked him how he could understand his thoughts, because although sometimes he thought in English, he mostly thought in Romanian. Axel didn't have a straight explanation for that.

He didn't know for sure, but he supposed that thoughts were streams of energy and his mind interpreted that energy. He could understand a thought in any language, but if someone spoke to him in any other language, but English or French, he didn't understand jack.

He got so lost in the thoughts of a statuesque blond beauty, who assessed all the men in the terminal in colorful terms, that he didn't notice the stare of a woman with chestnut hair.

She was pushing a cart in which she had stacked a few suitcases. Two small children clung on to her coat, afraid that they would get lost in the crowd.

Axel noticed her when she stopped before him and asked him something in Romanian. The only thing he understood was Victor's name. He shook his head, and then showed to the sign.

"Are you Liliana Rogoz?" he asked, obviously in English.

The woman nodded and said something in her language again, but Axel was so busy to assess her that he didn't dive into her mind.

"I'm sorry," Axel replied. "I really don't understand Romanian. Do you speak English?"

"Yes, I do," she replied in English after a brief hesitation. "I thought you still spoke Romanian. Your mother says she speaks to you in Romanian," her brow furrowed.

Axel smiled at her, and shook his head again.

"I'm not Victor," he informed her and she gasped softly. He put up his hand and soothed her in a quiet voice, "Now, don't be afraid. I'm a friend of Victor. He had a… let's say, an accident two days ago and is confined to his house. He sent me here to drove you and the kids back to his home, all right?"

She hesitantly nodded, although she wasn't sure if she should believe him and go with him.

Axel noticed her big chocolate eyes had widened and he picked on her fear immediately. He put the cardboard under his arm and showed her his hands, palms up.

"Look, I know it is somewhat frightening to go anywhere with me, and yes, you are right. You should be reluctant to go with a man you have never met. But let me point out that you never met Victor either. He told me at least that when we discussed your arrival here."

"That's true," she admitted. "I asked his mother to arrange a Skype session with him so we could talk and arrange things, but she kept saying he never found time," she shook her head, and disbelief gleamed in her eyes.

"Interesting," Axel interjected and his eyes shone with mischief.

"What's so interesting?" she tilted her head.

"His mother told Victor the same thing about you, whenever he asked to speak to you," Axel pointed out, and then, unable to refrain, he chuckled.

"I see… I wonder why," Liliana mused. "I noticed she was a shrewd woman when I visited… My parents moved back to my mother's birth village a few years after they retired, you see. My mom inherited some land," she waved her hand. "Anyway, I didn't think she would be so underhanded, though."

"Mommy," the little boy gave his mother's coat a firm tug. "When are we getting home?"

Liliana leaned toward him and brushed his hair. "Soon, baby, soon," she crooned.

"Look, I have an idea to put your fears to rest," Axel intervened, sweeping with his eyes over the three of them.

The children were as tired as their mother. The long fifteen-hour trip had exhausted them. Liliana had shadows under her eyes and looked pale.

"I will call my girlfriend. She's a policewoman. She will talk to the police dispatcher and tell them that you will call and that they should put you through to her. She will vouch for me, all right?"

Liliana pondered on his words and gave him a brief nod. At least that was more than nothing. Her other choice would have been to take a cab but she didn't even have an address.

Axel laid the cardboard on top of her suitcases and fast-dialed Leah.

"Hi, there, love," he said softly when she answered his call. "I found Liliana and the children at the airport, but she's a tad leery of coming with me... Yes, she's right, of course, I know... Well, I was thinking. Maybe you can call the police dispatch and tell them that Liliana will call in a couple of minutes. They should be able to put her through to you so you could appease any of her apprehensions... All right. We'll wait a couple of minutes and we'll call... Of course, not from my phone. I will have her call from one of the pay phones so she would be sure there's nothing fishy going on... Yes, indeed... Are you now? That's nice to know. See you there, then," Axel finished his conversation with a bright smile.

He replaced the cell phone in his pocket and directed them to a row of chairs.

"Let's sit for a spell. We'll give Leah time to call the dispatch first and then you will call and ask to be put through. She's lieutenant Leah MacKay, by the way," he nodded to Liliana after they sat the children on chairs near one of the pay phones. "Meanwhile, would you like something to drink, guys? There are a few places here from where I could buy something. No food, though. Leah's on her way to Victor's house and she has already bought a bucket of chicken and a few other things," he explained his refusal.

"Can we have something to drink, mama?" the girl asked.

Axel smiled at her. She was the very image of her mother. Although the children were twins, the boy was dark-haired and he didn't share his mother's coloring. Liliana and her daughter were fair, while the boy was dark-skinned. He reminded him of Victor and Axel made efforts to smother a chuckle.

"I have some Canadian dollars with me," Liliana said, opening her handbag.

Her eyes searched through the contents of her large handbag. She had bought it especially for that journey so she could stash more things inside. The downside was she couldn't find anything without digging into the bag for a few minutes.

Axel stilled her moves with a gentle touch.

"No need, believe me. It will be my pleasure to buy the drinks. I'll go just there," he pointed to a shop right across from them so she could keep her eyes on him.

Liliana nodded hesitantly and sat next to her children. Her glance followed Axel, but she leaned down and whispered a few words to the kids.

Axel bought three boxes of juice and a bottle of water. He imagined Liliana would prefer the water.

"Here you are, champs," he said when he returned, and handed a box of juice to each child.

The children snatched the boxes from his hands, and he chuckled amused. Liliana frowned at their behavior, but he waved her concerns away.

"I imagine I would be as thirsty as they are after such a long flight," he said softly. "You have a choice between juice and water," he showed the two to her.

"Water, thank you," she replied, taking the bottle from his hand.

Axel watched her drink greedily. Then, he glanced at his watch and said, "I think you can call 911 now," he showed her the pay phones nearby. "I will stay with the cart," he offered, when he felt her hesitation. "Ah, and you will need these," he handed her some coins. "You will probably get them back at the end of the call, but you might need them to start the call," he shrugged. "I don't really know, to be honest with you. I never use pay phones," he confessed.

She nodded, took the coins, and taking the children with her, she moseyed to the first available pay phone.

Axel watched her for a few seconds, and then, he sprawled onto one of the seats. He'd been on the road most of the day and tiredness had caught up with him.

Liliana spent about four or five minutes on the phone. Axel didn't bother to read her mind. He knew what Leah would tell her and he imagined Liliana would believe she was safe with him.

"So, everything's fine, now, I suppose," he observed when she returned.

"Yes, it is," she replied softly, and Axel noticed her throaty voice again.

"Then let's go. I take the cart, you take the children. We'll have to go down to the parking," he said in a very matter-of-fact voice, and pushing the cart, led them to the elevator.

***

"I'm afraid I've turned out to be a serious imposition on you and your boyfriend, lieutenant," Victor observed, reclining in his armchair.

He couldn't stand lying in bed anymore and despite the discomfort he felt, he preferred the armchair. He didn't feel utterly useless, sprawled in an armchair.

Leah stood by the window watching outside. She glanced at him with a frown.

"Be serious, you aren't an imposition for any of us. Imagine we wouldn't do anything if we didn't want to," she waved a hand.

"You've done more than anyone could have expected," he pointed out, and his eyes turned thoughtful.

Leah shook her head and her eyes swept over him. He had decided not to welcome Liliana dressed in his sweatpants, and now, he was wearing a pair of black jeans and a white t-shirt. They suited him. The stubby beard gave him the allure of a bad boy, but she doubted he was anything else but that.

His arms were folded over his stomach, but they still didn't hide his muscles. Leah imagined he worked out a lot or did some physical work regularly.

The sound of a car stopping in the driveway drew her attention back out the window again, just in time to notice that Axel was getting out of the car. He jogged around and opened the passenger doors.

A woman of about 5.7-feet tall climbed out, clutching a big handbag in her hands. She wore her thick chestnut hair in a coil at the nape of her neck. When she turned around, Leah's lips arched in a smile, and she glanced back at Victor.

"What?" he asked in a nervous voice. He didn't trust her catlike smile. "What did you see?"

"Well," she replied softly, "I think you might be in for a big surprise."

"What do you mean?" Victor inquired, unease creeping into his heart.

The lieutenant just shrugged, "I won't ruin it for you. You'll see soon enough."

She sauntered to the hallway, while Victor gritted his teeth. He never liked surprises, and this time, he had a bad feeling about the surprise his mother had prepared for him.

***

"Don't worry about the others, I will bring them in," Axel's voice came from the hallway.

Victor cursed his inability to go there and see what was going on. Yet, he wanted to recuperate fast, and that meant to keep his movements to a minimum for a while. Just going to the washroom required a lot of effort and sweat from his part.

"Do you know in which rooms I should leave the suitcases?" Axel spoke again, probably posing his question to Leah.

"No, I didn't think to ask him," she replied. "I suppose it would be all right to bring everything inside first and leave them in the hallway for the moment. We'll see what is what afterward."

Victor decided to stand up, although it was difficult and painful. He had just pushed his behind a few centimeters away from the armchair, that Leah entered the room with the children and Liliana in tow.

"What do you think you're doing?" she chided him, her eyes thundering with dismay. "Sit down, you fool. I'm sure no one would mind making your acquaintance while you're sitting," she continued, rushing to him and pushing him back down.

Victor fell down at once. He grunted and scowled at her, but he had to admit that the effort had already exhausted him. She wouldn't have been able to push him down with so little effort if he had been in one of his good days.

"I wanted to show you to the rooms," he groused.

"You can tell me, and I'll tell Axel," she retorted mulishly. "It's no need for you to stand up. Let me introduce you to your guests," she said, the same catlike smile on her lips.

'She's not a woman to trifle with,' Victor concluded, taking her smile at true value. That smile gave him chills.

"And don't you forget that," Leah whispered, leaning over him, proving to him that she wasn't above some mind reading if the fancy struck.

She didn't mind his frown. She straightened, her lips twitching with glee, and removed herself from his line of sight.

She waved her hand toward the door and said, "This is your guest, Liliana Rogoz and her two wonderful children."

Victor, who was still watching Leah, narrowed his eyes, just a second before he turned his head to the door. He had the feeling the policewoman was toying with him and he didn't understand why.

When his eyes fell on the woman in the doorway, his breath caught in his throat, and his mouth turned dry.

She didn't look like one of the women he would regularly date. Yet, her appearance, and especially her warm wide chocolate eyes, rendered him silent.

Liliana's smile faded under his scrutiny. She became restless when he didn't say anything for a minute or so and fidgeted with her fingers.

"I understand this is not the best moment for you to have guests," she said, and her throaty voice brought a sparkle in Victor's eyes.

'Yep, hook, line and sinker. Oh, mom, you knew I would go down hard,' Victor thought, and shook his head with self-depreciation.

Leah leaned over him, and in undertone she said, "It happens to everyone sooner or later, so take heart. Don't be a chicken," she chuckled.

She straightened and said, "I see Victor's just a bit poleaxed right now, but I can assure you everything's fine. He would be all right in a couple of weeks, if he takes it easy. Meanwhile," she turned her eyes back to Victor, "which is the room you chose for Liliana?"

"The bedrooms are on the second floor. The second one on the left is hers and the third is for the kids," Victor manned up and said.

He had spoken to Leah, but then he glanced at Liliana. In a hoarse voice, he added, "I didn't bother with furnishing that bedroom before. That came in handy, though. Now, I stashed two twin beds inside, a table and chairs for the children and two shelves. I don't trust bunk beds when it comes to children as young as yours, so… Anyway, besides that, I didn't know what else they needed," he confessed. "I haven't been around kids much," he made a wry face.

"I'm sure everything is fine. We will try not to bother you too much, I promise," Liliana reassured him in a haste, although she was far from being confident that the children wouldn't trouble him.

He waved her words away, "I am sure it won't be a problem. By the way, I have a housekeeper. She comes only on Mondays, but she made all the beds and I hope she left towels in the bathrooms. All rooms have en-suite bathrooms. If she forgot about the towels, look into the linen cupboard. It's right across from your bedroom," he explained.

Liliana just nodded, and looked down, not knowing what else to say. However, the kids continued to keep him under close observation.

Victor felt as if he were under microscope. He tried to smile at them, but he doubted that he had managed more than a grimace.

"All right, then," Leah clapped in a cheery voice, "let's take the suitcases upstairs to your rooms. I suppose you will want to wash your hands, because we will eat in a few minutes. Southern fried chicken. It's delicious," she said with enthusiasm. "Of course, if you're not vegetarian," she said, and dismay sounded in her voice. She hadn't thought of that before.

Victor knew she could extract the information from Liliana's mind if she wanted to, and now he believed Axel's words from the other day. Leah was polite and didn't pry. When it suited her. Just a few moments ago, she had read his thoughts without any compulsion.

Liliana shook her head, a smile tucked in the corner of her mouth. She liked Leah's demeanor.

"No, we're not vegetarians, so the chicken would be great, thank you."

"Everything's inside," Axel came into the room. "Now, I need to know where to move the suitcases."

"Oh, you've done so much already," Liliana hurried to say, and a faint blush covered her cheeks. "I will move everything."

"Huh," Axel scoffed. "I would be insulted, you know. Believe me, the exercise is good for me."

"Then let me show you to their rooms," Leah said. "You have to come with us and tell us which luggage to leave in your bedroom and which one in the kids' room," Leah addressed to Liliana.

Her words brought Liliana back to the present. Her eyes had been caught in Victor's intense glance. They had been watching each other like two contenders in a duel.

Axel shook his head and laughed. Then, he winked at Victor and left the room.

CHAPTER 10 – AN AWKWARD MORNING

The soft knock on his door didn't find Victor sleeping, even if it was just a little after seven. He was just gauging his strength and wondering if he should get out of bed or wait for a little while.

"Come in," he said, trying to scramble in a sitting position.

He tried to muffle his grunts, when the door opened. He disliked showing any kind of weakness and especially in front of a woman. He understood it was his vanity talking, but that wasn't enough to change his ways.

Liliana didn't come in. Only her head appeared shyly in the opening, her chocolate eyes giving him the once-over.

"I hope I haven't woken you up," she said quietly, staring at his chest.

The bed sheet had slid down and rested at his waist. She didn't dare to look lower than his abdomen.

"No, you haven't. I was already up," he replied in a haste.

He grimaced. He didn't like his slip of tongue. '*God knows what she's thinking now,*' he thought.

"I was thinking of making breakfast and wanted to know what you preferred," she explained her audacity of checking on him.

"Whatever you're making is fine with me," he answered with a wave of his hand. "The only thing I would insist on is coffee," he explained. "I always need coffee in the morning. The stronger, the better."

"So do I," she replied, and her lips arched into a smile. "I've already started on the coffee. Do you want me to bring your breakfast here? Probably, it's for the best," she assumed, her gaze sweeping over his body once more, and he felt like burning under the licks of her gaze.

"No, no need for that," he replied in a deeper voice. "I'll make it to the kitchen. Just give me about ten or fifteen minutes," he asked, and then scowled. "I don't know yet how fast I can move and how long it will take me to get there," he explained through his teeth.

"I can help you," she offered, although she didn't know whether she could bear his weight.

'*Yeah, sure,*' he thought. '*I can see you running away, and howling, as soon as I lose this bed sheet.*'

"I'll manage, don't worry," he waved her away. "I'll be there soon," he said in a dismissive voice.

"All right, then," she accepted his decision. "I've discussed with the children to be quiet and not disturb you," she thought to mention. "They might not be able to keep quiet all the time, but I will reinforce the rule from time to time. We'll try to bother you as little as possible," she said.

"Leave the children alone," he asked her in a voice that didn't broach any argument. "I'm not so sensible and I don't intend in sleeping my days away, even though I'm unable to move around much. There's also a fenced yard in the back. You can let them play there. No one can come inside and the children can't go out. The fence is high enough," he explained.

Then, he pondered on that thought a little more, his eyes on the bed linen. He glanced back at her after a few seconds.

"We should probably buy them a ball or something. I haven't thought of that," he mumbled, shaking his hand with annoyance.

He was upset with himself. He prided himself with his ability to foresee things, and this time, he had failed.

"Thank you," Liliana replied with a grateful smile.

Her expectations hadn't aimed very high when she decided to accept his hospitality for a while. Actually, her mother had insisted very much on her staying at Victor's house in the beginning.

She had a point, though. Liliana could save more money if she didn't have to pay for a hotel room. Her mother had also involved Victor's mother in the persuasion process and Liliana hadn't seen any way to get out of it. That woman could wear someone down.

Liliana had even feared that Victor would loathe her children. She knew he was a bachelor. That clearly meant he was hardly accustomed to children's antics.

By now, Liliana had already stepped in, and Victor's eyes swept over her. She wasn't on the thin side, but she did look enticing, with her round hips and breasts.

'It won't be easy living with her in the same house, darn it,' he thought. It wouldn't do to lust over his guest. *'Besides, she's a mother, for God's sake,'* he reprimanded himself.

Then, he grinned. He had noticed something cute. She had braided her hair in a hurry, and now, her braid appeared lopsided, resting over her right shoulder.

She hadn't bothered with makeup and she looked much younger than her twenty-eight years, as his mother had told him she was.

Then, she opened her mouth and said, "I will go out today and I'll buy them a ball."

That stirred him out of his reflection. A deep frown set between his eyebrows, he practically growled at her.

"Are you out of your mind?" he shouted at her. "You don't even know where you are and you want to get out and get lost?"

Her eyebrows shot up her forehead. She hadn't expected temper from him. He seemed aloof enough and she didn't think he would care what she was doing one way or another.

"I assure you I can manage very well by myself," she replied to him haughtily. "I haven't had you on my side so far to keep me from getting lost," she snapped back at him, her hands on her hips.

Victor forgot everything about his bed sheet and straightened some more, even though pain pierced through him at every move. He tried to stare her down, but it didn't seem to be working. Either the woman counted on the fact that he couldn't move fast enough to make it to her or she didn't give a fig about his anger.

"Listen, be smart about this. You're not back home where you know the surrounding areas. This is a huge city and even someone who's spent years in this town can get lost. Be smart and stay inside for now. I will see what can be done later," he said.

He put up his hand to stop any comment from her when she opened her mouth to contradict him.

"I'm not patronizing you, but you need to listen. Yes, in a couple of days, after you had a chance to see the neighborhood, you will be able to do whatever you want. I'm sure you will be able to find your way home then, even if you get lost. But this is not that day," he groused, upset that he had to explain at length such a basic concept. "If you don't like surprises, I advise you to get out, because I'm about to lose this sheet," he concluded his diatribe in a mean voice, sick of explaining himself to her.

Liliana's blush pleased him. She huffed, but she didn't contradict him anymore. She just turned on her right heel and stomped out of the door.

Victor grinned when she shut the door behind her. Then, remembering he had to get out of bed, he sobered enough. He didn't relish the pain which would wash over his body soon.

***

When he entered the kitchen, he had the impression he'd stepped into a different world. Liliana was nowhere in sight, but her twin children had already turned the kitchen into a mess.

196

Victor shook his head, and a grin spread widely over his lips. A veritable food war had broken out apparently, and now, the kitchen, which he remembered tidy and spotless, was covered in pieces of bread, bits of bacon and eggs. The cherry on top was the milk which had spilled on the floor. He had to watch where he stepped so he didn't lose his footing.

The little girl wore some of those bits of bacon in her hair, but nevertheless, she appeared to be a fierce little thing. Her brother hadn't escaped unscathed. The little imp, who looked like an innocent angel, had spilled her milk over her brother's hair and the boy also wore part of her omelet.

The children were still bickering about some imagined offences. An only child, he hadn't had the experience of such squabbles first hand, but he had seen his friends warring with their siblings often.

Victor shook his head again, and barely keeping his laughter at bay, interceded between the two children.

"Where's your mother?"

At his low and deep voice, the two kids practically jumped out of their skin. Both looked up at him with wide eyes, and as if they had been on the same wave, they looked around at the mess they had made.

"Oh, oh," they both whispered at the same time, and exchanged a fearful look.

"Where's your mom, kiddos?" he asked again, a smile flitting on his lips.

"Oh, my God," her voice came from behind him. *"Oh, my God,"* she repeated, enunciating every syllable, as if she couldn't find her words.

He turned his head to her and noticed that her skin was paper white. A second later, though, she turned scarlet, and her eyes thundered.

"I apologize for my children, Victor. I don't know," she said fast, but then, she had to stop and swallow. Tears brimmed in her eyes. "I don't know how they could do this when I explained to them, very clearly, that they should be on their best behavior," her voice shook, but she finished her apologies, and appeared ready to do battle.

The children had frozen already. They looked everywhere, but at their mother.

Victor sighed deeply and moved slowly to a chair, attentive not to step on the food lying on the floor. '*God, I feel so old,*' he thought, each step carefully taken not to jar anything inside his body.

Pain came and went in waves. He had decided not to continue with the painkillers. He knew it was a sound decision, although there was a price to pay.

Liliana hurried to help him, but he shook her hand off his arm when he understood her intention. He threw himself on a chair, grunted, and then, he turned to her. He stared her down, but although she still felt ashamed because of her children's behavior, her gaze didn't shy away.

"Look here," he began to explain. "First of all, I don't want any help. I need to function by myself. The day I'm not able to move around under my own steam, it's the day you can put me in the ground," he groused. "Second, they're children. I can't expect that children don't move, make noise or make a mess. Yes, they seem a little unruly, but, what the heck, I don't really mind," he said in a gruffly voice. '*I did worse than that,*' he remembered. "You're with the cleaning duty, after all," he grinned at her now, and shrugged.

She rolled her eyes, but the corners of her mouth lifted. She seemed relieved that he hadn't combusted on spot. The kitchen was a fright sight, indeed.

"No," she replied in a very severe voice, "they are on cleaning duty. You will clean everything, you hear me, and then, you will go and clean yourselves."

Liliana also frowned at the children for good measure, and they started picking up the pieces of food off the floor immediately.

"That's mean, you know," Victor said in English so the children wouldn't understand him.

Yet, the children turned their curious eyes to him immediately. Baffled by their gazes, he looked at Liliana inquiringly.

"They understand English, Victor," she sighed. "I wouldn't have brought them here without making sure they spoke at least a little, the basic, you know. Apparently, they're good at languages, though," she shrugged her shoulders. "They learned much more than I expected. Anyway, you need to know that speaking in English won't prevent them from understanding."

"I see," he replied pensively, his gaze sweeping over the two kids. "You promised me some coffee, if I remember correctly," he looked back at her, ready to change the topic.

"Of course," she said and rushed to the cupboard to take a cup for him.

That morning, she had spent a couple of hours to familiarize herself with the downstairs. She hadn't looked inside the drawers in the den or in the dining room. That would have meant breaching his privacy.

However, she had checked all the cupboards in the kitchen and the pantry.

She poured him a cup of hot coffee and brought it to the table.

"Do you take sugar or milk with your coffee?"

He shook his head, but he didn't look at her. He was busy checking the weather outside. It seemed they would have another warm day, although they neared the end of September.

"Liliana," he glanced back at her, "would you mind taking my coffee and food to the table on the patio?"

She shook her head and immediately snatched his coffee cup to take it outside.

"I'll put the food on a plate for you immediately. I thought to wait for you to come downstairs before putting it on a plate, and it seems to have been a smart move. Otherwise, your breakfast would have joined the rest on the floor," she observed with a grumble.

Of course, she took another occasion to look daggers at her children. They were smart enough not to look back at her.

Victor just snickered and followed her outside through the French doors. When he walked, he felt only a slight faintness, and he was grateful for that. The pain hadn't subsided, that was true enough, but he had feared the weakness the most.

Liliana put the coffee cup on the large table on the patio and watched him walking slowly, as if he had been afraid not to jolt something inside his body. He sat down on a chair carefully, and pain painted visible lines on his face.

"Are you okay?" she asked in a worried voice.

He left the impression that he was about to kneel over and she was afraid she wouldn't be able to help him up. He towered over her and wasn't rod thin.

He just nodded and gritted his teeth. Apparently, his trip down the stairs had already taken a lot out of him that morning.

"I'd like to ask you something," he looked up at her. "I would do it myself, but I'm tapped out."

"Don't worry, just tell me what you need," she replied in an impatient voice, and her gaze turned back to the house.

Liliana's thoughts were still at the kitchen and the disaster her children had produced. She wanted to clean it as fast as possible.

Victor might not say a thing for the moment, but she didn't believe he wasn't upset with what Maria and Lucian had done. Anyone would have popped a vein at that sight.

"I think I left my cell phone, lighter and cigarettes on the night table in my room," he replied.

Displeasure shone briefly in her eyes when she heard about cigarettes. It took only a second and she tried to cover it, but Victor noticed the flicker of annoyance.

"You don't like smoking," he ventured to guess, in a dry voice.

She shook her head briefly, but made sure to specify, "It is your business, not mine, though."

He just shrugged, as if it hadn't mattered to him one way or another whether she liked or disliked his habits. However, he couldn't keep his mouth shut.

"Well, I'm in the process of quitting, so don't get in a huff. Plus, I won't smoke in the house with the children, so you don't have to worry about secondhand smoke. However, I *do* need a cigarette right now. It might take my mind of my pain a little," he grumbled, and tried to find a better position on the lawn chair.

Then, he gave up, and with a grunt, stood up, pushing into the table with all his might. Liliana watched him with astonishment.

He moved to the other side of the patio where he had arranged a lounge seating, with a sectional sofa, a few armchairs, an ottoman and a low table.

"I think I'll sit here," he said, sprawling on the cushioned sofa.

Indeed, it felt more comfortable than the chair he had just left. He could adjust his body on the sofa, so he didn't sit in a rigid position.

Liliana just nodded and brought the cup of coffee to Victor. She placed it on the low table, right in front of him.

"I'll bring your things from upstairs and when I come back I will bring your food. Of course, meanwhile, I'll send the kids to their room to ponder upon their behavior," she assured him.

She wanted to prove to him that she took her responsibilities seriously, but he interrupted her.

"Don't punish them for that," he waved his hand. "They went through that long flight and are in a new place. I think it's normal they misbehave a little. You can let them come outside and play," he told her. "Oh, I remember now," he said, and his face lit. "I have a badminton set with everything. We won't install the net right now, but they can play without. If you go downstairs to the basement, you will find the rec room.

The badminton set must be on one of the shelves on the right," he explained to her.

"I don't know," she hesitated.

"What don't you know?" he asked in a quarrelsome voice.

He didn't like where she was going with that line of discussion. He was sure she already thought of trouble.

"They might break a racket or…"

"So what? There are four in the set, so no big deal. Stop worrying about everything. It's not like their heirlooms or anything, for God's sake," he thundered. "If I think well, I haven't even used them once. I don't even remember why I bought them," Victor shrugged.

"If you really don't mind," she probed him hesitantly.

She knew the children needed some active occupation. They had been cooped for far too long and the results could be seen in the kitchen. They needed to use up some of their energy.

"I don't mind. I'm not wasteful but I'm not attached to things either," he made his reasons clear.

Liliana just nodded briefly and went back inside. Her throaty voice carried away and reached his ears when she addressed the children.

Victor grinned. She had probably told them about the badminton set because they were cheering.

Still with food in their hair and their messy clothes, the children gushed outside and threw themselves at him, very vocal in their gratitude.

Victor grumbled and bit his lower lip to mask the sliver of pain provoked by their jarring.

"All right, all right. Enough now. Go and clean yourselves and then, you can play," he said, trying to pry them off his thighs.

However, at the moment, his strength didn't match theirs. Each child had clung on to one thigh with all their might by now, and didn't want to let go. Liliana returned with his things just in time to see a resign scowl on his lips.

"Are you fine?" she rushed to him. "Maria, Lucian, let go," she bellowed to the children, but her words fell in deaf ears.

She left Victor's things on the table near his coffee and proceeded at unfastening her children off his legs. All the while she kept apologizing, and Victor closed his eyes and shook his head.

"Enough already," he snapped, when he couldn't take it anymore. Her eyes widened and shot up at him. "Stop apologizing," he groused. "I'm sick of hearing excuses all the time."

Liliana was shocked into silence. Yet, his outburst had also a secondary effect, which he welcomed with all his heart. The imps let go off his thighs and he breathed with relief.

CHAPTER 11 – AT A SNAIL'S PACE

Victor had finished his helping of bacon and eggs when the children came back out. Their faces and clothes didn't show any trace of their earlier war.

Victor noticed that Liliana had found the badminton set. Each child had a racket in their tiny hands and they chattered like magpies. It was evident that they couldn't wait to play, and he laughed up his sleeve.

They skipped down off the patio, and at the girl's prompting, they stopped somewhere in the middle of the yard. Maria measured the distance from them to Victor with a critical eye. She wrinkled her button nose and Victor's lips twitched.

'Probably, her mother had read them the riot act,' Victor thought with amusement, very attentive to what the children were doing.

Liliana didn't seem the kind that would listen to his words as if he had read the gospel. He didn't expect her to take his arguments at heart anyway.

After she made sure they were far enough away from him, the little girl turned to assess the distance to the flowerbeds. After a few moments, she seemed satisfied because she signaled her brother that they could play.

Victor's lips twitched once more. The little girl turned out being every bit as bossy as her mother. Liliana might have driven him crazy with her continuous apologies, but he had sensed the steel beneath the delicate package she presented.

He lit a cigarette and sipped from his coffee, watching the children play. The ring of the phone seemed to come out of nowhere and made him wince.

"Dobrota," he answered curtly, his voice bordering on rudeness.

"I see your mood hasn't improved yet," Axel chuckled.

"Yeah, it hasn't," Victor admitted with a growl. '*As if yours would if you were in my place,*' he locked his teeth.

"We're on our way to your place, by the way. And when I say *we,* that doesn't mean only Leah and I," he warned Victor. "One of her people will come along too. Is it all right?" Axel asked in a considerate voice.

However, they both knew that his question was superfluous. If they already were on their way to his house, whatever Victor had said, wouldn't have mattered.

"That's no skin off my nose," Victor shrugged.

He wasn't fond of dealing with the police on a regular basis, but he knew he didn't have a choice in the matter right then. Anyway, he had decided to take it in stride.

"Good to know, old man," Axel chuckled. "By the way, the guy that's coming with us knows nothing of what Leah or I can do, so don't slip," he cautioned Victor in a very serious voice, forgetting about his usual laid-back manner for a moment.

"Got it," Victor replied and rudely disconnected the call.

Then he thought better and sent a message to Axel, asking him to buy a ball for the children. He didn't look forward to another disagreement with Liliana about her going out, and thought to counter any kind of argument from her.

Satisfied that he had solved that problem, he picked up his cup of coffee and sipped again, sighing contentedly.

"Would you like some more?" Liliana asked.

His eyes narrowed. She was right there, almost touching him.

'I haven't even heard her steps, darn. How long has she been standing there?' he wondered, dissatisfied with himself. *'You're slipping, Victor boy,'* he admonished himself.

He glanced her way with suspicion in his eyes, but she didn't give any sign that she had heard his phone conversation. She just waited patiently with the coffee carafe in her hand.

"Yes, please," he said. "But you don't need to wait on me," he thought to mention belatedly.

It didn't feel right to have her attend to every single whim of his. His offer for her and her children to stay there didn't come with strings attached, even if his mother had twisted his arm to make that *'offer'* in the first place.

He wouldn't have thought of doing that. Yes, he would have helped her to find an apartment and counselled her about what was what, so her transition be easier. But he wouldn't have gone as far as to bring her in his proximity.

"I wouldn't if you would be able to do it yourself," Liliana replied dryly, unfazed by his bear-like behavior. "For the moment, you aren't," she remarked very matter-of-factly.

Her eyes didn't leave his, in an effort to show to him that he couldn't scare her away. She poured some more coffee in his cup, leaning over him.

"Would it bother you if I stayed here for a spell?" she asked, once she finished and straightened.

"Suit yourself. You can stay anywhere you want," he shrugged with a light frown, waving his right hand around. "By the way, Leah, Axel and another detective are on their way here," he told her.

"I should take the kids inside then," Liliana murmured, her gaze directed onto the children.

She dreaded calling them inside and being a kill-joy. She knew it couldn't have been easy for them to leave everything behind and move into another country.

In the beginning, when she explained her intentions to them, they had asked questions about when they would see their friends and grandparents again. Closer to their leaving, the questions had stopped, and Liliana worried because she didn't know what the kids were thinking anymore.

"Not on our account," Victor made it clear. "*We* will go inside if it's necessary. This weather won't last for long, I think," he continued in a far-away voice.

He tilted his head toward the sun, enjoying the warm strokes on his stubby face. He hadn't shaved for a few days, but it wasn't the first time, so he didn't mind it.

"Let them have some fun outside for now," he concluded, reclining a little more on the sofa.

"All right, then. I should make some more coffee if the detectives come, shouldn't I?" she glanced at him inquiringly.

"If you want to, yes, why not? I'm sure they would like some. But if you have other plans…"

"Not, not really," she shook her head.

Liliana didn't have a clear plan for that day. She still suffered because of the jet leg and couldn't order her ideas.

Victor didn't match her expectations, and his accident put an unexpected spin on the entire situation. The man had offered to house her and her children, and she couldn't turn her back on him in his hour of need, regardless how much he tried to push her away.

Liliana would have liked to wander through the town for a while, but she didn't want to have a full blown-out scandal with Victor. He had been adamant earlier when she mentioned going out.

"I promised my parents to call them after our arrival," she said with some insecurity in her voice, "but I don't know how to go about. I'm sure they already worry because they knew when the plane was supposed to land. It's already been several hours since our arrival."

"Knock yourself out," Victor pushed his cell phone to her. "Just dial 011 before the number," he advised her. "And when I am not available, there's a landline in the house. You can use that, as well," he said, and leaned farther back, closing his eyes, enjoying the dance of the sunrays on his face.

"How much will it be?" she asked and bit her lower lip.

She had come with some money, but not much and she had to make sure it would last until she found a job.

His eyes opened at once and he scowled at her.

"I won't take your money," he groused. "Anyway, I have a special plan," he lied, flipping his hand. "You can call your parents without qualms," he assuaged her fears.

Liliana glanced at him sideways. Something in his posture told her he was lying through his teeth, but she couldn't call him a liar to his face.

She sighed. She had to call her parents — probably, they worried already. As she didn't have any other choice, she picked up his phone and put the call through, sitting down in an armchair next to Victor's seat.

Victor wondered that she didn't go away so he wouldn't hear her conversation, but didn't ponder on the matter too much. It wasn't something important to him.

***

Victor was still sprawled on the sofa outside, watching the kids bickering, a smile tucked in the corner of his mouth, when the detectives and Axel came. Surprisingly, he enjoyed the children's antics.

He hadn't felt like moving, and because of that, only a numb pain bothered him. Probably, because his entire body turned senseless after he had kept still in the same position for a long while.

Leah and Liliana walked out of the house first, chatting quietly. Axel and another man, Victor had never met before, came afterward. Axel headed straight to Victor and elbowed him, which brought a grimace on his lips.

"I see you've got some more color in your face," Axel noticed with grin. "Sorry, I have some business to attend," he said, and lifted a bag from Toys R Us.

First, he showed to Victor what was inside, and Victor approved his choice. Then, he strode to the children who had almost come to blows.

"You missed," Maria groused and stomped her foot furiously.

She had braced her small fists on her hips and stared her brother down with a ferocious scowl, but Lucian didn't look intimidated.

"Huh, huh," he chanted. "I didn't miss. You didn't catch it," he pointed out, poking her chest with a finger.

Maria's eyes narrowed to slits. She was ready to jump him, the ferocious grimace on her face turning nastier, when Axel reached them. He shook his head and chuckled.

"Whoa, champs, no need to come to blows. I'm bearing gifts for you," he intervened, shaking the bag he had in his hand.

His last few words caught their attention and they turned to him like one. Their attuned reactions amused Axel to no end.

He had noticed their similar responses the previous evening, as well. The children might not have looked like twins, but they did react that way.

"Victor told me that you needed a ball," he said, and without further ado, he opened the bag and took a white and red ball out.

The cheers that followed were deafening.

"I take it you like it," Axel remarked dryly. "My hearing won't ever be the same," he thought to mention, and the kids grinned mischievously at him.

Lucian snatched the ball from his hand, throwing the badminton racket to the ground. Maria gasped, unpleasantly surprised by his rudeness.

"Mom will have your hide," she shouted, and immediately picked his racket off the ground. "You haven't even thanked Mr. Axel for the ball," she pointed out.

"Just Axel, no Mr.," Axel intervened and ruffled the girl's chestnut hair.

The little girl's hair matched the color of her mother's hair as well as its thickness, but she kept it short, pixie-like. It felt silky under his fingers, and he enjoyed its texture.

"Give me the rackets. I will take them to the table there," he pointed with his thumb back, toward the grown-ups, huddled around the lower table in the lounge corner.

She thanked him with all the politeness her mother had instilled in her, and then, she ran to play ball with her brother. Axel, shaking his head with delight, returned to the others.

"They're something else," he thought to mention when he reached the table.

Victor just nodded briefly. He agreed with Axel. The kids were two rascals, although the education Liliana had stubbornly drilled into them was visible.

"We should have thought about some games, as well," Axel mentioned. "Children get bored easily," he pointed out.

"I have games in the rec room," Victor said in a hard voice.

He didn't know why, but he didn't like that Axel was trying to take over. The children were his guests after all.

Axel just glanced at him and shook his head, to let him understand that he was wrong, and Victor scowled at him. He loathed the way Axel took strolls through his mind whenever his mood struck.

Liliana leaned over him and asked, "Do you want some more coffee?"

"Yes, if there is still some coffee, thank you," he nodded, and suddenly, his eyes zeroed in on her cleavage, which was right in front of his eyes. It was difficult to miss it. Liliana wore a top with a low neckline.

'She does have an impressive rack,' he thought, and then, he shook his head with dismay. He had no business in noticing her breasts.

Axel chuckled and everyone looked at him with curiosity. Leah shook her head at him and Victor practically growled when he understood that Axel had taken a new incursion in his mind.

Suddenly, realizing that Victor was ogling her breasts, Liliana blushed violently, and she straightened at once. She fumbled with the carafe and poured coffee in Victor's cup, spilling only a few drops, which she wiped with a napkin immediately.

"It's almost eleven," she noticed. "Would anyone of you care for some sandwiches?"

"I told you that you don't have to wait on me," Victor snapped at her.

"I wasn't waiting on you," she replied haughtily.

Liliana braced her left hand on her hips and her eyes shone with annoyance. She stared him down, mutiny sparking in her eyes.

Victor hadn't thought that those silken eyes could turn steely. That surprised him.

'Well, they can. Note to myself – never underestimate a woman.'

Liliana didn't like what Victor implied, and he hadn't done that for the first time. She had the distinct feeling that he made efforts to keep her at arm's length. She didn't understand why because her actions didn't have any ulterior purpose.

"I have to feed lunch to the children, so I will make lunch anyway. Besides, we have guests in the house, if you haven't noticed," she replied, annoyance ringing in her voice.

"They're not guests," Victor glowered at her. "They're here with business," he hissed through his teeth.

"Does that mean you're against offering them some sandwiches?" she bit back, sick of his round-about answers and looking for a straight one.

The other three watched the discussion between them with interest. Their gazes shifted from Liliana to Victor in the same rhythm with their replies.

Liliana had felt conspicuous in the beginning, but she decided that if he didn't mind that the other three overheard their exchange, she wouldn't either.

She, for one, knew that when someone stepped into the house, the host laid something on the table.

"Of course, not," he retorted. "I was only thinking that you shouldn't bother yourself if you had other things to do," he specified gruffly.

"Don't assume that you know what I want or have to do," she replied wryly.

She also shook her head to drive her point home. Her eyes sparkled with annoyance.

"I will make the decisions when it comes to my actions," she pointed out.

"I'll keep that in mind," he mumbled and dismissed her without another glance.

Liliana strode across the patio, her back straight, and one hand fisted at her side. Victor watched her furious stride out of the corner of his eye.

Axel grinned, shaking his head. When the pointed tip of Leah's ankle boot made contact with his shin, he turned inquiring eyes on to her.

"What?" he mouthed and flipped his hand.

Leah just shook her head to him once more, to make him understand that he had to quit goading Victor into reacting. Victor might have been hurt for the moment, but he didn't leave the impression he would take Axel's interference for long.

Axel wasn't dense. He could see, as well as Leah, that Victor didn't appreciate Axel's free trips in his head. Yet, Axel seemed impervious to Victor's discontent.

Leah commiserated with Victor. She understood his reaction very well. No one would have liked to have their mind probed all the time. That was an inexcusable breach of privacy.

"Let's get cracking," she said. "Time's flying away and we haven't even started," she specified, pointing to her watch. "So Mark? What exactly did you find out?

Victor must hear everything, so he could help us," she explained patiently to her subordinate.

It wasn't the first time she had done it that morning. She had already explained the situation to Mark twice before.

Mark could be as stubborn as a mule when he wanted. Now, he didn't like Victor's involvement in their work, although the man had not pushed his way in. Leah had decided to include Victor in their investigation because he had already started working on the case and his help had proved valuable.

As expected, Mark scowled. However, he turned on his iPad and opened the file he had prepared for the meeting.

"We have followed up on the seven cases you already investigated," he said, glancing at Victor. "As you already suggested, the first two didn't bring any light on the case. Indeed, no one could prove they were murders and not accidents. Without witnesses and any forensic evidence, it would be difficult to make a case," he shrugged, and his mouth tightened in a hard line.

"If we had known where to look then," Leah explained in an apologetic voice, "maybe we would have found something to support our theory. The officers called to the scene in both cases didn't have any reason to suspect foul play," she turned her palms up.

"I know," Victor nodded. "I checked them both and if I hadn't known something was fishy because of all the other cases, I wouldn't have suspected anything either. That is why I pushed them aside and moved to the others," he pointed out.

"Well, the following three cases you investigated are promising, indeed," Mark nodded. "I don't really know how the police missed them. Especially that one with the cabbage," he said and shuddered. "Ugh, terrible way to go," he grumbled.

Victor remembered that case very well. It would have been difficult to forget it. The thirty-five-year-old woman had supposedly slashed her veins while trying to thrust a huge kitchen knife into a cabbage. She was making preserves at that time.

The theory was that she had missed the cabbage, and the knife had pierced the wrist of the hand with which she held the cabbage in place. A bloody business.

Her husband claimed he had come home to find her on the floor in a pool of blood, the knife still protruding from her wrist. The officers who arrived at the scene didn't question his innocence. They considered it to be an open-and-shut case.

"How the coroner could have dismissed the other bruises on her arms, no one understands," Mark pointed out. "Luckily, we still have the photos before the autopsy and the bruises are there, telling their story."

"But there must be much more than the bruises," Victor said in a stubborn voice. "I know that the woman was killed and the insurance money cashed," he turned his palms up in a sudden gesture. "But there must be more," he insisted and shook his head. "Something I haven't dug out yet, unfortunately. The broker must have received part of the insurance money because otherwise it wouldn't have made sense for him to be involved, and he is involved. He sold far too many policies of that kind, not to be involved. So it stands to reason that he had something else to gain as well. Now the problem is how he could coerce the husband to pay in this instance, let's say. Once the husband was exonerated, no one would have looked his way twice. If the husband did the killing himself, by the way. Someone else might have helped. And killing doesn't come cheap."

Mark glanced at him, victory in his eyes. Dobrota might have begun the investigation, but his own people had found the focal point.

'God, how young and stupid he is,' Victor reflected, taking note of the satisfaction in the detective's eyes. *'As if it matters who found what. I'd have thought that what mattered was to put a stop to the crimes.'*

He practically rolled his eyes, and then sensed Axel's amused smile. He scowled at him, but Axel put up his hands and chuckled.

"I didn't do it this time," he said, convinced that Victor would catch his meaning.

And he did. Probably, Axel knew what was going on inside his head because of the expression on his face.

Mark's eyebrows shot up, though. He didn't know what Axel was talking about, and his statement didn't make sense in the context.

He didn't think that Axel would confess to any possible murders. He didn't like the man, but he had to reckon that Axel was anything but stupid.

"Well?" Victor prodded Mark.

Mark glanced at him sideways, not understanding what he wanted, and Victor sighed. He looked at Leah almost begging. His look implored her to take the lead.

"Mark, go on. What's the connection we found? Tell the people. Can't you see they're waiting?" she nudged Mark to continue.

"Oh, yes," the young detective blushed slightly. "Anna asked our forensic accountant guru to take a look at our broker's business. Of course, based on what he can check without having to ask for a warrant," he explained.

Victor noticed that Mark's hands carried a second conversation on the side.

"Anyways," Mark continued, "our guru determined that Smidgen conducts the financial brokerage side of his business with only one individual. Supposedly, this individual provides loans, which he recalls within a month, with a specific interest. Now, more interesting…" Mark said, and then paused for effect.

That made Victor lift his eyebrows. A grin perched on his lips. He appreciated Mark was in his thirties, yet he behaved like a man in his early twenties, quite very early twenties.

Leah laughed in her sleeve. She knew Mark well. They had been working together for quite a few years now, and she had learnt to take his quirks in stride.

Now, seeing the play of emotions on Victor's face, she could reassess Mark through fresh eyes again, and his actions amused her, as they had entertained her in the past.

Victor understood Mark had stopped for effect. Yet he didn't continue, as it was expected.

Victor looked up at the sky, as if he were asking for divine intervention. Axel grinned when he saw his reaction, but decided to intervene.

"What's so interesting, Mark?" he asked.

Mark grimaced. He had waited for the insurance investigator to ask the question. He needed to hear him say *please*.

"It seems that Gunther had information for Mr. Dobrota, indeed," he grumbled.

CHAPTER 12 – BATTLE OF WILLS ON ALL FRONTS

"Let's forget about all these formalities," Victor held an olive branch out to Mark. "You can call me Victor, as everyone else," he invited him.

His voice sounded pleasant enough. The shadow of a smile appeared on his lips, even though it did not reach his eyes.

Mark looked at him sideways and wrinkled his nose with displeasure, sign he didn't appreciate Victor's gesture.

'He thinks he can sweeten the pot, eh,' Mark mused with distaste. *'Not with me. I can't be bought with so little.'*

Victor interpreted his look correctly and shrugged. *'As if it bothered me.'*

Leah just shook her head, a distinct signal for Mark that he should reconsider his behavior. She was sick and tired of his juvenile grudges, first against Axel and now against Victor.

Mark pretended not to see her gesture. *'She can't say a thing if I can't see,'* he thought childishly.

"I'm hungry," Maria tugged at Victor's sleeve.

Victor grimaced, but turned to her. That was the second time that day that someone got near him and he didn't hear a thing.

Unexpectedly, a smile appeared on his lips. The little girl's face was red because of her exertions. Of course, a few streaks of dirt marred her creamy skin.

"Your mother should be here in a minute. She said she would make some sandwiches. Maybe, you should go inside and wash your hands and face so you could eat, all right?" he replied to her in a gentle voice.

"Good then," she said, and calling for her brother, she ran into the house through the French doors.

The boy left the ball behind and followed her like the wind. It became more evident that Maria was the appointed leader between the two of them.

"You're good with children," Leah noticed, a playful smile on her lips.

Victor just grunted. He didn't want to think of things like that, especially in relation to Liliana's children. Not that he'd ever thought of children.

That very moment, Liliana came out of the door with a tray with bowls and plates. Victor's eyes laid squarely on her and he frowned.

He was left with the impression that he had been very clear. He had told her without ambiguity that she shouldn't go through all that trouble.

"I thought a dumpling soup would go just fine with the sandwiches," she explained to everyone, a warm smile crinkling the corners of her eyes.

Liliana was very careful to avoid Victor's eyes. She had noticed his frown when she appeared on the patio, and she didn't feel like going through another discussion with him again.

She wondered what was going on. If she thought well, she had been in his house for less than twenty-four hours and they had already had a series of disagreements and for no reason, after all.

Liliana was also furious with him, because she refused to understand that someone wouldn't offer lunch to a guest, even if the guest had come with business.

She couldn't believe that living in a foreign country could have changed him so much. His mother was a very attentive hostess and Liliana was convinced that she had taught him to be the same.

Liliana laid the tray on the table and set a bowl with soup before each one of them. Then, she put the plate with sandwiches in the middle of the table and a stack of plates next to them so everyone could help themselves. She laid some napkins in the middle, as well, and then she set the spoons on the napkins.

"If you need anything else, let me know. Is it all right if the kids and I eat at the table there?" she glanced at Victor, pointing to the other table a few feet away.

"Yes," he answered curtly, through his teeth, trying hard not to shout at her again.

Yet, at the same time, his eyes continued to drill into her. They smoldered with quiet fury, which worried her somewhat.

"Thank you," she said politely. She was bent on not letting his anger determine her actions. "Where are the children?" she asked, her voice a tad higher than before, when she realized that they weren't in the yard where she had left them.

Her eyes widened, clear sign that she was scared. She worried that something had happened to them and no one had noticed, as they were busy with other things.

"Haven't you seen them? They must have passed by you when they ran inside," Victor wondered, his eyes glimmering with bewilderment. "They have just gone inside to wash their hands and faces. They want their lunch," he specified.

'Oh, all right," Liliana replied with relief. "Then, I will go and bring their food outside as well. Thank you," she said and strode in a hurry to the house.

Victor sighed. He had forgotten how polite people in his part of the country were.

Yet, it didn't sit well with him that she kept thanking him when he didn't do anything in reality. He just lay around, like a lump, unable to move more than a muscle.

"Wow, dumpling soup," Mark exclaimed, eyeing his bowl.

He snatched a spoon and started delving into his bowl, his eyes rounded with excitement.

"Have you eaten any before?" Victor inquired in a mildly annoyed voice, and lifted his left eyebrow.

Mark shook his head and spooned some of the golden liquid into his mouth.

"Then, why the heck, are you so enthusiastic?" Victor couldn't keep his mouth shut. "It might be awful, as much as you know," he commented with sarcasm.

Mark stopped for a moment, baffled, but then shrugged.

"Because I am hungry. But now that I tasted it, I can see it's yummy. Try it," he invited him in an excited voice, waving his spoon around.

Victor grimaced, He tried to avoid the drops coming off Mark's spoon, and his annoyance with the man became more obvious.

He rolled his eyes, sighed again and replied, "I know how dumpling soup tastes. I imagine it is good. Liliana couldn't have made a mess out of it, even if she had tried. Anyway, as a rule, women in my part of the country do know how to cook," he mentioned, picking up a spoon, as well.

He spooned some of the golden liquid and shoved the spoon into his mouth. It did taste good, and he nodded with satisfaction.

"Well, most of them," he revised his answer, thoughtfully. "I have an aunt, you see. No matter how hard she tried — and she did, no one can say differently, not even the dog accepted her food," he shook his head, while Axel laughed like a loon.

"Really? Not even the dog?" he asked as if he couldn't believe him.

"Yep. My uncle cooked in their house. He was very fond of good food, you see, so he had to learn how to make it if he wanted to eat," Victor explained in a deadpan voice.

"This here, this is good," Mark said, pointing his spoon to his bowl, He didn't seem to address to anyone in particular. "Too bad I like blond women," he mumbled, but Victor heard him.

He leaned over the table, without paying any attention to the stabbing aches crossing his lower abdomen, and looked straight into Mark's eyes.

"Don't even think about it," he warned him through his teeth, his eyes hard and threatening.

Axel elbowed Leah, and she nodded almost imperceptibly. Of course, she had noticed Victor's territorial behavior. Axel needn't bother to point it out to her.

She also noticed that Mark froze, his spoon halfway to his mouth. She barely stopped a chuckle in her throat. But she did cough conspicuously a couple of times.

"You were telling us about something that Gunther had for Victor," Leah said tactfully, hoping to stop any kind of blows between the two men.

Not that she expected Mark to exchange blows with Victor, but she wasn't so sure about Victor's temper. He appeared furious enough to react. The empath in her was capable of saying that he fought hard to control his impulse to flatten the detective.

"Oh, yes," Mark jumped at the chance to divert the conversation. "It is possible that Gunther had something with him when he came to meet you," he told Victor. "I think the killer took the information after he finished the job. In Gunther's coat pocket, we found a shredded piece of hard paper that surely came off a white disk casing. It was soaked in blood, of course. Anyways, he kept another disk at home. The forensic team almost missed it. Gunther had taped it under his desk in the den. There are all sorts of transactions on the disk. Everything is neat. He wrote down everything: policy number, face amount, amount for the loan and date when the loan had to be paid. There must be electronic traces for everything," he concluded, and helped himself to some more soup, sighing in contentment.

"We can use that file to determine how much went to whom," Leah pointed out, tasting the soup as well. Her eyes closed in bliss. "She is a good cook," she said.

"You're a lucky bastard," Axel chimed in, as well, and then chuckled when Victor practically growled at him.

"Now, we have to determine how each death took place," Mark said, waving the hand holding the spoon again, which made Victor cross his eyes. "And of course, who did the killing," the detective added.

"Plus, we have to prevent a few more killings," Leah pointed out. "We asked the two insurance companies to verify and total the number of policies of this kind that were sold during the last six months. We start from the premise that all the deaths take place in less than six months, and hope we aren't wrong," she explained, and then, she helped herself to a sandwich. "But to think they would wait a longer period..." she shook her head with apprehension. "Imagine, we wouldn't ever conclude this case," she continued with dismay.

"That's a good starting point," Victor approved. "Maybe, you should talk to the two claim adjusters I dealt with. They must know other claim adjusters in the city who work for small companies. And you can get in touch with the others. They could check if anything like that happened with policies in other insurance companies," Victor proposed, and everyone, Mark including, nodded.

"That's a good point," Leah said, after she swallowed the piece of sandwich she was chewing. "We should ask Anna to do it," she turned to Mark, who promptly reached for his cell phone.

He didn't have the time to dial Anna's number. Leah's phone rang and she answered.

She listened for a couple of minutes, a deep scowl on her face, and then she glanced at her watch.

"All right, we'll probably be there in thirty minutes, depending on the traffic. Keep the officers on site and bring a forensic team in," she ordered and disconnected the call.

"We have a new *'accident'*, she said with a frown.

She shoved her phone back into her handbag with a shake of her head. Her facial expression bordered on deep annoyance.

Then she spoke to Victor, "When we found that file at Gunther's house, we checked to see who was alive and we drew a list with the names of the people insured. That list was made known through all the precincts. We thought that at least thus, if an accident took place, the officers wouldn't write it down just as an accident and would call for us. Which they did. One insured life had just had an *'accident'*, she concluded in a tired voice.

"I was afraid of that," Victor said, shaking his head, and his mouth turned into a flat and hard line.

"We have to go," Leah told the other two, ready to stand up and leave, her handbag gathered in her lap.

"Yeah, yeah, let me finish my soup," Axel mumbled his displeasure. "No more than two minutes. I am sure nothing will change in two more minutes," he pointed out and sank his spoon in the soup again.

Mark supported his proposition and shook his head vigorously in denial. Then, he started spooning the soup as if it had been no tomorrow.

Both Leah and Victor exchanged amused looks. They knew somebody died, but they needed to keep a distance and be prepared for what would come.

CHAPTER 13 – DISCONTENT AT A CRIME SCENE

When Leah stepped into the victim's house, with Axel and Mark in tow, she couldn't believe her eyes. Several people were trespassing the crime scene without any worry that they could destroy important evidence. They were milling around as if they had been in the food court at the mall.

She hardly stopped a groan, but her eyes narrowed to slits, throwing arrows right and left. Her hands fisted so tight that her nails scratched the skin of her palms.

Leah looked around for the person responsible for that flagrant breach in procedure, ready to chew them up and spit them out. What happened there wasn't just a violation of the rules and disrespect of her orders, but blatant disregard for their own uniform.

She stomped inside the house, without hiding her anger. She hadn't even reached the middle of the hallway that silence fell behind her.

Axel and Mark followed her closely. Both shared her indignation and astonishment. It wasn't as if the officers hadn't been warned out about the possibility of having a crime in their hands.

Axel mused and his lips arched in a sardonic grin. He had noticed the reaction of the uniformed police officers when their eyes fell on Leah with panic.

Why they hadn't thought she would come was beyond his comprehension. She'd been notified about the *'accident'*, after all, and she had informed them that she would be there.

The state of the crime scene upset Axel, as well, but that didn't prevent him to enjoy probing a mind here and there. It was enlightening to see such burly men afraid of a slip of a woman.

Leah stopped only when she entered the kitchen. There, a detective was talking to the coroner, unaware that Leah had arrived at the scene and stood in hearing distance.

"Eh, anyone can see it was just an accident, doc, but you know women. They must make a mountain out of a molehill," he said with biting irony.

"Are you sure about that, Mike?" Leah asked in a deceptively calm voice from behind him.

When her words reached him, the officer winced and turned to her. His pinched mouth showed his consternation. He wasn't very thrilled that she heard what he had said.

By now, he had a reputation among his colleagues. Everybody knew about his views concerning his female colleagues.

He had already been reprimanded a few times for his misogynistic opinions and didn't want to be called on that again. He didn't need another reprimand on file. For the last three years, he hadn't seen a promotion because of the previous reports in his file.

"Detective Leah MacKay," he murmured with dismay.

Yet, he couldn't control himself. As always when he was in her presence, his eyes swept all over her body leisurely. The fact that he had a wife at home didn't make him blind.

That was the look of a man checking out a woman, and that didn't sit well with Axel. He strode forward purposely until he was shoulder to shoulder with Leah.

His charcoal eyes had turned hard in the blink of an eye, and he stared the man down, without flinching. The metallic flicker in his eyes and his belligerent stance warned the officer to back off if he valued his skin.

Axel was a big man, both in height and in built, and his stance was foreboding. Mike readily understood that he should reconsider his actions and treat the lieutenant politely. He nodded, an excuse at the ready in his eyes, which pleased Axel.

Mike winced inwardly. He loathed that he had to step back. He was a big man, as well, yet Arnett, whom he had met before, towered over him and his presence made the officer sweat.

Mike had never understood why he was so wary of Arnett, but he preferred to give him a wide berth. That way of action just seemed smarter, and no one could say that Mike's mind didn't work well enough, especially when it came to the preservation of his own hide.

After she made his acquaintance, Leah had never considered that Axel would represent a threat to anyone, but she had to admit that the man was imposing enough. He had never used his size to impress or cower her, though.

She pretended she hadn't noticed the power play between the two men and said in an even voice, "So, Mike, you think I exaggerate because women are prone to do so."

Mike made a face, thinking of the lecture the chief would deliver to him when he heard about his slip of tongue. This time, he might not even get away with only a reprimand. He had been told to watch his mouth or else.

He ran his fingers through his short hair, drawing a deep breath. He thought he should smooth things over and he tried to explain his words.

"I didn't mean it that way. I wanted only to point out that this situation here," he said, pointing to the body on the floor, "couldn't be considered anything but an accident."

"And why's that?" Leah inquired, staring him down unnervingly.

"The guy died because of an airway obstruction. More specifically, he probably ate his lunch too fast, and he swallowed a bone," the detective explained and waved again toward the victim's body.

The victim, a sturdy man, had fallen near the table, fingers curved close to his neck, as if he had tried to pry his throat open, but didn't get there in time.

"I see," Leah murmured. "And yet, I'd like to see for myself," she replied sweetly, and her tone of voice brought beads of sweat on the officer's forehead.

He had a bad feeling. The lieutenant was too composed and unafraid that she had made a mistake.

Knowing the lieutenant quite well, that could mean only one thing — he was the one who had erred. Worse, he hadn't taken care to keep the scene pristine because he didn't suspect that anything was amiss.

'*If this is really a murder, I'm in deep trouble,*' he practically groaned. The chief's reprimand loomed over him with dark certainty.

Sympathetic, although he knew the man didn't deserve it, Axel patted him on the shoulder, and shook his head with regret. His mouth had turned into a flat line, as if he commiserated with the detective.

Axel's gestures stunned the officer's mind for a second, and then, he fisted his hands. He didn't need his pity. He stepped aside so Axel couldn't touch him anymore. Axel just shrugged, unconcerned with the detective's dismissal.

"Doctor, I understand the man died because of an airway obstruction," Leah hunched near the coroner, who was still checking the body. "Besides that, can you see anything else?" she inquired, her eyes searching the arms of the victim.

Apparently, the victim liked to have his lunch shirtless. Probably, because he spilled his food. She noticed the traces of food on his chest and abdomen. They drew the map of a bizarre land.

Yet, that didn't present much interest to her. Her eyes swept over the spots, looking for something else more important.

The tattoos on the man's beefy arms fascinated Leah. They coiled around the impressive biceps, climbed over the man's shoulders and descended on his chest.

"The tattoos would make it difficult, but not impossible to visualize any kind of bruises on his arms. But I would rather check his neck and cheeks, if you think this is a murder," the coroner explained when he noticed her fascination with the victim's tattoos.

Leah glanced at him inquiringly, and the coroner decided to explain.

"You see, he must have been restrained in order to shove that bone down his throat. But whoever did that had to keep his mouth open and his head still, as well. At least two strong men were necessary for that," he pointed out, just in passing. "Anyways, I suppose there must be some pressure points here, on both cheeks and the back of his neck."

"With that beard," Mark remarked, shaking his head with displeasure, "you can't see a damn thing."

"We'll have to shave him, that's true," the coroner nodded. "But now that I finished with the front, and we have already taken all necessary pictures, I'm thinking of turning him over. Then, I can verify his neck."

"All right, do it," Leah agreed, and even helped him to turn that mountain of a man over.

The doctor brushed the sloppy hair off the man's neck, and sure enough he found the signs showing that a large hand had put pressure on the man's neck.

"It's a crime, all right," the coroner sighed.

His words stunned Mike for a few seconds. Then, he messaged the back of his neck with nervous gestures.

Axel couldn't keep his curiosity at bay and made a brief foray in Mike's mind. He read a string of foul words crossing the detective's mind and rolled his eyes.

He was satisfied though because, at least, the detective didn't say anything out loud. Axel wouldn't have appreciated such a language in Leah's presence.

"All right," Leah straightened. "When you finish the post-mortem let me know, doc," she asked the coroner.

The doctor just nodded his assent and signaled to the morgue technicians to load the man into a plastic bag. Leah watched the procedure pensively, and then, she turned to Mike.

"I believe the wife was the beneficiary of his life insurance, if I remember correctly. Do you know where she is?"

Mike pointed to the back yard, and at the same time, he ruffled his hair again. His face showed signs of exhaustion and defeat all of the sudden. His cheeks lacked color and his eyes had turned dull. He needed a few moments to find his words.

"She's out there with a uniformed policewoman. She was crying and wailing…"

"Did she say anything?" Leah inquired, although she knew she would ask questions to the victim's wife herself.

"Just that she put the lunch on the table and he insisted on drinking a beer, which they didn't have in the house. Apparently, he bullied her into going and buying him some. She was away for about fifteen minutes. When she returned, the man was on the floor, already dead. She lost her control for a few minutes, shocked to find him like that. But then she thought of calling 911," Mike recited the story in a flat voice.

He still didn't recover after the coroner's verdict. His heart had fallen in his boots, waiting for Leah's reproaches.

"I see," Leah said. "I will go outside to speak to the wife. Bring the forensic team in here to search the kitchen. I don't think they can find anything in the rest of the house now, but at least the kitchen wasn't vandalized," she said dryly, and strode to the back door, which, apparently, opened into the yard.

CHAPTER 14 – THEORY AND REALITY

"So now we know that they needed at least three strong men for this last crime," Leah finished her explanation.

She leaned forward and helped herself to one of the slices of cake Liliana had left on the table. It was her third slice, but she couldn't have enough of them. The combination between the apricot jam, the nut filling and the chocolate icing was compelling.

About twenty minutes before, Liliana had passed by and presented them with the cakes piled on a platter. Leah had invited her to stay with them, but she had refused to remain on the patio.

First, she had glanced at her children playing the ball in the yard, and then, she had glanced at Victor askance for a few seconds. The arrows her eyes shot at him didn't go unnoticed.

Her glance conveyed the fact that she found him sorely lacking and in dire need of a dress down. Afterward, with her lips pursed, she had straightened her shoulders, and sauntered toward the French doors of the house, her head held up.

Victor's blue eyes had turned dangerously darker for a few moments, and his mouth had flattened into a hard line. No one doubted that something had happened between the two of them. It was clear that none was very happy with the other.

Leah's curiosity increased by the moment, yet she didn't want to ask indiscreet questions or to probe Liliana's or Victor's mind. She imagined Victor would say something if he wanted them to know what was going on.

After all, earlier that morning, she had warned Axel not to hunt after any kind of thoughts in Victor's head. Her dictate had soured Axel's mood for a little while, but he had recovered soon enough. She relished that he wasn't the kind of man who would let anything upset him for long.

"You were saying?" Victor asked Leah, feigning ignorance.

He had heard her just fine, but it would have been hard to miss the curiosity building in her eyes. He didn't feel like going into details about what had happened between him and Liliana that morning. He didn't know what to make out of their last argument.

"I said that three strong men must have been involved in the last so-called accident," Leah repeated patiently, although her fingers flexed.

Axel grinned. He guessed Victor's game and he suspected that Leah did too. Yet, she didn't want to let him feel awkward so she played the game.

Only Mark curled up his lip. He still tattered on the border about Victor. He wasn't sure whether he accepted Victor's involvement in their investigation, although he had offered them some good pointers. He was a civilian, though, and in his opinion, civilians shouldn't be involved in law enforcement work.

"That means we have the broker, the money loaner and at least three people involved in this affair," Victor mused. "But you know what I wonder?" he asked, and then, leaned forward to help himself to one of the cakes.

He had waited enough for that. His willpower went just that far. They were his favorite dessert, and he had missed them. His mother had him hooked on them since childhood, and he hadn't enjoyed one since he last visited his natal home, and that happened some time ago.

He always kept himself busy and hadn't had a vacation in four years. He had spent those last few years rearranging his new life in Toronto. He had bought the house, gone to school to take his private investigator certification and he built a clientele.

'*I'm due for a vacation, for sure,*' he mused. '*Next summer, probably.*'

He bit into the cake and when the flavor exploded onto his tongue, he practically sighed in pure bliss.

"What?" Mark asked impatiently, eyeing the cakes with suspicion. One would have thought he suspected that an illegal substance had been mixed in the composition of those cakes.

Mark had a sweet tooth, but, a creature of habit, he wasn't keen on trying new things. Right then, he failed to understand all the fuss over those cakes.

Leah and Axel had already nibbled three or four each. Victor had just taken his first, although his eyes had kept sliding to the plate with cakes for the past twenty minutes. If he had to go with the expression on Victor's face, those cakes were something else.

That decided Mark to try one, as well. '*I won't die, after all,*' he thought, and cautiously, he chose a smaller slice and shoved it into his mouth.

Then, he understood what the fuss was about. He chewed fast, grumbling, and snatched another piece in short order.

The other three watched him with amusement and Victor shook his head. '*Have I ever been so young?*' he wondered. He couldn't remember. His life had been full of events and experiences and he had lost something of the baggage along the way.

"You were saying?" Axel prompted Victor, unwilling to witness Mark's gluttony.

"Well, I wonder how the wife knew where to go. To whom she should speak to. I don't see the broker advertising that side of his business, you know," he waved his hand with impatience.

"That's a good question," Leah replied. "I wondered about that too."

"Maybe you should check the others," Victor proposed. "The beneficiaries of the other policies," he specified. "There must be a common denominator somewhere."

"And if there isn't?" Mark intervened peevishly, speaking with his mouth full.

He had already checked a few of them and hadn't found that they had anything in common. He didn't think someone else could uncover something he couldn't.

"No, there must be something somewhere," Victor contradicted him mulishly. "It doesn't make sense otherwise," he shook his head. "What do you know about the wife of the last victim?" he turned to Leah.

"She's a homemaker. She goes to church every Sunday and has a group of friends with whom she passes her time. The husband used to be a truck driver and was on the road most of the time," Leah read her notes. "But, interesting enough," she said, looking up, "some of the neighbors mentioned serious scandals coming from their house whenever he came back home."

"Then how come no one reported them?" Victor asked with a doubtful look in his eyes.

He knew the law in Ontario and he didn't see the police stand by and let a man abuse his wife.

"They said the guy was a bully and they were afraid. In their opinion, even if the police had arrested him, he would have still come back after a while, and they feared his retribution," Leah shrugged. "It happens sometimes, you know," she observed.

"Yeah, that might be a reasonable possibility," Victor nodded. "Did they say what prompted those scandals?" he inquired, curiosity etched on his features, and an inquisitive light shone in his eyes.

"The guy thought his wife… let's say, entertained other men while he was away," Leah explained with an impish grin.

"And was he right in his assumptions?" Victor prodded some more.

"Oh, yes," Axel answered, and bobbed his eyebrows to Victor.

"How do you know?" Mark asked and looked at Axel askance.

When they discussed with the woman no one said anything about any love affairs on the side. He would have remembered.

Axel shrugged, and to Mark's dismay, winked, "It was there on her face, Mark. Not difficult to see," he replied with conviction.

Victor bit his lower lip not to burst into laughter. He imagined how Axel '*had read*' the woman's face.

"So, maybe you should look for those other men, who knows," Victor proposed and opened his arms. "One of them might be the relation you are looking for. You don't have anything to lose," he pointed out.

"Only time," Mark groused out. "It's a waste of time to look for some men just because Axel '*read her facial expression*,'" he added in a quarrelsome voice.

"No, it is not," Leah replied quietly. "Call Josh and ask him to see to it," she ordered the detective.

Mark pursed his mouth, but couldn't refuse a direct order from his superior. Anyway, he was grateful she hadn't asked him to do it. His plans didn't involve overtime.

He put the call through to Josh, and at the same time, he took the chance to grab another piece of cake and stuff it into his mouth. He was hooked.

Leah shook her head and gave him a dirty look. Mark hurried to chew and swallow. Suddenly, he remembered she didn't like to see someone talking with their mouth full.

Maria and Lucian ran by them, laughing. Maria said something to her brother, but Leah didn't understand, as the little girl talked in Romanian. They ran into the house, but their laughter still reached the patio.

"I was thinking of getting a search warrant for the broker and the money lender," Leah turned to Victor.

"Based on what?" Victor asked in a very business-like voice.

"Hearsay," she replied with a shrug. "Based on what you told us. We have probable cause, you know that," she explained.

"Maybe you do. But you will tip your hand, I think," Victor explained. "I doubt it is a good move," he shook his head. "Maybe you should try something different first," he said in a barely audible voice, somewhat preoccupied with something else.

"What?" Leah asked, leaning forward to hear him better.

She sat in an armchair across from Victor and she needed to hear him.

"I was wondering," he looked back at her. "If those people didn't even know they were insured?"

'Now, that's a thought," Axel jumped into the discussion, very interested in the new direction Victor indicated.

Even Mark concluded his discussion with Josh immediately to listen to what Victor was saying. It wouldn't do to be left aside.

"Why do you think that?" Leah asked, rubbing her hands together, as if she had the feeling that more work would be thrown her way.

"Well, I shopped around these last few days, let's say. It's not like I could do much, you know, being cooped inside and unable to move around freely," he opened his arms. He showed to the laptop he had left on the table and continued, "I checked the market for life policies and prices. I also read a few studies and checked statistics, you know," he gesticulated. "Just to have a clearer idea," he shrugged his shoulders.

He didn't feel those piercing aches at every move anymore, and now, he compensated for all the hours he couldn't help it and had to keep still. Otherwise, he wasn't very exuberant in his gestures.

"I learned a thing," Victor said quietly. "People between eighteen and forty, forty-five, let's say, lean toward a different type of insurance, not this one," he shook his head with conviction.

He glanced at each of them and noticed the confusion on Mark's face and curiosity on Axel's. Only Leah kept a neutral mien. He decided to explain some more.

"Yes, this policy is a guaranteed issue, but mostly either old people or people with medical problems look into this kind of coverage. It comes with higher premiums, you see, but it goes up to the end of the insured person's life and doesn't require medical tests… Let's take the people I investigated before you started your inquiry," he addressed Leah directly.

She didn't show much interest, but she didn't look as if he annoyed her. That encouraged him to develop his theory.

"I don't think any of them was over forty-five or sick. No one could be included in any of those two categories. So why would they choose that specific insurance when they had other options? Better options, you know?" he inquired.

He shook his head and flipped his hand. He had clearly made up his mind.

"No, I don't think those people chose that specific policy. I don't think they even knew they were insured," Victor shook his head once more.

Leah and Mark stared at him. Apparently, they needed a little more explanation.

"You should check with some of the people who are still alive and have a policy on their life," he indicated. "You'll see that I am right," he nodded. "These should be two important avenues for your investigation, I think. First, you must find out if they knew that they had a life policy on their head. If they didn't, then you must question the beneficiaries. And then, you will find out how the beneficiaries knew where to go and purchase such a policy, and more important, in the absence of the insured person. They will give you information when they see they are about to be arrested for insurance fraud, at least."

Now, all of them looked at him confused. He admitted that probably they didn't know how the insurance industry worked.

"As far as I can see," he explained to them, "such policies require the presence of the insured person and their signature on the contract. Of course, when you discover how those people were capable of buying insurance on someone without their knowledge, you will find out how they knew who to talk to in order to have the insured person killed. Everything else will fall into place," Victor stressed out.

Then, he leaned back, in search of a more comfortable position on the sofa. He was on the mend, but still had twinges of pain now and then.

Leah seemed to ponder on his words for a few moments, and then, she nodded. He had a valid opinion.

"You have a point here, Victor. Perhaps, if we refocus our investigation on the people who are still alive, we might conclude our investigation faster and put the criminals and murder instigators behind the bars," she agreed with him.

"Of course, if any other '*accident*' happens, we still must investigate it," Axel mentioned.

He didn't relish the thought that someone who instigated a crime would go on unscathed, and would also benefit from the proceeds of their crime.

Victor nodded his agreement and chose another piece of cake.

Maria and Lucian came out of the house again, badminton rackets in their hands. With hesitant steps, they approached Victor.

"We're bored. We played cards and Monopoly, although it is no fun to play just the two of us," Maria mentioned. "We want to play badminton, but mommy said we need your approval," she explained.

Victor ruffled her hair and nodded.

"Yes, you can play badminton if you want. You don't need to come and ask me every time. I gave you those rackets, so they're yours. It's not my place to approve or disapprove of what you're doing. What your mother says counts. If your mother allows you to play badminton or come out into the yard, you may. My permission is unnecessary," he explained in a very matter-of-fact voice.

Both children looked at him sideways, as if they hadn't believed him, and he pursed his lips.

"What now?" he asked, impatience ringing in his tone.

"Nothing," Maria chimed in fast. "We're playing there," she pointed to the other end of the yard, and they ran away.

"I'm dying of curiosity here," Axel said after the children couldn't hear him anymore. "Something's going on and I need to know what," he practically begged Victor.

"You mean to say you haven't found out yet?" Victor asked in a dry voice.

Axel shook his head vigorously, and glanced at Leah.

"No, I promised, you see," he bobbed his eyebrows, and tilted his head toward Leah to clarify his statement.

Mark looked at him askance. He didn't understand what the man was talking about, but he felt it was important to catch the meaning of his words.

"I see," Victor murmured. "Well, because you were so considerate, I will tell you, although I don't find any pleasure in doing that. You know I couldn't move at ease during the last few days. So I asked Liliana to answer the phone, if I wasn't there. This morning, when

I showered, my mother called," he explained, and glanced away.

Something made him feel uncomfortable, and Axel leaned forward, bracing his elbows on his knees. He rested his head in his hands, all ears.

"Today, I turned forty," Victor confessed and the other three gasped.

"You rascal. And you said nothing," Axel jumped to his feet.

In his enthusiasm, he smacked Victor over the shoulder, hard enough to make him groan. Everyone else winced when the slap echoed in their ears.

"Sorry," Axel made a face. "Didn't mean to maim you," he chuckled, a little mortified because of his lack of attention. "I wanted just to congratulate you," he clarified his behavior.

"Thank you, I think," Victor replied dryly, and a smile appeared on Leah's lips. "Anyway, my mother called to congratulate me. She talked to Liliana, of course, and told her it was my fortieth birthday," he grimaced. "Immediately, that put the notion in her head that we should celebrate. Which in her translation meant that she would bake a birthday cake and cook a feast," he rolled his eyes. "Of course, I forbade it."

"Why?" Leah inquired softly, lacing her fingers together.

"Because she's not a hired housekeeper in my house, that's why," Victor snapped at her.

"I see," Axel said. "You're afraid she would think that you would let her stay here only if she takes care of certain chores," he nodded.

"My point exactly," Victor replied, flipping his hand.

"That's why the little girl didn't believe you when you said you couldn't approve or forbid anything," Mark concluded.

"Probably," Victor mumbled, feeling flustered with their interrogation.

"Anyways," Axel intervened, intending to bring the discussion back to Victor's birthday. "It's your fortieth, man, you should celebrate."

"Maybe," he replied pensively. "I was thinking to load them into my car and drive to Harbourfront. Sometime around five or five thirty… Reserve a table at the Irish Pub there, for instance… Take a stroll on the promenade," he said with some hesitation and looked at Axel for any ideas. "They haven't gone out of this house since they arrived and they're itching to see the city," he turned his palms up.

"Not a bad idea, Victor, my friend," Axel approved of his plans. "But you know what would be better?" he grinned.

"I see you can't wait to tell me, so…" Victor said in a dry voice and opened his arms.

"Invite all of us. We'll celebrate together. We're friends, after all," Axel threw a meaningful glance at Victor. "And if you have other friends…"

"Not really," Victor shook his head. "I have a few pals here and there, but I'm not close to the ones in Toronto."

"All right," Axel accepted his answer. "Then, invite us. And when we've finished eating in the Irish Pub and taking that stroll, you are talking about, we can go back to my place. I have a condo right there on the Harbourfront. We can have a drink, talk, something else than shop…" Axel looked at Victor inquiringly.

"Why not?" Victor embraced Axel's proposition. "Let's do it. You're in, right?" Victor looked at the others in turn.

Mark turned his head to the side, pretending he was looking at the children.

"I was talking to you, too, Mark," Victor said.

Mark's eyes shot to him with bewilderment.

"You would invite me," he stated, but his eyes had already bugged out.

"Yes," Victor laughed. "I invite you as well. Are you free? We'll meet there, at the Pub, at five thirty."

A shadow of regret flitted on Mark's face and he shook his head.

"I have a date," he revealed.

"Interesting," Axel whistled. "Who's your date?"

"Axel," Leah admonished him in a quiet voice.

"What? I was just asking," he protested.

"Bring your date," Victor replied quietly.

Mark glanced furtively at Leah, and both Victor and Axel whispered in unison, "Oh, oh."

Leah mused, and asked Mark in an insistent voice, "Who is she that you're so evasive?"

Mark swallowed hard and looked down, reminding her of a child caught with his fingers in the cookie jar.

CHAPTER 15 – TRUTHS AND DISAPPOINTMENTS

They climbed down the car in relative silence. It had been that way between the adults since he announced that they would be going out that evening.

Liliana immediately snatched Lucian's hand in hers. Maria was outspoken, but she listened more when she was told not to wander away.

Liliana always counted on her to stay by her side. She was more concerned that her son would wander away and get lost somewhere. He had a listening problem. In Liliana's experience, most males did have an issue with listening.

However, after he locked the car doors, Victor noticed her gesture, and he reached out for the little girl's hand. Her hand felt strange in his. Her fingers curved around his thumb, and made him grin.

Then, Victor took the lead and showed them the way to the Irish Pub. The restaurant overlooked the front of the lake and it was known for his good and hearty cuisine, but also for the view.

After some serious thinking, Victor had made a reservation for five-thirty in the evening. He wanted to give the detectives time to get home and change.

Even Mark had accepted the invitation in the end. He had fussed a little at the beginning, but he had given in and pointed out that he needed time to go and get his date.

Victor still remembered that the man hadn't accepted the invite graciously, though, and that gnawed at him, although he didn't take it personally. Apparently, Mark still had some apprehension concerning Leah's meeting with his date.

Interesting enough, he hadn't cracked under the pressure. He had refused to reveal who his date was.

Victor had noticed the exchange of looks between Leah and Axel. Definitely, Axel wanted to extract the information from the detective's head, but the lieutenant forbade him to do so. She could be very stern when she chose to.

Liliana had also looked at him in a strange way when he informed her about the reservations he had made. He wondered if he shouldn't have talked to her beforehand. Probably he should have invited her, instead of telling her, but it was already too late to consider all of that now.

Anyways, he had told her about his plans in front of the children and they had immediately rallied behind him. They had practically howled with pleasure because they were finally going out of the house. Given the circumstance, Liliana hadn't had the choice to refuse his invitation, but her black gaze had told him what she thought about his underhanded manner.

He hadn't had any ulterior reasons, though. Or at least, not conscious reasons. He hadn't done it on purpose. However, the feeling that he hadn't acted quite right kept bothering him.

Yet, he couldn't regret what he had done because, in the end, everything worked out just fine.

He didn't find any use in apologizing either. *'What's the point in apologizing after the fact?'* Victor was a very practical man and he didn't waste time with something that seemed nonsensical.

On their way to the pub, both Liliana and the children turned their heads everywhere. That time around, his birthday had fallen on a Saturday, and the Harbourfront was packed with people who wanted to take full advantage of the atypical temperatures they enjoyed that year.

There had been a slight drop in the temperature after the day Liliana landed in Toronto, but it was insignificant. The temperature was much lower from where they came. Even the children wore only t-shirts over their blue-jeans.

"Luci, look there," Maria shouted, turning her head toward her brother. "Boats. Mommy, we can go on a boat," she practically skipped, and Victor grinned.

"I don't know," Liliana hesitated. "We'll have to see. I don't know if they are for the public or…"

"They are," Victor interrupted her. "We'll look into that," he looked down at Maria. "Right now, we're going to have dinner. When we finish, we'll check their booths," he promised to her, and the girl rewarded him with a huge smile.

They moseyed around the groups of people and finally got to the Pub. A few people were waiting before the hostess's desk, hoping for a table. Victor elbowed his way until he reached the hostess.

"I have a reservation under Victor Dobrota."

"Oh, of course," the young woman smiled at him, showing a row of white teeth. "Some of your friends have already arrived and they're waiting for you at the table," she informed him.

Grabbing two menus off her desk, she invited them to follow her with a wide gesture.

"You said you wanted a table outside, right across from the water," she said inquiringly, and Victor nodded.

Always smiling, she sashayed between the rows of tables until they reached the one that Victor had reserved. He noticed that they had actually joined two large tables together to accommodate all of them.

Leah and Axel were already seated, and Axel stood up as soon as Leah whispered to him that Victor was there. They all exchanged a few words, and the men sat down after the children and Liliana chose their chairs.

To Liliana's surprise, Maria announced that she wanted to sit next to Victor. Not to be left aside, Lucian chose to sit between Maria and Axel. Feeling very conspicuous, Liliana accepted the chair next to Victor. She avoided his gaze when he held the chair for her, as she didn't want to see what he was thinking of that arrangement.

They had barely sat down when a waitress appeared at their table, a notebook in her hand.

"Would you like to order now or would you prefer to wait for your other friends?" she asked, her eyes sweeping over the empty chairs.

Victor glanced at everyone, and with the children's exception, who seemed willing to be done with their dinner as soon as possible, so they could speak about boats afterwards, everyone decided to wait for Mark and his date.

"We'll wait a few more minutes," he informed the waitress, and chuckled when Maria's groan reached his ears.

After the waitress left, he turned to the little girl and spoke to her in English, not to be rude.

"Don't worry, we'll have enough time to speak to the people with the boats, if they are still open at this hour. If they aren't, we'll come back tomorrow," he assured her, but the little girl pouted and crossed her arms over her chest.

"Did I hear the word *'boat'*?" Axel inquired.

"Yes, they want a cruise," Victor explained. "We'll check the booths there," he said, pointing with his chin in the direction of the cruise booths lining the shore. "Probably, we should do it now, while we're still waiting for Mark," he proposed.

"No need," Axel shook his head, and his words claimed the children's undivided attention. "Leah and I had already decided to gift you this bottle of whiskey for your birthday," he took a boxed bottle out of a bag he had laid at the foot of the table. "This bottle also comes with a cruise on my power yacht tomorrow morning," Axel said and bobbed his brows, making everyone smile.

However, at his words, the children cheered loudly, and Liliana's face turned scarlet. She burnt with embarrassment. People from other tables turned to them and some shook their heads with disapproval.

"You shouldn't care," Victor whispered in her ear, and then, he turned to the kids. "All right, we'll accept Axel's gift and go for a cruise on the lake tomorrow. But no more cheering, now, all right? Your mom doesn't seem to be fond of that," he winked at them, and they laughed.

"You'll have to put some more clothes on you tomorrow, though. It seems we'll have a drop in the temperature for the next couple of days," Leah explained to the children. "We'd have arranged for the cruise afterwards," she explained to Liliana apologetically, "but we have to work and we don't know what the weather will be like next weekend."

"So what?" Lucian replied, wrinkling his nose. "We're fine with cold," he pointed out.

"How long is it until tomorrow?" Maria chose to ask Victor and he rolled his eyes.

"Long enough for you to have your dinner and a good night sleep," he replied dryly.

"You don't talk to us like other people do," the little girl observed, scrunching her nose.

"Meaning what?" he asked gruffly.

He knew he was lacking any experience in dealing with children, but he entertained the illusion that he hadn't done so badly with them.

"Like we're small and understand zilch," she replied, nodding vigorously.

"Ah, so you don't mind, then," the truth dawned on Victor.

Maria shook her head and then, she patted his hand encouragingly.

"No, we don't. Continue to do so," she ordered in a very serious voice, and then she announced serenely, "The other man is here."

"Mark?" Leah inquired and turned her head to the promenade, when she noticed the direction of Maria's gaze.

She had expected him to come from the street and that was why she had chosen that specific chair. She wanted to lie her eyes on him as soon as he had arrived. When she found him in the crowd, a few feet away, her eyes widened and she gasped.

"Oh, no, he didn't," she whispered, and her voice mirrored her incredulity.

"What happened, love?" Axel asked. "Oh, that's Mark and his date," his eyes also found the man.

Mark strolled leisurely along the promenade, his fingers entwined with the fingers of a tall, willowy woman. The wind ruffled her purple thick hair, and she laughed at something Mark told her.

"Do you know her?" Axel asked Leah, his eyes always on the couple.

Mark and his date seemed to be taking their sweet time to get to the pub. They didn't rush their steps and they seemed deep in an amusing conversation.

"You know the Klavdya case," she turned her head to him inquiringly.

Axel nodded, a grin on his lips.

"It would be difficult to forget it, love, don't you think?" he drawled, and then turned to the others. "That's when the two of us met," he mentioned. "Now, tell me," he asked Victor in a very demanding voice, "what man would forget such a thing?"

Victor just shrugged, unwilling to share his opinion. He'd never been in Axel's shoes to know what he was talking about.

"Anyway," Leah intervened in the conversation, stressing the word, "Klavdya's son works for a video-game company or something of the sort," she said with a shrug. "And that's the receptionist that works for the same company," she pointed out, and her head tilted in the couple's direction. "We met her when we went to ask Aleksey questions about his mother."

"Oh, I see," Liliana murmured. "And is that forbidden?" she inquired.

"I hope not," Axel burst into laughter. "Or the two of us would be in serious trouble," he said, wiggling a finger between Leah and himself.

"Oh, shut up," she slapped his arm. "It's not that," she turned to Liliana. "But that woman didn't seem willing to give Mark the time of the day. She treated him as if… he hadn't even been there. I'm just surprised that he… let's say, charmed her to the last," she explained.

"Ah, now, I get it," Victor chuckled. "Maybe the man has hidden talents, who knows?" he said with a shrug, his eyes always on the couple.

His eyes brushed past the two other men behind Mark and his girlfriend. He had felt somehow forced to watch them.

The reddish sunset rays reflected in the shiny skull of one of them. Yet, the two men seemed deeply in a discussion and he dismissed them immediately.

Mark and his girlfriend disappeared from view, and with another cursory survey of the crowd, Victor returned his attention to his guests at the table.

A few moments later, the hostess led the couple to their table and a very scarlet Mark introduced Jen to them. They sat down, in the middle of Axel's guffaws. Mark's embarrassed face invited to laughter, or at least to some ironic smiles.

Leah asked Axel to stop and proposed that everyone checked their menus to order. The waitress's eyes had already bored into them for some time.

"Where's your present?" Lucian asked Mark, and the man looked at him wide-eyed.

Liliana gasped and her hand covered her throat in mortification. Her eyes drilled bores into the little boy, but he didn't seem to care.

Victor leaned over Maria's head and whispered to Lucian, "Here, presents are not compulsory, kiddo, so give the man a break. I consider his presence as a present," he thought to add.

Lucian looked askance at Mark and shrugged. He will definitely not invite him at his birthday.

Victor read the child's thoughts in his eyes, and his lips twitched. The boy was at the age when presents mattered the most. He still remembered some of those years.

He opened his menu to choose what to order, when his nape pricked. His eyes narrowed and he looked up and towards the shore of the lake.

It looked like more people had come out for a stroll in the evening. In spite of the crowd, Victor had the feeling that he saw the top of that shiny skull he had noticed behind Mark earlier, but couldn't be sure. His brows knitted and his mouth flattened into a hard line.

"Is something amiss, my friend?" Axel whispered over the children's heads, in a voice meant not to alarm.

"I don't know yet," Victor replied in the same calm voice.

The head had disappeared completely and he shrugged. He didn't know if there was any threat, but that prickle of awareness made him more determined to pay attention from that moment on.

***

"He didn't die, boss, I'm telling you," the man with the shiny head said, a cell phone at his ear. "Smidgen must have killed someone else," he pointed out.

"That man must die. The police can obtain a warrant based on hearsay. Without him, there's no basis for a hearsay warrant. We don't need the cops sniffle around our business, Tom," the harsh voice from the other end of the line replied.

"I'll take care of everything tonight, boss," the man promised, and disconnected the line.

CHAPTER 16 – ONE ATTEMPTED MURDER AND ONE KILL

When they arrived back home, Liliana was exhausted. The lengthy dinner in the Irish Pub had been full of laughter, but it had also been a harsh eye-opener for her.

She had thought that she would come to Canada and be able to found a job soon. *'They did request that I had certain degrees and experience, after all.'* Now, to her dismay, she found out that nothing like that mattered. Without experience in Canada, no one would hire her.

If only Victor had pointed that out to her, she would have nurtured a glimmer of hope. She didn't understand him and his actions, but she had the acute feeling that he had been against her coming into the country since the beginning.

Yet, Jen also supported his opinions. Apparently, she had immigrated a few years back and had a few stories to tell.

Jen looked like a teenager and Liliana was stunned when she found out that the girl was already twenty-seven, only one year younger than she was. Her name was Jana, but the friends she had made in Toronto called her Jen, and she started introducing herself as Jen, as well.

Jen had come from Serbia. She had thought she would find a job in her field at the time, but she couldn't.

She started working for the video game company, as a receptionist, and studied to become a paralegal, a completely different profession from what she had trained for, back home. She had only one more session before she graduated and obtained her diploma.

Jen's story depressed Lilian. Now, she understood that she had to go back to school if she wanted to find work in her field or, at least, to be able to find a good job.

'How the heck will I attend school and take care of the children at the same time, if I don't have a job?'

That was a conundrum. She knew she didn't have enough money to support them for a lengthy period of time.

The waitress came when they finished their dinner and provided a supplementary shock to her. She asked if they wanted separate bills and, for a moment there, Liliana forgot how to breathe.

Her fearful gaze shifted to Victor. The waitress had stunned her so much that she couldn't even voice her concerns.

She had taken some money with her that evening, but she didn't think she had enough to cover what she and her children had ordered. She had thought to have some money with her if the children saw and wanted something during their stroll.

The thought that someone would invite her in a restaurant and ask her to pay the bill at the end of the dinner, had never crossed her mind. Such things never happened back home.

Luckily, Victor asked the waitress to bring the bill to him. He made it very clear that only one bill was needed, and the others were his guests. Liliana sighed with relief.

Mark eyed him with distrust for a few moments, but Leah and Axel seemed to know and understand Victor better. They didn't show any reaction.

Jen just smiled at him and said, "Wow, and to think I was about to refuse Mark's invitation to dinner. I didn't know I would get a free meal out of it, you see. I get my paycheck soon, but until then, I have to watch my expenses," she mentioned.

"I wouldn't have asked you to pay," Mark turned hard eyes to her, which was something to be seen. Mark left people with the impression that he was nothing more than a teddy-bear.

Yet, sometimes, he was just sick of the way Jen kept dismissing him. He hadn't ever taken her somewhere and asked her to pay her way. So, he didn't understand why she would find necessary to say something like that.

If he hadn't fallen hard enough for her already, he would have looked around for some other easy conquests. Jen was a handful at times. *'All right, most of the time.'* With his demanding profession, Mark would have preferred some easy banter and a bit of sex thrown in between.

His thoughts were written all over his face. Axel and Leah preferred to admire the lake, but Liliana still remembered how Jen had bitten her lower lip, ashamed of her words.

Yes, all in all, it had been an interesting evening with interesting people. They strolled for an hour and spent a couple of hours in Axel's condo, where the children actually fell asleep. Victor and Axel had to carry them back to Victor's car.

Liliana sighed deeply, and Victor, glanced at her after he turned off the ignition. His eyes swept over her face and took note of her ringed eyes.

"Tired?" he asked with a whimsical smile on his lips.

"Exhausted," she replied in a dry voice.

He chuckled and nudged her chin with his thumb, "Well, you're going to bed now. You'll be all right in the morning."

He got off the car and opened the passenger door in the back. He leaned inside and lifted Lucian in his arms.

"I'll take him. He's heavier than Maria," he said, straightening up and turning back to her. "If you are too tired, and I think you are, you can wait here, and I will come back for the girl," he told her.

"I couldn't ask-," she started, but he interrupted.

"Yes, you can. Just wait here, and I will be back in a moment," he replied gruffly, and strode to the front door.

He braced his knee on the doorjamb and propped the boy onto his thigh. Then, he took his key out of his pocket, unlocked the door and entered inside, rushing to the stairs.

When he reached the children's room, he turned on the light, pressing his elbow on the switch. Lucian didn't stir at all, and Victor grinned.

His eyes swept over the beds and he laid the boy on the bed he judged to be his. He imagined that the one with several plush teddy-bears belonged to Maria.

When he returned downstairs, Liliana was leaning on the car's hood, her eyes closed. Something close to tenderness stirred inside him, and he pushed it aside with determination. He didn't have time for nonsensical things like that.

Victor put his hand on Liliana's shoulder and she opened her eyes immediately. Her heavy chocolate gaze felt like a fist in his chest, and he made an effort to find his voice.

He handed her the car keys.

"After I take the girl, you close the door and push this button here, all right?"

Liliana nodded, and Victor leaned over Maria and gathered her in his arms. *'Yep, I was right. She is feather-light, not like her brother.'*

He nodded to Liliana, and she closed the car doors. Then, she pushed the button, as he had indicated. Satisfied, hearing the sound of the lock engaging, he gave his head a shake, inviting Liliana to precede him into the house.

He laid the little girl on her bed and straightened. He glanced back at Liliana, who had stopped in the doorway.

"I think they can sleep one night without getting undressed. Let's just remove their shoes," he proposed, and in a few seconds, Maria's shoes were off.

Meanwhile, Liliana took off Lucian's shoes, and covered him with the blanket. She kissed his forehead, then came to Maria, brushed her hair off her forehead, kissed her and pulled the blanket up to her shoulders.

Both left the room, Liliana turning off the light on her way out. She didn't close the door completely, but left it ajar.

Victor looked at her, ruffled his hair, and then abruptly said, "Good night."

He didn't wait to hear her answer. He hurried to his own room and closed the door behind him quietly. It wouldn't do to tempt fate.

Liliana just shook her head, looking after him with confusion, and then went to find her own bed.

***

When Liliana's shaky fingers touched the door knob, ready to burst into Victor's room, the door opened and startled her. She had only the time to see Victor's fist coming toward her face, before she opened her mouth to bellow her outrage.

Midway to the target, the fisted hand opened, and Victor covered her mouth tightly with his large palm, so she couldn't make a sound. His hand covered almost half of her face.

"Shush," he whispered in her ear. "I thought you were someone else. Of course, I won't hit you. What are you doing here?" he took his hand off her face.

"I think I heard someone getting into the house through the French doors," she whispered back, and although he couldn't see her, he could feel her trembling next to his body.

"You've got good hearing," he whispered back. "Now, take my cell phone," he said and handed her the cell phone he had put in his pants pocket when he got out of bed and pulled his sweatpants on.

"Take the kids and hide in the walk-in closet in the fourth bedroom, the one that's empty. Call 911 and tell them to hurry. Give them my address, 24 Geraniums Street M4P 2A5. Now, go," he pushed her away from him, and listened to her quiet steps going toward the children's room.

Victor started down the stairs, his ears straining to hear the slightest noise coming from downstairs. He had heard the sliding of the French doors because they were right under his bedroom, and he knew the noises he would hear in the night. That wasn't one of them.

Yet, he didn't know how many people had come into the house and which their intent was, although he doubted they had come to congratulate him on his birthday.

He reached the bottom of the stairs without any encounter. He was content that his body had almost recovered completely. Two days ago, he wouldn't have been able to fight anyone.

He leaned his back on the wall, keeping still for a few seconds. A slight noise came from the den, and then he caught some whispers.

Victor leaned forward and turned his head around the corner. The blinds which normally covered the

French doors were open. The moon bathed the living room in a silvery light.

Two shadows came from the den and stopped just two feet away from Victor, who tried to breathe quietly. The moonlight shone over the shaven head of the man he had seen on the Harbourfront earlier. His eyes became hard and unforgiving.

Now he understood that Mark had been followed and that was how they found him. Probably, they had thought him dead before, and hadn't cared about his whereabouts until then.

"I'll go upstairs first and stab him," the man with the shiny skull said to the other one, who was a tall, wiry guy, with reddish hair. "You follow after me and kill the bitch," he ordered in a hard voice.

His hand went to the waistband at the back of his pants. He took out a butterfly knife and opened it with a flicker of his wrist.

Victor had seen that type of blade in the past. He frowned. He knew what such a blade could do. Then, his eyes narrowed, and a cold determination steeled him.

The second man, the carrot-haired guy, who was supposed to go and kill Liliana, took out a gimlet knife. The grimace on his lips proved he didn't have any qualms to take a woman's life.

They both crept toward the stairs, and Victor flattened his body to the wall. The first one appeared in sight.

'*Aha, so the first will be the carrot man,*' Victor noticed, and an ugly scowl contorted his lips.

Victor's fist made contact with the man's face and dropped him to the ground. A satisfied smile claimed

Victor's lips when the guy fell to the floor like a dead weight, and remained there, unmoving.

Shiny Ball, as Victor had taken to calling the other, attacked with the blade at the ready, but only nicked Victor's arm. The knife blade slashed through the superior layers of muscle, but didn't lodge into the arm.

Victor decked and thrust his knee into the man's midriff. He followed immediately with an elbow to the man's jaw and threw him to the floor.

The man had managed to hold on to the knife and now was scrambling to find his footing. They matched in height and weight, and Victor suspected the man was as stubborn as he was.

Victor rushed to him, grabbed his wrist, and with a sudden move, he twisted his hand to an unnatural angle. The wrist broke with a crunching pop.

The knife slid from the man's fingers and a groan of agony escaped his lips. The smell of his acrid sweat attacked Victor's nostrils, but he didn't react. He had felt that smell before and even on himself.

The man stumbled a few steps back. White-faced, his lips pinched because of the pain, the man still tried to attack again. He thought of rushing Victor and level him with a good kick in his private parts.

Yet, Victor read his intention in his eyes and sidestepped. He didn't give the man any second to recover from his surprise, and drove one of his big fists in the man's eye. He had actually aimed at the temple, but the man had refused to comply with Victor's intentions and moved to the side.

However, Victor's fist landed him to the ground again. A second later, Victor hunched near him, and planted his elbow into his liver, with all his strength.

That ended the fight. The man wasn't able to draw a breath into his lungs and began wheezing. Victor knew from his own experience that his attacker was out for the count and didn't present a danger anymore. He straightened and breathed deeply.

Suddenly, hushed steps sounded close to him on the hardwood flooring, and instinct made him turn and confront the new threat.

The carrot man, he had decked earlier, attempted to drive the short-bladed dagger into Victor' chest, but Victor dodged the blade.

His chest remained unscathed, yet the blade plunged into his left arm, right into the biceps. Victor read the man's intention of pulling the knife toward the elbow. He wanted to sever the artery, which would kill Victor and leave the other three upstairs in the two men's hands.

'Not a good day for you to die, Victor boy. You must find a way to remain standing," he thought with sarcasm.

With a hard stare, he closed his fingers over the man's hand, which grabbed the hilt, and he crashed it with all his might.

Victor groaned when the blade twisted in his biceps and jarred him. He fought to pull the blade out and his opponent fought to pull it down towards his elbow.

His adversary's onion breath stirred Victor's nausea, and his head pounded. He drove his knee hard into the man's groin, hoping to dislodge his fingers off the dagger.

The man stepped back, crying out in agony, but he took the blade with him, pulling it out of Victor's arm, and causing suction in the process. Blood gushed out of the arm, spraying the carrot man all over his face and clothes.

Victor howled at his turn. Sweat beaded his forehead and he tried to wipe it off with his right forearm. Then, he noticed he was bleeding there, as well.

Apparently, Shiny Ball had done more than nicking him. He had slashed the muscle, although superficially. The adrenaline, rushing through his veins, had prevented Victor to feel anything before.

He didn't think he could use his left arm much, but the other one still helped him. With one eye on the wiry man, he tried to flex his right arm. It was painful, awkward and didn't have much force. Probably because he'd already lost too much blood.

The carrot man found his legs under him, although his face was still contorted in pain. He adjusted his hold on the hilt, and with a cry, he lurched toward Victor, ready to shove the knife into his neck.

Victor thought to break his wrist, as he had done with his mate, but after they fought for a few minutes, while the knife kept advancing toward his neck and even pinched him a couple of times, he understood he couldn't do it. He didn't have enough strength left in his right arm.

With a bellow, he also closed the fingers of his left hand on the man's wrist. Sweat poured in his eyes, and a lock of hair had fallen over his left eye. His entire skin felt clammy and cold.

He tightened his teeth, and then, he dug deep inside himself to gather his last reserves of strength. With another bellow, he pushed the hand with the gimlet knife away from his throat and plunged it into the man's neck.

Carrot man's eyes widened in shock. A gasp flew off his lips and he staggered on his feet. His fingers were still locked on the hilt of the knife, but he fell to his knees.

He continued staring at Victor, who was breathing heard, his eyes on the man on the floor. Then, the man slid on one side and gasped once more. Blood gushed out of his mouth and he gurgled.

The man was done. Victor knew the signs, and he turned around to watch the other one. Moonlight shone in the blood drops on the floor, but there were too many shadows in the room. Victor hit the switch and he winced when his eyes fell on Liliana, who was standing on the stairs.

The fingers of her right hand were coiled around her neck and her other hand pushed against her midriff. Her eyes glimmered with tears and their pupils had turned the color of dark chocolate.

CHAPTER 17 – AWE AND TRUCE

"Why are you here?" Victor asked her in a hoarse voice, looking at her. His eyes lingered over her disheveled appearance.

Liliana had been exhausted when she took to her bed that evening, and she didn't bother with braiding her hair. Now, she looked thoroughly tumbled, and even though Victor was aware of the multitude of aches pulling at his body — hard to miss those, the male in him still responded to her appearance.

"I thought I had told you to remain upstairs, ensconced in the walk-in closet with the kids," he mentioned in a mean voice.

"I wanted to make sure-" she began to say, but he interrupted her.

"What? Did you think you would handle the situation better than I could?"

Liliana shook her head, and the fingers at her neck quivered. She had seen part of his last fight and what she had witnessed still shocked her.

The moonlight had fallen right on the two men who were fighting. She had barely stopped the screams in her throat whenever the blade slashed Victor's skin.

Now, she took note of his savage eyes and the tension in his muscles. Victor's wild eyes didn't scare her, but the sight of blood dripping on the floor from his left arm, which he kept at some distance from his body, did.

"Then what?" Victor snapped when she didn't answer fast enough to satisfy him.

His patience slipped away and adrenaline wore off. He made note of the fear in her eyes and felt disgusted with his behavior, but something pushed him to be mean to her.

"You just wanted to join the fray, is that it?" he bit off in a dry voice.

"Victor, shut up," she shouted. "You're badly hurt, you fool. Instead of talking nineteen to the dozen, you'd better sit down somewhere and let me take a look at your wounds," she said with dismay, when she observed that his neck and the other arm bled as well.

"Where are the kids?" he asked, as if she'd never said anything.

Liliana looked up the stairs with concern in her eyes, and then confessed, "I left them in the closet and told them not to move until I came to get them."

"Then go and get them, and then, put them to bed. They had enough excitement for one night. I have to bind this guy's hands," he pointed to the man still wheezing on the floor. "He shouldn't be able to react for at least a couple of hours, but I prefer to err to the cautious side."

Liliana shook her head, but he didn't pay any attention to her and started to the closet in the entry hallway to look for a rope or something. He didn't get to take more than two steps that the siren of a police car sounded not far away.

He turned his head to Liliana, "At least, you've called the cops, I see."

She nodded and sighed with exasperation. "I also called Leah," she mentioned. "I found the phone number on your phone," she explained.

"At least that," he grumbled and that fired her up.

"What the heck do you mean? I've done nothing wrong," she pointed an accusing finger to him.

Victor noticed with satisfaction that the tears had disappeared from her eyes, and now, her eyes sparkled with fury. Yes, her anger was directed toward him, but at least she didn't look as hurt and scared as before. He could take her anger, but he didn't fare well with her tears.

With an effort, Victor grinned and said in a much kinder voice, "Go and put the kids to bed. I'll take care of the police."

Liliana looked after him for a few seconds, and shook her head over his stiff gait and tight shoulders. She followed him by sight until he disappeared in the hallway and shook her head again. Then, she ran upstairs to take the children out of the closet.

Victor opened the front door exactly when the police cars stopped in his driveway. His eyes shied away from the lights, and he cursed. They needn't try so hard to wake the entire neighborhood.

Axel's car stopped right behind the three police cars, and Leah immediately opened the door and rushed out of the car.

"Is everyone all right?" she ran up the stairs to Victor, and when her eyes fell on his appearance, she gasped. "Oh, my God, you've been hurt again." She shook her head in disbelief and her lips pinched.

Axel came behind her and his eyes smoldered with fury. He just nodded to Victor, his eyes travelling up and down his body.

"Just tell me the other one is worse," he said quietly, a light bordering on savage in his eyes.

Victor nodded briskly and invited them inside with an abrupt gesture.

"One's dead, one's alive," he told them, and both looked at him as if he were crazy.

"You fought two guys with knives," Leah observed in an uncertain tone of voice.

She looked pointedly at the wounds located on his neck and his biceps. She had guessed that knives had been involved given the appearance of the wounds, but she was convinced that she misheard him. He couldn't have fought two armed men, and especially not after his last brush with death.

"Yes," he replied, and waved them inside again. "They're both in the living room. You can see for yourself."

Leah stared at him for a few more seconds, and then turned to her fellow police officers.

"We have one dead suspect and one still alive, but hurt. Of course, Mr. Dobrota is hurt as well, as you can very well see for yourselves. Have you called the paramedics?" she inquired, without asking the question to anyone in particular.

"Yes," one of the officers answered. "The ambulance must arrive in a couple of minutes," he mentioned. "I think I hear them," he tilted his head to the side, listening to the noises in the night.

"All right, then. Call the coroner, as well, and stop the sirens and the lights. The neighbors didn't ask for that," she ordered and then stomped into the house, followed by Victor, Axel and three other officers.

"How did they find you?" Axel wondered.

"I saw one of them on the Harbourfront earlier, although I didn't know who he was at the time," Victor explained. "They followed Mark and probably, they saw me there. I should have been careful and check my back when I drove back home," he growled. "An amateur mistake," he chastised himself.

"You couldn't have known," Leah patted his arm, and when he flinched, she apologized. "I don't know where someone could lay a finger on you without hurting you," she commented, her eyes sweeping over the blood that covered almost his entire bust, and had dripped onto his legs.

"It's not all mine," Victor grumbled, and waved his hand between the two men on the floor. "The one there is dead. I didn't have a choice," he said in a quiet voice.

Axel came next to him and touched his uninjured shoulder. Victor turned to him inquiringly, and Axel whispered, "She knows, don't worry."

"I didn't worry," Victor snapped. "I had to protect myself, no matter what. They already had plans to kill Liliana. I heard them when they came out of the den," he pointed to the room the two thugs had searched before coming after him. "If I had died, she wouldn't have survived. Plus, I couldn't be sure that they wouldn't kill the children afterwards," he explained with anger, and his pale face turned scarlet with molten fury.

"If it was self-defense, and it does sound like self-defense to me, you shouldn't worry," a man's voice came from behind, and both Victor and Axel turned.

"Oh, Mike, hi there," Axel greeted him with amusement. "Demoted to the graveyard shift?" he asked in a malicious voice.

"Arnett," Mike replied, and his voice told Victor that the detective hated Axel. "I see you're still joined at the hip with our lieutenant," he noticed.

"And don't you forget that," Axel replied in an easy-going manner, yet his eyes bored into the other man.

Mike nodded, suddenly uneasy under Axel's scrutiny. He strode to one of the uniformed officers and whispered a few orders. Then, he joined Leah.

"I asked the forensic team to come," he told her.

"That's good," she replied, but she kept busy analyzing the scene.

Mike's eyes swept over the living room, and shaking his head, he observed, "This Dobrota is something else. Imagine, to be attacked by two men with knives and to get out of it alive, able to tell the story."

Leah caught the open admiration in his voice, and her lips arched into a smile. That was the type of thing that impressed Mike. This time, she was impressed, as well. Few people would have come out alive from such a deadly confrontation.

"I'd like to speak to that one," she pointed to the man still gasping on the floor. "But he doesn't seem to be able to catch his breath," she expressed her exasperation.

"Probably, he caught a serious blow to the liver," Mike assumed. "He might need a little time before being able to say anything," he shrugged.

"I think I would prefer that you ask the necessary questions from Dobrota," she glanced at Mike. "I don't want anyone to think I favored him or something."

"Not a problem with me," Mike nodded. "But no one would say that you favored him. He was definitely in self-defense. There is no case against him."

"That's what I think, as well, but…" she shrugged.

"Got it. Don't worry, I will take care of it," he nodded again and returned to Dobrota.

'I forgot Arnett is here, as well,' he scowled when he saw Arnett talking to Dobrota, near a window.

He still approached the two men, and when Axel gazed at him inquiringly, he put up his hands and said, "The lieutenant ordered me to ask a few questions. She prefers that I discuss with Mr. Dobrota."

"It makes sense," Axel nodded and turned to Victor. "I think that you need to have those cuts and nicks seen by a professional first," he noticed.

"I'll take a look at them," Liliana's voice came from behind him, and her tone didn't allow any opposition.

"He was talking about a professional, though," Mike explained.

"I am a professional," she gritted out, and Victor's lips twitched.

"She is, you know," he chimed in, to save the detective's skin. Liliana seemed ready to do battle.

CHAPTER 18 - WHEN ONE VALUES THEIR SKIN

A knock on his door stirred Victor awake and he groaned. The movement had awoken the multitude of aches, his body had contended with since he took to his bed. He felt as if someone had poured liquid lava everywhere on his skin.

"Yes," he bellowed, mostly to cover the groans which crowded in his throat.

The door opened and Liliana entered the room. Her appearance reminded him of the first morning, she had spent in his house, but with a notable difference. This time, she hadn't remained behind the door.

Liliana sauntered to the bed. She leaned over him, and her cool hand rested on his forehead for a few seconds. She nodded satisfied, and then, she reached for his wrist. She checked his pulse and nodded again.

"You're not worse for the wear," she said, and a light amusement chased away the concern on her face.

"Is that why you woke me at this ungodly hour? To tell me I am fine?" he asked heatedly, although he was far from disliking her ministrations.

She sighed, shook her head, and then said, "Why would I have expected that you would be in a different frame of mind this morning?"

Victor sneered, and she put a hand on his chest, to smother his upset. She straightened and pushed her braided hair over the shoulder. Victor's eyes watched attentively every move she made.

"First of all, it is not an ungodly hour, but noon," she specified in lecture mode, her gaze pinning him down.

When her words registered, Victor frowned and reached for his cell phone on the night table. He couldn't stop a groan and put up his hand when Liliana moved to help him. He snatched the phone and checked the time. When he saw the hour, he frowned and cursed.

"Why didn't you wake me up before this?" he shouted at her and pushed the bed sheet aside with impatience.

When her eyes rounded in shock, he remembered he always slept in the nude, and pulled the bed sheet back over him swiftly.

"Sorry," he muttered. "It went clean out of my mind," he explained.

"It's not a problem," Liliana waved his concern away. "Anyway, if you don't need my help," she said, and then, pausing, she glanced at his face, just in time to see him shaking his head in denial, "then I'm going back downstairs. The detectives and Axel are here," she continued. "That's why I came to wake you," she explained and retraced her steps back to the door.

"Why not earlier?" Victor asked, still upset with himself that he had slept the morning away.

"You needed your sleep," she said softly, turning her head back to him.

"You went to bed at the same time," he pointed out in a stubborn voice.

"Yes," Liliana nodded, "but I didn't go through the wringer first," she pointed out, and this time, she didn't give him the time to answer. She strode out of the room, closing the door behind her quietly.

Victor muttered a few choice words under his breath, and then, got out of bed, his movements eliciting groans and curses, more appropriate for the ears of a drunk sailor.

He decided to take a hot shower, hoping to appease his mistreated muscles, and gritting his teeth, he trudged to the bathroom. A glance in the mirror assured him that even if he was still alive, he looked like death warmed over.

***

With measured steps, consequence of his previous night's activities, Victor went out onto the patio where the detectives congregated.

His yard faced the south and it always felt warmer there than on the other side of the house, so it wasn't a wonder that they chose to sit outside. Most of the Canadians he knew tried to take advantage of the sun as much as possible.

He knew that the detectives had gathered on the patio because their voices had reached him through the window when he got dressed — another endeavor that had taken an eternity.

They had been waiting for a while. It had taken Victor almost half an hour to finish his shower and pull on some slacks and a polo shirt.

'If they didn't want to wait, they should have called before,' he shrugged inwardly and stepped out onto the patio.

Axel's eyes shifted to him immediately, and he stood up to greet him.

"Hey there, buddy, is everything fine?" he asked and thumped him on the shoulder.

Victor couldn't swallow a deep groan, and beads of sweat sprinkled his forehead. He fisted his hands, and his blue eyes darkened. If he hadn't been so run down, he might have answered in kind.

"Oh, I forgot again," Axel apologized, a faint blush powdering his cheekbones. He rushed to take Victor's arm and lead him to the sofa, where he might have felt more comfortable.

Victor scowled and pulled his arm off Axel's grip. Yet, he accepted the seat on the sofa and sat down with a muffled grunt.

'One more adventure like the one I had last night, and I'll kick the bucket,' Victor observed very matter-of-factly. A body could take so much beating, after all.

"How are you feeling?" Leah asked him with concern in her eyes.

'Do you really have to ask?' Victor mused with sarcasm. It wasn't as if anyone could miss the black rings around his eyes and the paleness of his skin.

"Probably, I'd better not ask," she remarked, interpreting his dark glance accurately.

Victor shrugged and hissed when a stabbing pain reminded him of the wound in his biceps. Luckily, the slashes on his neck had been shallow. Otherwise, he wouldn't have been able to move his head either.

Victor heard Maria's laughter from the other side of the yard. He glanced her way, just in time to see her taunting her brother because he had missed to catch the ball.

He smiled with satisfaction. At least, they didn't suffer after the night's ordeal. They bounced back up. It mustn't have been easy for them to be taken out of their beds in the middle of the night and stashed in a closet.

Victor turned back to his *'guests'*. The number of detectives had increased. Mike had joined Leah and Mark, and now, he watched Victor in awe.

Victor winced inwardly. He had always disliked blind admiration and he didn't see a point in being kept in high regard right then.

"So, what's the verdict?" he asked, his voice void of interest.

He was interested, all right, but not when he could have slept a little more. He couldn't avoid what would come, so he didn't see the point to rush and meet his fate.

"You have nothing to fear," Mike hurried to tell him. "I presented my report and the Crown Attorney agreed with me. He decided that it was an open-and-shut case. You were in self-defense and didn't use inappropriate or excessive force given the circumstances."

Victor nodded that he understood. He knew that not always someone in his situation was lucky enough not to go through extensive interrogation and subsequent trial.

"I'm sure I have to thank you," he said to Mike, who shook his head.

"No, you don't. I asked questions and I analyzed the scene. It was obvious you hadn't done anything wrong. Even the weapon used in the killing didn't belong to you. Plus, your blood was on the assailant and it was covered with his blood afterward. That nailed it. You were hurt first, and quite badly, considering the amount of blood found on the dead guy's body. It stands to reason that you had to respond with deadly force," Mike pointed out. "I would have done the same," he smacked his fist onto the table top.

Victor acknowledged his words with a nod. It felt like a weight off his shoulders. He knew that most of the time, someone in such a situation was charged with something, especially if they used a weapon they had in their possession. He hadn't, but one never knew how facts could be interpreted.

"Thank you, though," he repeated. "Have you got anything out of the Shiny Ball?" he asked Leah.

"Shiny Ball?" Axel smirked. "Well, I think it's an accurate name," he observed. "It suits him."

Leah shook her head at him, and then replied to Victor.

"Imagine, he'd been singing since he recovered. It took him some time," she admitted. "That was some blow you delivered," she shook her head.

"Better incapacitated than dead," Victor grumbled.

"I hope you don't have any serious remorse about the guy who died," Axel intervened in a serious tone of voice.

"I can't," Victor replied in a dry voice. "He would have killed me and them," he pointed his chin to the children playing on the other side of the yard. "I can't have any remorse, just relief that everything ended. Have I preferred that I incapacitated him without killing him? Of course," he said, opening his arms. "But it doesn't make sense to play the *'ifs'* right now," he replied drily, and then, he turned to Leah again. "So, what did he say?"

"Oh, he gave us enough," she told him. "Of course, after a visit to the hospital. They had to fix his wrist. You broke it, you know," she mentioned.

"Enough to do what?" Victor insisted, watching her steadily. He knew he had broken that bloody wrist and didn't care about what the doctors had done to the man at the hospital.

Moreover, he didn't believe that the detectives had come with the intention to pay a courtesy call and they didn't mean to tell him anything. It wouldn't have made sense to bring Mark and Mike along.

"We had two search warrants issued this morning," she informed him. "One for the broker and the other for the so-called businessman who loaned the money. Our people are sifting through the papers now. As Shiny Ball, as you like to name the guy, gave us also information related to some of the *'accidents'*, we arrested both the *'businessman'* and the broker in the morning."

"At least the *'accidents'* will end now," Victor noticed, and Axel approved with a nod.

"Shiny Ball will testify that Smidgen, the broker, planned and killed Gunther and, of course, attempted to kill you too," Mark thought to add. "Last night, the order to kill you came from the other one, Donald Stanton. That's the businessman's name," he explained.

"I hope you are hungry," Liliana's low voice came from behind him. "It's almost one o'clock," she noted.

Victor turned around fast, and pain washed through his body. He flexed his fists, not to grunt loudly and his hard eyes landed on Liliana's face.

"You're unbelievable," he grumbled. "After last night, you still found the nerve to cook," he shook his head, as if he couldn't believe it.

"Children don't care about last night. They still ask for food, no matter what," she replied with sarcasm. "You need food as well, so shut up and get ready to eat," she said, putting a big bowl with soup on the table.

She turned around and sashayed back to the house to bring the small bowls, spoons and bread. Leah and Axel immediately stood up and followed her, intending to help.

"We should go, too, I think," Mark whispered to Mike, who nodded, ready to stand up.

"It's not necessary," Victor remarked. "Between the three of them, they should make short order of everything. Just relax for a while," he invited them, and then, he proceeded to do just that.

***

"So, you have cause to arrest both Smidgen and Stanton," Victor observed, helping himself to another bun from the basket Axel had put on the table.

They had already finished the soup and started on the second course, which consisted of meatballs, mashed potatoes and salad. The kids had already had their lunch apparently, but they still came by and snatched a meatball and a bun each, to everyone's amusement.

This time, Leah had convinced Liliana to sit and have lunch with them. Liliana already knew enough about the case and the previous night, when she tended to Victor's wounds she had proven she wasn't squeamish.

"More than enough," Mike replied, and then forked some mashed potatoes. "How do you make them so creamy?" he asked. "My wife's mashed potatoes are lumpy," he complained.

Victor practically growled. The detectives had become once more too concerned with food and forgotten about the purpose of their visit.

"I whip them with butter and milk," Liliana revealed. "I think the milk is the secret," she admitted.

Victor rolled his eyes. It was as if they had been at a bloody reunion with the purpose of exchanging recipes. When Axel burst into laughter, he glowered at him, and Axel put his hands up.

"Come on, it's funny," he told Victor, and his reply brought a blush in Mike's face.

Liliana just shook her head and continued eating. Since the beginning of the lunch, she had avoided glancing at Victor. She didn't want to see his disapproval, if he did disapprove of what she had set on the table.

"Could you expend on that *'more than enough'*?" Victor asked in a churlish voice.

Mike glanced at him inquiringly. He didn't understand what upset Victor, but replied, "When we told him that we can prove that the so-called accidents were actually crimes, he confessed to a few, counting on leniency. He also told us who ordered the crimes, that's why we had probable cause to arrest the two others."

"And on Monday morning, we'll organize the lists with the other policies that Smidgen sold," Mark intervened, after he took care to swallow, so Leah wouldn't lash out at him. "We contacted the claim adjusters and they promised to have the lists at the ready. Then, we will check and see who was aware that they had life insurance and who wasn't."

"We can arrest the beneficiaries for insurance fraud, at least," Leah pointed out. "We will probably make some of them talk and tell us how they found out about this scheme."

Victor nodded satisfied that they took his recommendations into consideration. It was more than he had expected.

"You still have a lot to do, though," he noted, and Leah approved with a shake of her head.

"Yes, it will take some time, but at least we have arrested the brains behind the entire organization," she said. "Now, it is a matter of determining how guilty the others are and of course, if possible, to arrest the instigators of the other crimes that have already taken place."

"That will be difficult," Victor conceded. "You have very little evidence, and no one will confess to murder if there's nothing to coerce them."

"But we can determine if the signatures on those policies belonged to the people insured, as you said,"

Mark pointed out. "There must be a piece of paper somewhere with their writing," Mark said in a stubborn voice, and Leah had to hide her smile.

Now Mark embraced Victor's opinions and advice all-heartedly. It took only a bloody fight to change his perspective.

"Are we going on a boat today?" Maria's question came from next to Victor.

Victor narrowed his eyes when he remembered the cruise, and he turned to the girl.

"You promised," she stressed out, and a shadow of a smile flitted on his lips.

"Maria," Liliana intervened, "Victor was hurt last night. We'll have to go some other time."

Victor noticed the disappointment in the girl's eyes, and her pout. He glanced at Axel to see what he thought, and Axel shrugged.

"It's up to you," Axel mouthed, so the child wouldn't hear him.

"We'll go today," Victor said. "Axel doesn't seem to mind."

"Yippee," both children cheered, and Victor grimaced.

"When?" Maria asked immediately.

Victor looked at Leah and Axel for an answer.

"We covered everything, I think," Leah shrugged. "I think we could go after we finish lunch. What do you think?" she turned to Axel.

"It's perfect for me. Do you want to come?" he asked the other two detectives.

"Not me," Mike shook his head. "My wife has her heart set on a movie this afternoon, so I will have to go home."

"I bought tickets for Jen and me at Mirvish Theatre so I can't come either," Mark opened his arms. "But I am enjoying this lunch," he thought to mention, with a smile for Liliana.

"There's also dessert," she told them.

Victor turned to her, shook his head and said, "You've been a busy bee today, I see."

"People react differently," Liliana rebuked him. "When I'm tense, I cook. Plus, the kids expect a dessert on weekends," she shrugged. "Being a mother doesn't stop because of something that happens out of the blue," she snapped at him, and stood up to go inside.

"I didn't mean-" Victor tried to apologize, but she shook her head and left.

"She'll be back," Maria stroke his forearm. Luckily, she had chosen the one without cuts. "She's just gone inside to bring the dessert. And I want some," she said and sat next to Victor, waiting patiently for her mother to return with the dessert.

Victor chuckled and ran his fingers through her short hair.

"Why don't you keep your hair long, like your mom?" he asked her, curiosity etched on his face.

"Because mom doesn't have someone who pulls her hair," she replied dryly. "Lucian always took advantage. Now, he can't," she replied and lifted a shoulder.

CHAPTER 19 – GRAVE THOUGHTS FOR A CRUISE

Liliana was leaning on the rail, looking in the distance. She didn't notice the ducks playing in the water or the other sails out on the lake. Deep in her thoughts, she pondered on what she should do.

She didn't worry about the children. Axel had made them wear life-saving jackets and both children had been pestering him with questions since they set sail. In the beginning, she worried that the man would get sick of all those inquiries, but he didn't seem to mind.

"What's with that gloomy face?" Victor's words intruded in her musing, and she glanced at him with a shrug.

"Just thinking," she replied quietly.

"About?" he insisted, unwilling to let the subject drop.

He braced one elbow on the rail and tilted his head toward her to see her face better.

"What I should do."

"About what?" he groused impatiently. It was frustrating to get a straight answer from her.

Liliana turned her face to him and her gaze searched his eyes. She didn't understand the man most of the time. At times, he seemed so remote that nothing would touch him. There were also times when he appeared angry with no reason at all. After the first couple of days living in his house, she had given up finding a logic in his actions or behavior. Yet, she found him a very interesting specimen.

"It's been almost a week since we came here," she pointed out. "I have to think of what I must do. I can't just live in a limbo, as a guest in your house," she shrugged.

"Well, I'm sure it has been more eventful than you expected," his mouth set in a hard line. "You've had enough to cope with."

"Not really," she admitted in a soft voice. "You're the one who had a lot to cope with. I've just watched from the sidelines," she explained.

"I see," he observed with hesitation. "And what are you thinking of doing?"

"I'll have to check my options. I can't abuse your hospitality more than a couple more days. I will have to find a job, I think," she replied with indecision. "I will probably have to get some education in another profession because I don't see how I could go through medical school and work and take care of the kids," she added with regret.

"First, we should check what you need to do in order to obtain a medical license. I don't think you have to go through the entire training. You might be looking only at about one year or maximum two years of training, if not just a few exams."

She laughed bitterly and shook her head.

"What now?" Victor inquired with a frown between his brows.

"I don't have the financial means to support myself and the children for more than a month or two. I can't even think of a year or more," she explained, and the corner of her lips curbed down.

"What expenses do you foresee? Yes, we will have to look into a school for children, probably a kindergarten, I think, considering their age. And tomorrow, because the school year has already started. But you'll afford that, I am sure," he replied very matter-of-factly.

"That's nice and good, but I also need to pay a rent for an apartment and put food on the table and…" she started enumerating in a rush, ticking every item on one of her fingers.

"Whoa, whoa, whoa. Just slow down for a moment. You don't need an apartment. There are enough rooms in my house and no one uses them," he pointed out.

"But I can't abuse…"

"That's no abuse," he cut her off, slicing the air with his open palm. "The rooms are empty. Someone should live in them."

"But I still need to pay-" she started but stopped abruptly when his gaze turned forbidding.

When he noticed she didn't continue the sentence, a smile flitted on his lips.

"Smart girl," he observed, a dry amusement in his voice, which made her scowl at him. "Now don't turn all Valkyrie against me," he chuckled.

"If I don't pay, I have to do something in return for you," she replied in a cross voice.

"Unfortunately, not what I want the most," his words came out of his mouth before he could think what he was saying.

When he realized what he had said, Victor looked at her askance, hoping she didn't catch his meaning.

"What do you want the most? I might be able to oblige you," she replied, not understanding what he was talking about.

His eyes widened, burned with a weird light, and he pressed his lips.

"Come on, I'm sure I can do what you need," she insisted.

Victor started coughing to hide his reaction at her vehemence. Liliana looked at him confused.

"Are you all right? What happened?" she asked, already touching his throat.

Victor flinched under her touch and took a couple of steps back. He shook his head and tried to contain his cough.

Then, keeping her at bay with his outstretched arm, he said, "Nothing, I am fine. Just dandy," he added for a good measure. He shook his head again, and then made sure to say, "No, you needn't do anything. You've done enough so far. What, with your cooking and your patching," he pointed out showing to his biceps. "You don't need to pay me anything and do anything."

With those words, he stalked away. Liliana looked after him annoyed, as well. She couldn't understand the man at all.

Leah approached her, her lips arched in a smile.

"Is everything fine?" she asked Liliana.

"I don't know," she replied with frustration. "Maybe you can make more sense out of this, because I, for one, can't," she decided to share with Leah. "I was just talking to him, you know. He said we could remain in his house, but he didn't want any money from me," she waved her hand with agitation. "I asked him what he wanted, and he said that he couldn't ask for what he wanted, or something of the sort," she continued, suddenly unsure of her accuracy. "Anyway, when I told him I could oblige him and give him what he wanted, he burst into coughing and stalked away," she explained, outrage very keen in her voice.

To her consternation, Leah burst into laughter, shaking her head.

"Don't start you too," Liliana groused through her teeth. "Usually, I am not so dense."

"I apologize, but both of you are so funny, I can't refrain from laughing. What he wants is you. It's plain to see. How you can't see it, I don't know," she expressed her bafflement. "And it is also clear that you're interested. Again, I don't know how he can't see that," Leah pointed out in a very practical manner.

Then she strode to Axel, who welcomed her sliding an arm around her and hugging her to his side. Liliana's eyes had widened and her hand had flown and rested at the basis of her throat when she heard Leah's words.

Now, dumbfounded, she stared at the woman who settled in Axel's embrace. Leah's words put everything in a new context.

Liliana shook her head. She couldn't believe she hadn't understood it yet. But truth be told, Victor was different than the men she knew and she couldn't make head or tails of his actions and words.

She felt Victor's eyes on her and she turned her gaze at him. His pupils had darkened, and the intensity she read in them made her shiver. She laced her fingers tightly, until her knuckles whitened. Now that she understood the meaning of his earlier words, she found herself floating in an ocean of indecision.

CHAPTER 20 – WHEN IT RAINS, IT POURS

By Friday, the kids had stopped complaining about going to kindergarten. Victor had already resigned himself to loud mornings by then, though. He hadn't thought there was any way to get them out of the house in the morning without them taking a lot of potshots at their mother.

On Wednesday, he had decided that he would drive the children to the kindergarten alone. They didn't dare to be so vocal with him, and at least, that ensured that he had some peace and quiet. He had assumed the drive duty ever since and hadn't regretted once.

On Friday, driving back home after he had left them at the kindergarten, Victor thought of calling Leah or Axel and find out what was going on with the case.

They hadn't called since Tuesday, when they informed him that he had been accurate in his assessment.

The people insured had no knowledge of those policies. The police started rounding up the beneficiaries for questioning, and Victor couldn't wait to learn what they had discovered.

After he parked his car, he strode inside, enjoying the warmth of the day. The temperatures were still high enough, and he thought of taking advantage of the weather and drive Liliana and the children to Niagara Falls the following day.

He dropped the car keys in the bowl he had set on the hallway table just for that, and not seeing Liliana around, he took out his cell phone. He speed-dialed Axel on his way to the den. He thought it was more likely that Axel would answer his call. He assumed that Leah might still be busy with the interrogations.

"Hey, there," Axel's voice greeted him. "How's it going?"

He had just opened his mouth to reply when a hard voice barked at him from the door to the dining-room, "Turn it off and put your hands up."

Victor looked up and saw the indigo copy of the carrot man, aiming a pistol at him. His eyes flickered with annoyance. If it wasn't one thing, it was another.

In a calm voice, which was far from how he felt, he replied, "Hold your horses, I will turn it off."

He pretended to turn off the phone, but pressed the speaker key instead. He hoped that Axel would understand what was going on and take some action. More important, he hoped that he had already heard the man's voice and wouldn't say anything to disclose that the phone was still on.

He didn't even think of stuffing the phone back into his pocket, but asked, "What do you want?"

The man advanced toward him, with a grim face. His scowl darkened his pale face and his eyes glowered at Victor.

"You took my brother's life, I will take yours," he said very straightforwardly. His mien showed as much emotion as if he spoke about the weather.

Victor backed away a few steps, gauging his chances, but the man stalked him with the patience of a hunter.

"An eye for an eye, I gather, eh?" Victor observed mildly, and the man nodded curtly. "You know I didn't have a choice, though," Victor tried to reason with him, although he doubted he would succeed.

"You had a choice — to die. You should have died, not him," the man shrugged. "Anyways, I don't care anymore. You will die today. But first, I want to see you squirm," he announced his plans, a sneer on his lips. "Where's the woman?" he asked in a firm voice.

"What woman?" Victor asked.

He feigned disinterest in the conversation and even went as far as to check his nails and the back of his hand, as if they had been of utmost importance to him.

"Don't play stupid. I want the woman first. I checked around, but I haven't seen her. So, where is she? Anyways, we'll wait for her to make an appearance first. Killing her will make you squirm. Too bad, it won't last long," he said with regret. "I'll have to kill you soon afterward. But at least, for a few seconds, you will have known my wrath," he nodded with satisfaction, when he saw the dark twinkle flash in Victor's eyes.

Victor tried to order his thoughts. So far, Axel hadn't said a thing, which meant he was aware of what was going on. He had probably put the phone on mute, because not even a light breath came through the line. He didn't think Axel had disconnected the call.

He couldn't imagine where Liliana had gone. She had ventured out of the house a couple of times during the last few days, but she didn't go very far. She always kept close to the area. She didn't dare to take longer trips because she didn't know the city.

However, she hadn't said anything to him about going out. Victor only hoped she wouldn't come home before Axel could intervene.

"Now, kneel there," the carrot man barked pointing with the gun to the floor. "And put your hands behind your head," he thought to add.

Victor shook his head in refusal, and the man scowled.

"Why would I comply?" Victor asked. "You will kill me anyway, so there's nothing for me in obeying your orders," he shrugged.

"But I can shoot you just enough to keep you alive for a while," the man growled.

"So what?" Victor retorted.

"So it will be more painful for you while you wait for the death to come," the carrot man pointed out.

"Considering that I will die soon enough, pain doesn't bother me. It's inconsequential," Victor replied with indifference, and that made the other man grit his teeth.

"I will shoot you in the belly. That would be a long and painful death. Now, kneel," he bellowed.

"Not necessarily," Victor contradicted him, always in a calm voice, meant to grate on the other one's nerves.

"What?" the shooter shouted, enraged with Victor's continuous refusal to obey his orders.

"I was just saying that shooting me in the belly doesn't necessarily mean that I will have a long and painful death," Victor explained patiently. "It depends where the bullet travels, you know. And that's not something you can plan beforehand. I might just well instantly die," he pointed out.

"Are you out of your mind?" the man shouted again, in bewilderment.

"No," Victor shook his head. "I'm very sane. But I also know what a bullet can do. In theory, I mean. I haven't had such an experience yet. That you want me to suffer doesn't automatically mean that I will," he shrugged again, yet always surveying the man attentively.

He could swear that his attacker was very close to blowing his gasket. His face had contorted and his eyes had turned wild.

Victor didn't know whether he had a chance to get out of that situation alive, but he hoped either to drive the man so mad that he would attack him physically, forgetting about the gun, or that he would gain enough time for Axel to arrive and help. He was confident he had already let Leah know about what was going on.

"You are a wacko," the man said and raised the hand with the pistol. "I think I'd better shoot you now and wait for the woman afterward. I might have some fun with her first, before killing her, I mean," he smirked and Victor saw red.

The man released the safety trigger and decocked the pistol. He stretched his arm, his mien cold and indifferent now. His index started to press the trigger.

Victor resigned himself. He would probably die in the next second. He was aware that even if he had attacked the man, he wouldn't have had time to get to him before the bullet had sawed him down. Yet, he knew he had to try, so he sprung forward, dropping the cell phone to the floor.

However, in that very moment, barefoot, so she wouldn't make a noise, Liliana rushed out of the den with one of Victor's huge technical dictionaries at the ready. With a shout that would have made a warrior pride, she hammered the man over the head with it.

The man's head snapped to the right at the impact. His finger pressed the trigger though, and the bullet crossed Victor's arm, always the left one, which hadn't had a chance to heal yet.

The bullet followed an upward trajectory, across the biceps, and came out of Victor's arm after it travelled only an inch and a half through his muscle. Then, it lodged itself in the wooden frame of the living room.

Stunned, Victor just grunted and stared at the woman, who was breathing hard now. She had paled, and her chocolate eyes shone vividly.

Liliana kicked the gun from the man's hand hard enough to throw it a few feet away, and then, she ran to Victor, "Are you all right?" she asked, her voice trembling with worry.

Victor looked at her as if she'd lost her mind. Surely, the woman could see for herself that the bullet had gone through his arm. The blood must have gushed out. He had felt it.

When she reached him and her shaky fingers touched his biceps, he flinched. The bullet had hit very close to the wound left by the knife a few days ago.

He shook her hand off him and rushed to the man who started to stir. He slammed him down with a heavy fist in the temple, and the man blacked out with a groan again.

Victor sighed with relief, and then, looked up at Liliana who had frozen on the spot.

"Bring me something to tie his hands," he asked her softly. Her eyes still looked wild.

Liliana nodded and ran to the hallway closet. She came back with a rope after a few moments, and handed it to him.

Victor noticed she was still shaking. The adrenaline had worn off, but he knew that wasn't the moment to comfort her.

He had hardly restrained the man's hands when the sound of car doors slammed shut reached his ears.

"I suppose Leah and Axel are here," he remarked in a dry voice, and with a grunt, he straightened up.

He grimaced when he felt the sting of the new pain, which, of course, joined the countless others to torment him. At least, he had got used to the previous ones during the last few days.

"By the way, where were you?" he turned his head and asked her on his way to the door. "He told me that he hadn't found you when he came and searched the house."

"I was in the den. I was doing some research on your laptop when I heard the noise he made. His housebreaking wasn't very stealthy," she wrinkled her nose with disgust. "The man lacks basic skills," she shook her head. "Anyway, I closed the laptop and hid under the desk," she shrugged. "I know, not very smart, but there was no other place in sight. He should have found me immediately, but I think he just checked the room at large. I heard him going upstairs afterward, but I didn't know if I had had enough time to run out of the house, so I remained there, until he decided to shoot you," she explained.

"I see," Victor murmured and shook his head. "Well, I probably should thank you," he grumbled. "Although, that bullet still found me," he added and left the room.

Behind him, Liliana gasped her outrage loudly. She couldn't believe his lack of gratitude.

***

"We were just looking for him, when your call came," Leah explained apologetically.

The uniformed officers had handcuffed the man and taken him outside to the police car. Meanwhile, Liliana had patched Victor again under the paramedics' eyes.

"He was the third man who took part in the killings," Leah said.

"I understand," Victor said with a nod. "I don't blame you for anything. I just seem to have a string of bad luck," he shrugged.

"Well, you've been stabbed, punched, shot... You name it," Axel intervened in a dry voice. "Yeah, I would say you have had a string of bad luck, indeed. Hopefully, it's ended."

"And yet, you survived, every single time," Mark noticed in awe, and Victor rolled his eyes, disgusted with the young man's admiration.

He didn't see anything worth admiring. He ached everywhere and had lost more blood than he cared to imagine. He turned his head from the detectives and ruffled his hair with impatient fingers.

His eyes fell on the concealed bar he had set in the den, and decided to treat himself with a glass of whiskey. He deserved it after all.

He opened the bar and took out the bottle Leah and Axel had gifted him with, for his birthday.

"Does anybody else want any?" he turned to them and asked, lifting the bottle so they could see it.

The detectives shook their heads with regret. They were on duty and couldn't partake in alcohol.

"Yeah, probably not a good offer for you right now," Victor mumbled. "Sorry guys, but after the last couple of weeks, I think I do need a glass, even if you think I'm rude," he said and poured a generous portion into a tumbler, which he also took out of the bar.

"Are you sure you don't want to go to the hospital?" Leah asked, worried that Victor had been injured too many times lately.

Victor shook his head, "Liliana stopped the bleeding… Of course, making everything hurt much more in the process," he thought to add gruffly, and a scowl claimed his lips, although he knew he was just mean. "She put some antibiotic locally, so I'm covered."

"I also thought he should go to the hospital to get checked, but he's as stubborn as a mule," Liliana's voice came from the door.

After she had finished patching him again, she decided to make some coffee and didn't want to listen to any of his arguments against her endeavor.

'As if she wanted me to be wide awake so I could enjoy my aches better,' he reflected with resentment, and his lips turned into a scowl.

Liliana put the tray with the cups onto the desk and poured coffee in each of them. She invited the detectives to help themselves to sugar and cream, and then, she straightened and turned to Victor.

When her gaze fell on the glass with whiskey, she scowled and stomped to him. She snatched the glass out of his hand exactly when he tried to sip some more, and the whiskey sloshed out of the glass and splashed him in the process.

"What the heck?" he exclaimed, livid, wiping his face off.

His eyes widened and an ugly glower set on his face. He couldn't believe she had had the audacity to snatch the tumbler from him.

"You don't drink alcohol in such a situation, you fool. You've just taken an antibiotic and a painkiller. I didn't push the matter to have you go to the hospital, but that doesn't mean I will stand aside and let you kill yourself," she replied angrily, and poured the whiskey in the flower pot on the windowsill.

"That's plastic," he observed dryly. "The plant," he clarified when she looked at him with bewilderment.

Liliana blushed violently, but then she shrugged, "I don't know much about plants and gardening," she muttered. "But I know about that," she pointed to the dressing she had applied to his arm.

The detectives had a hard time keeping their laughter contained. Mark stared at some invisible spots on the ceiling, and bit his lower lip. It wouldn't do to burst into laughter right then. Victor might want to have his head.

Victor glowered at Liliana some more, then turned to the detectives.

"So what now?" he asked.

Then, to their amazement, he started out of the door. With no connection to what he had just said, he threw over his shoulder, "Let's go out onto the patio. There isn't enough space for all of us in here."

In a couple of seconds, he had left the room and the detectives still looked after him, stunned by his behavior.

Liliana sighed and sauntered to the desk to put the cups back on the tray and take them outside to the patio.

"Don't bother," Axel stilled her movements. "We'll take the cups with us."

When they came outside, Victor was already seated in his regular spot on the sofa, his legs stretched in front of him and his arms folded on his stomach. He looked at them with defiance, his mien belligerent, and his eyes hard.

"So," he asked after they sat down as well, "what other attacks should I expect?"

"None," Leah replied with conviction.

"Are you sure?" he asked again. "Because if you are not sure, I will send Liliana and the kids on a prolonged vacation out of the province. I won't have them in harm's way again," he declared with determination.

"We're not objects to be sent away," Liliana observed in a hard voice. "If you want us out of your house, we'll leave, but that…"

"Have I said anything about wanting them out of my house?" Victor interrupted her, but he asked the question to the others, not to her. "I said I wouldn't keep you in harm's way," he stressed out, turning to her and staring her down.

For a moment, nonplussed, Liliana didn't know what to answer, and Axel took advantage of the silence.

"Yes, we're sure, Victor. Every single person involved in this case is arrested. We were just looking for the twin of the carrot man, but now, he's out of circulation, as well. You can go on with your life without fearing that someone else would come after you," he explained patiently.

"So the case is closed?" Victor asked with skepticism. He didn't believe for a second that they could have closed the case already.

"No, it isn't, of course. But what's left is to gather all the people who bought those insurance policies and instigated to murder," Leah specified. "Which means that Axel told you the truth. You're not in danger anymore. The guys doing the killing are behind bars."

"So can I drive the kids to Niagara Falls tomorrow?" he asked, and Liliana's eyes widened.

"How do you want to drive with that arm?" she asked with disbelief.

He just waved his hand to show that her question didn't merit any attention, and Axel shook his head.

He leaned over Victor and, shaking his head, he whispered, "You should learn how to choose your battles, Victor. Like me."

Yet, Leah heard his words and fixed him with narrowed eyes. Axel just shrugged, as if he hadn't done anything wrong.

***

Victor drove Liliana and the children to Niagara Falls only after two more weeks. He had underestimated the stubbornness and steel backbone of a woman from his birth country, but he had promised himself not to do it again.

He had given in and allowed her to cook for him so she wouldn't feel indebted, but he didn't budge and refused everything when it came to doing laundry and cleaning. The line had to be drawn somewhere.

After a few outings with the children, he gathered the courage to ask her out, just the two of them, on a date. He had steeled himself for her refusal, but her acceptance shocked him more.

He grabbed his chance, and Leah and Axel were called in to babysit. His boldness stunned Liliana, which he considered a good thing. She didn't find the words to counter his plans.

The date went fine, according to his standards. He had chosen a nice restaurant, where they could enjoy a good dinner, dance and listen to good music.

Victor could have done without her outrage at the end of the evening, though. He didn't understand why she went in a huff when he stared that guy down.

The man could see she was with Victor. She had refused his invitation to dance and he still insisted.

Victor didn't think he had overreacted. He had just staked his claim. Now, he just had to move slowly, patiently, until he had everything. He knew how to go after what he wanted, after all.

NOTE REGARDING TORONTO MUSIC GARDEN

TORONTO MUSIC GARDEN was designed by internationally renowned cellist Yo-Yo Ma and landscape designer Julie Moir Messervy, in collaboration with the City of Toronto's Parks and Recreation department. This garden is a reflection in landscape of Bach's Suite No.1 in G Major for unaccompanied cello, BWV 1007. Each dance movement within Bach's Suite No. 1 in G Major for unaccompanied cello, BWV 1007 corresponds to a different section of the garden:

PRELUDE represents an undulating river scape with curves and bends. The first movement of the suite depicts a flowing river. Granite boulders from the southern edge of the Canadian Shield represent a stream bed with low-growing plants softening its banks. The entire ensemble is overtopped by an alley of native

Hackberry trees (Celtis occidentalis), whose straight trunks and regular spacing suggest measures of music.

ALLEMANDE represents a forest grove of wandering trails. The allemande, an ancient German dance, is interpreted here as a Birch forest with various contemplative sitting areas, that move higher and higher up the hillside, culminating in a rocky vantage point that looks over the harbor through a circle of Dawn Redwood trees.

COURANTE is depicted by a swirling path through a wildflower meadow. Originally an Italian and French dance form, is interpreted here as a huge, upward-spiraling swirl through a lush field of grasses and brightly-colored perennials that attract birds and butterflies. At the top, a Maypole spins in the wind.

SARABANDE is a conifer grove in the shape of an arc. This movement is based on an ancient Spanish dance form, and its contemplative quality is interpreted here as an inward-arcing circle, enclosed by tall needle-leaf evergreen trees. The garden's centerpiece is a huge stone that acts as a stage for readings, and holds a small pool with water that reflects the sky.

MINUETS – this segment is represented by a formal flower parterre. This French dance, contemporary to Bach's time, reflects in the symmetry and geometry of this movement's design. A circular pavilion is designed to shelter small musical ensembles or dance groups.

GIGUE is reflected in giant grass steps that dance you down to the outside world. The gigue, or "jog", is an English dance. Its rollicking music is interpreted as a series of giant grass steps that offer views onto the harbor. The steps form a curved amphitheater that focus on a stone stage set under a weeping willow tree. Shrubs and perennials act as large, enclosing arms, framing views out onto the harbor.

Source:

http://www.harbourfrontcentre.com/venues/torontomusicgarden/

BONUS - GRETA GARBO CAKE RECIPE

Ingredients

For the sheets: 500 g flour, 2 eggs (optional), 200 g margarine for baking, 1 teaspoon of baking soda brewed with one teaspoon of vinegar, a little salt

For the filling: 200 grams ground nuts, 200 grams sugar, apricot jam 400 or 500 grams

Icing: 200 grams sugar, 3 tablespoons cocoa, 3 tablespoons oil, 4 tablespoons water

Preparation

Mix the ingredients for the sheets well and spread 4 sheets.

The ground nuts are mixed with the sugar for the filling and left aside.

Grease a pan with margarine and flush with flour.

Place the first sheet into the pan, spread a thin layer of jam over it and sprinkle the nuts mixed with sugar. Do the same thing with the second and third pastry sheets. Place the last sheet over the last layer of filling.

Place the tray into the oven heated at medium heat (350F or 190C). Leave it in the oven for 30 minutes. After the cake has been removed, let it cool down, and meanwhile, prepare the icing.

Place all the ingredients for the icing into a pot. Put the pot onto the stove and stir often with a wooden spoon. When the icing starts boiling, continue stirring for a couple of minutes. Take it off the stove, and spread it over the cake immediately, using the wooden spoon to spread it everywhere. This should be done quickly because the icing will harden.

Leave the cake in the pan overnight, and in the morning, cut the cake in squares, slices, whatever shape you want.

Duration: 1 h

AUTHOR'S BIOGRAPHY

Born in Europe, some time ago, the writer started loving books very early. The next step was easy: writing became a dream and a purpose.

She enjoys writing and baking - these two work very well hand in hand, and she enjoys spending time with her dog - or at least most of the time, as he is a hellion.

One trip to Scotland made her lose her heart to a beautiful country and extraordinary people. That is why she chose a Scottish detective to promote some of her crime stories.

BOOKS BY ROXANA NASTASE

Mayhem on Nightingale Street – McNamara Series – Vol I

Scents in the Shadows – McNamara Series – Vol II

McNamara Series – Box set (Vol I and II)

A Suitable Epitaph

A Churchgoing Woman

An Immigrant

Forthcoming:

Relative Bonds – McNamara Series – Vol III

Table of Contents

Thank you for taking the time to read the MacKay – Canadian Detectives Series Book One, including the novels **A Suitable Epitaph & An Immigrant**.

If you enjoyed it, please consider telling your friends or posting a short review. Word of mouth is an author's best friend and much appreciated.

Thank you, Roxana Nastase.

To hear about future releases, please, subscribe to my newsletter on:
www.roxananastase.weebly.com.